in an awful way

SNYDER-CARROLL

also by s. snyder-carroll

The World of Kurt Vonnegut: A Hot Mess
On the Edge of Dangerous Things

and

available soon

Click...Kill

For my patient and loving husband

Author's Note: Though some facts about places in the novel are accurate, others are figments of the imagination. Furthermore, resemblances to actual persons living or dead are coincidental.

Cover Art/ Interior Design: Harriet Snyder

Cover Design: Jill Kohut

Acknowledgements

My sincere gratitude to my consultants, Nicole Genna and Seena Rich, for their insight and encouragement; to my readers, Claire and Sam Jefferis, Renee Roberts, Paul Stewart, and especially Joseph T. Carroll, who assisted in getting several key scenes right; to my parents, Julia O. and Russell J. Snyder, and all my family members for their continuing patience, interest, and enthusiasm; and to Jill Kohut for straightening out the cover.

Also, special thanks to Eric Brown and the Palm Beach Writers Group for welcoming me into their circle and providing information, inspiration, and the sort of camaraderie a lonely writer needs.

Play List:

Cooke, Sam. "Another Saturday Night." Lyrics. Ain't That Good News. RCA Victor, 1963.

Irons, William J. "Sing with All the Saints in Glory." Lyrics. The United Methodist Hymnal Number 702. 1873.

*"The heart is deceitful above all things,
and desperately sick;
who can understand it?"*

Jeremiah 17:9

Prologue

As she was about to put the old shaving kit on her table at the Silver Nugget Flea Market, Hester Randal opened the case and stared at the gleaming razor.

Decades ago, while shopping for an anniversary gift for Al, she'd come across it in Moon River Antiques. It was impractical and extravagant; but when she picked it up, she liked how it had weight to it, how its double-edged blade looked sharp enough to slice open her young husband's skin, if he wasn't careful.

Despite this potential for injury and thinking it really was a classy sort of gift, Hester purchased it and that night presented it to Al.

He tore the wrapping off, tossed it on the floor, opened the case, and asked, "Is this some sort of joke, Hester?"

"No, it's an old razor," she said, smiling expectantly.

"No kidding." The features of Al's striking face shifted into a scowl. "I can see that, but what the hell am I supposed to do with it? It's archaic, and, quite frankly, looks fucking expensive."

"Well, I thought you'd like it…I thought it was something unique, something for the man who has everything."

"I am far from having everything. We are far from having everything. Have you seen our bank balance lately?"

"Okay, Al," Hester said. "It was expensive; but it's our first anniversary, and I saved up for it on my own."

"What do you mean 'you saved up for it on your own'? Are you hiding money from me, Hester? And how expensive is expensive anyway? Don't tell me this thing is solid gold?" He took the razor from the case and held it up to the light. "Geezus Christ, Hester, what in the hell were you thinking?"

"I was thinking you'd use it every day and think of me fondly when you did."

"Me, use this thing? Christ, you might as well have flushed whatever money you spent on it down the toilet. I'm not giving up my electric razor. Didn't anybody tell you it's 1976, not 1876?"

So after she tried to use the thing herself and nicked up her legs pretty badly, Hester shoved it under the bathroom sink where it remained for the duration of her marriage. But could she ever really forget about it? Hell, no. It was like a ragged tooth, a sore pimple, a scab that wouldn't heal. Her mind kept going back to it, back to the fact that Al was a bastard to please.

Now she stood staring at the implement as a scorching wind blew down Goat Hill across the empty lot and kicked up more dust. The stifling heat on this August afternoon was sapping Hester's last ounce of strength.

She fingered the edge of the blade. Yes, the razor was a finely-crafted object, alright, but she should've known better. She sure should've known better in more ways than one.

The only two men in her life with whom she'd been intimate and both of them ended up breaking her heart.

Was she really that stupid to have picked such losers? Or was she such a loser that she deserved what she got?

Or, and here was the possibility she could live with, had she been duped?

Her college boyfriend Arty Kendall and her husband Al Murphy had turned out to be a couple of lying, cheating phonies, all good looks on the outside—so freaking beautiful it'd made her weak—but on the inside, rotten to the core.

God, it made her queasy to picture herself with them, to remember their naked bodies, their hands touching her, their tongues in her mouth, themselves inside her. She'd let them in and paid the price. Arty had been in her life only briefly, dropped one big bomb on her and disappeared. Unfortunately, with Al, it'd been a hell of a nasty, protracted war before she gathered her wits and withdrew.

Thank you, God, all of that is in the past. And she was hoping against hope she could keep it there. For the present she'd have to learn to make her way alone in the world. She'd always been afraid of being alone, but lately she'd been trying to accept it as the natural course of things. You came into the world from somewhere all by yourself, and you'd go out the same way. Such comforting thoughts didn't stay with her long, though, especially in light of the fact that so far she was already screwing this whole being alone thing up.

Hester sighed and closed the case. Gold was at an all-time low, still she hoped to sell the shaving kit for more than the hundred and forty she paid for it three decades ago. Making even one dollar would help her feel less like the sucker she'd been. And, hell if she didn't need that dollar. Look where she was, setting up at a flea market, sweating like a pig, and flat broke. How had she gotten into such a bind?

Hester closed the case and dusted it off with the corner of her shirt. The clouds over the Delaware River had thinned, and the sun blinded her. She squinted and turned away.

That very night so many years ago, she should have taken that blade and slashed ungrateful, arrogant Al right across his face. That gruesome inspiration never entered her mind at the time...but it did now.

And why hadn't she left him? Why had she wasted all those years hanging onto an illusion? Hell, why hadn't she at some point used that blade on her own wrists?

Why not use it now? Why not take the blade into the woods...?

Hester had plenty of excellent reasons to call it quits, but she had to admit it, she was terrified of the ultimate alone, of being stone-cold dead.

And, call her crazy, but in the back of her mind she kept telling herself she'd find something to live for.

She just had to...

One

The in-between time was over for Hester Randal. She stood by the wall of windows in her Lambertville condo watching the muddy Delaware River slog along. The sun hadn't yet risen above the hills so this would be the coolest part of this August day, the day she was going to get her life together. For too long she'd dwelt in the gloomy past. Time to come into the light. Time, like Oprah said, to live her "best life."

Hester lifted her mug and inhaled the aroma. God, if she didn't love the smell of coffee. She drank hers black and strong, a mixture of Chock Full o' Nuts and Lavazza, more flavorful than anything Starbucks could dream up. She'd enjoy her coffee, then suit up for a run before the humidity had a chance to suck the life out of everything. Later, she'd get off her butt and go look for a job.

There, she had a plan.

"Shall we gather at the river, where bright angel feet have..." Her singing was interrupted by the nerve-racking ringtone of her cell phone. "Polaris." Her ex-husband Al—she liked thinking about him as being X'ed out of her life—had installed it for her. As soon she got off the phone, she'd figure out how to get rid of the freaking nuisance.

"Hello," she said.

"Just a courtesy call, Mrs. Mur..."

"It's not Mrs. anything. It's Ms., Ms. Randal," interrupted Hester. She recognized Lou's whiny voice.

"Yeah, right. Well, anyway, I gotta have that rent by Monday, or I'll be forced to hacksaw your lock off and put ours..."

"Wait a minute, Lou. I..." Hester tried to interrupt again, but Lou talked right over her.

"…on your storage unit as per the contract that you, yourself, signed."

"But, please, it's already Thursday and there's been trouble. I'm in a bit of a financial…"

The connection went dead.

"*Forced?*" she thought. *Who's going to force him to do what? He's the effing boss. He knows I'll pay him as soon as…as what?*

Who was she kidding? She had no money, and how long would it take her to get some kind of work? But she couldn't afford to lose what she had in storage.

Hester drove north on River Road in the direction of Lou's Storage Center, her mind whirring. Begging the man for an extension would be gut-wrenching. He was always such a smartass.

Then it came to her. The Silver Nugget. A gift-from-the-gods idea. She'd get a table at the Silver Nugget Flea Market on Saturday and sell enough of her stuff to pay Lou. She had plenty of experience buying things at a flea market. How hard could it be to get on the other side of the table and sell?

What a goddamn great idea.

Hester felt better for about a half a minute before her heart thumped and her palms got sweaty. She pumped the air-conditioning up, but perspiration beaded on her forehead and dampened her armpits.

Every last goddamn thing she had in storage was irreplaceable. How could she part with any of it? Collecting had been her second career. She taught English, and she collected stuff. Those were her two passions. So what if Al thought it was all junk and hadn't let her put any of it in the condo? She'd packed it up and put it into storage; but that didn't mean she didn't love it, all of it, every last piece of it. Each acquisition had been a sort of conquest, each object like a trophy. And when they lived in the old Victorian, everything had a place and everything was in its place.

The upstairs front room, she'd made it into her library. She never bought new books, preferring to rescue used ones at yard sales where they were a heartbeat away from turning into trash. She'd pick one up, let the book fall open to a page, and read the last sentence on the left. If she liked that sentence, she bought the book, took it home, and recorded the sentence in a notebook. Someday, she'd use these sentences for something, what she didn't have a clue, but she liked recording them and thinking about them. So far her favorite was by George Eliot, page 396, the 1977 paperback edition of "Adam Bede": "Another day had risen, and she must wander on."

Wander on. It would make a good title for a story about herself.

Al hated this room, never went in it, and when he saw Hester heading there with a bag or box, he'd explode. "No more books! If you buy another book, you have to get rid of one you already have. I'm not allowing you to build another shelf in this house, and don't start stacking them all over the place. You have a problem, Hester, and you better start dealing with it."

Hester's books weren't a problem. "For God's sake, Al, I'm an English teacher," Hester argued. To her reading was like breathing. Books were her air, her oxygen. She had to have them so she kept her mouth shut and began sneaking them past her husband.

When they sold the Victorian and moved to the condo, she dismantled her library, packed up her books and all her other beautiful things, and had it all trucked up to Lou's. She had to lie to Al about everything going to the Goodwill.

No, she wouldn't take any of her books to the flea market. As a matter of fact, now that Al was gone, when she had time, she'd bring them to the condo; and when she got a job, she'd have lots of shelves built for them.

As for the rest of her stuff, well, getting rid of even one thing would be like gouging out an eye or severing a limb. Depending on what it was, it might even be as bad as ripping her heart out or giving up her first-born, if she'd had one.

At times, though, her attachment to these inanimate objects did baffle her. Was Al right? Did she have a problem?

No, her ex-husband always made her doubt herself, and now she was so over him and over letting his insidious accusations ever influence her again. Her belongings were magical. They kept her from being…a nobody.

But Lou had her over a barrel. If she didn't come up with the rent, he'd get it all.

Her head pounded, her mouth was dry. She couldn't let that happen. She'd sell what she had to, to keep the rest.

Hester stood in front of her open storage unit reading the labels she'd put on the sides of the boxes trying to make a decision. Out of the corner of her eye, she saw Lou skulk up alongside of her.

"Yeah," he mumbled half-under his breath, "I heard all about your trouble. Read it in the Trenton Times. The State yanked both your pensions. Looks like your husband, big Mister Vice-Principal, is gonna do some time too."

He shifted his rotund body from one foot to the other and folded his thick arms across his barrel chest.

"Yeah, Mrs. Murphy…I mean, Ms. Randal, I really do feel sorry for you. With a husband like that you must've had a terrible life alright. Too bad you didn't leave his sorry ass years ago. Then maybe that innocent student of yours, what was her name?" He scratched the side of his head. "Nina, that's it, Nina Tattoni. That girl would still be alive, and everybody in the world wouldn't be looking at you like you're some pervert's accomplice. How could you have stayed with that sicko? Why somebody ought to write a book about how sick all of it was.

"First, he knocks up one of his own students. What kind of a vice-principal is that? Screwing around with a teenager? In his own school, for Christ sakes? Then he does nothing and lets the poor pregnant kid fend for herself. Years later, he's back doing it with his own daughter."

Here Lou paused to wipe his nose on his sleeve. "And she's only fifteen or maybe sixteen at the time? Doesn't even know the poor girl's his own flesh and blood until she's dead. Worse than one of them Greek tragedies. You know as well as I do, he killed her. Broke her neck, didn't he? My, my, my, what a sick bastard.

"Damn, I really do feel goddamn sorry for you, but…" And here he widened his stance, shoved his hands in his pockets. "…you are already three months behind, and we got policies here that we got to stick to. You understand, don't you?" He shrugged, coughed up a chunk of phlegm, and spit it almost right at her feet.

Hester's first impulse was to defend Al, say how he had no idea Nina was his child. How could he have known when…but she stopped herself. What the hell was she thinking? Defend Al, the cheater, molester, the man who talked out of both sides of his mouth, and had gotten away with too much for far too long? No, she had looked the other way and was only getting what she deserved from Lou. Lou wasn't sorry at all about locking her out of her storage unit. He was only thinking exactly what everybody else in the Tri-State area was—Alexander Murphy was a disgusting creep; and the fact that his wife *finally* divorced him didn't mean she hadn't been a creep too.

"Really, Lou, I understand. You don't have to explain. I'll have the money by Monday. I promise."

"Put it in an envelope and slip it in the slot on the door." He turned to leave.

Hester spoke to his back, "No hard feelings. Right Lou?"

She expected to hear him say, right, but he said nothing. She watched his fat body hump its way back to the office. She wasn't accustomed to being disliked and it made her feel like a piece of dirt.

For hours Hester went through her neatly stacked boxes and filled her minivan. She was worn out and disheartened as she jammed the last carton in. She'd seen the backs of the vans of the pack rats and flea market dealers stuffed to bursting with the junk they were going to peddle. She'd looked down her nose at their grimy vehicles, at their loads of filthy boxes and garbage bags. Never would her car look like that, never would she be reduced to a life like that. But as her Odyssey hit a pothole while she sped back to the condo, and all her stuff noisily shifted behind her, she realized she should've never said never.

Two

Friday morning the temperature was well into the eighties by the time Hester mounted the treadmill in the rear corner of C&R's Fitness Center. The place was packed, and she was grateful to be in a spot where she might not be noticed. The last thing Hester wanted these days was to be recognized and approached and questioned by even those friendly people she had once enjoyed chatting with. She had nothing to say. The tragedy she lived through and was trying to recover from was inexplicable so she increased the elevation and mph's and punished her body hoping the pain might stop Lou's mean words from ringing in her head.

Even with the air-conditioning blasting and the fan blowing on her, Hester felt like she was running through the Mojave. Sweat poured off her. Shit, she'd be glad when autumn arrived...or would she? Wouldn't September only remind her of school and the fact that she'd never teach again? *Never.*

First thing, when she plead guilty to not reporting Nina's death and disposing of her body, the State of New Jersey yanked her certification and small pension. So school would start in a few weeks without her, and that was hard medicine for Hester to swallow. For the first time in her adult life she was unemployable, and broke.

Al had always handled their finances. Her paycheck went into an account. Al paid the bills, made the investments, and gave Hester an allowance. After Nina's death Hester promptly filed for divorce; and Al moved out of the condo, agreeing to end their marriage amicably.

"I've put you through enough hell already, Hester, haven't I?" He offered her an incredibly favorable settlement: the condo, the trailer in Pleasant Palms Trailer Park, half the money in their joint bank account which he would deposit into a savings account in her name only, and alimony of forty-eight thousand dollars a year. All this was dependent on Hester waiving the mandatory eighteen month separation. She signed the papers quickly without hiring an attorney. She was through with Al Murphy, the sooner the better.

Hester, however, didn't adjust well to being alone. It was as though she were adrift in a leaky row boat, no oars, no pail. All she could manage was eating, exercising, and watching TV. Bills stacked up on the kitchen counter. Periodically, she glanced at them as she shoved them in a drawer. Okay, they looked official and important, but she'd get to them later. Then one day when she couldn't fit another in, she knew it was time to start taking care of business. She went to the bank to move money from the savings account Al had opened for her into a new checking account.

"Sorry," the teller said, "but no deposits have been made into your savings account since the initial deposit."

"Well, that's alright. I guess this whole process will take time. My ex-husband must be a little behind," said Hester. "What's my balance?"

"Let's see. Fifty-one dollars and twenty-six cents."

Fifty-one dollars! Hester damn-near fainted.

She took out her cell phone and punched in Al's number. She'd deleted him from her contacts, but she would never forget his number.

He picked up.

"I'm at the bank, Al." Hester's voice was firm. "Where in the hell is my money?"

"I needed it." Al's voice was gruff. What else was new? "You have no idea, Hester, what this has mushroomed into for me. Because of you my reputation, my whole life is ruined. Nina died because of the fucking hurricane, because the goddamn tree fell on the trailer and broke her neck. Do you hear me? I never hurt that girl. Jesus, I spent my fucking life as an educator, a vice-principal, a damn good one. I would never do anything to one of my students.

Look, I'm fighting this thing to the bitter end if it takes every dime I have. I know you framed me, you vindictive cunt. Nina was not my daughter because I never touched her mother, Jennifer. Never! So you can forget about getting anything out of me. The State took my pension, my benefits, everything! And you expect me to worry about…"

He ranted like a madman, blamed Hester, claimed she made the whole thing up, paid people to manufacture false results.

"…and don't ever contact me again. I'm getting rid of this phone, rid of you." The line went dead.

Oh, it was a nightmare, but now, at least, she could move on with no illusions.

Thank God, I have the condo, free and clear. The thought dissipated as a new worry replaced it. She slowed the treadmill to a walk. The mortgage might be paid off, but what about assessments, taxes, insurance?

Her heart was a fist beating her up from the inside out. Headband drenched, eyes stinging, she stopped the treadmill and wiped her face.

Alexander Bruno Murphy was a liar. She had to remember that. The DNA didn't lie. She had to remember that too.

She went into the empty locker room, sat on the bench, lowered her head, and watched her sweat spot the grey floor.

By the time she got back to the condo, Hester made the decision to walk into Lambertville that very afternoon and knock on doors. She could learn to be a waitress or sales clerk in one of the cafes or shops. Why not?

She turned on the television, kicked off her sneakers, and tried to relax with Hoda and Kathie Lee for a few minutes.

Too many commercials, her mind wandering where she didn't want it go. She was hyped-up so she went into the bathroom to shower, but when she got there, she started rummaging under the sink.

She'd try it. Why not? Maybe it would calm her down. Like Doctor Oz said, orgasms were good for you. They gave women a "sense of well-being." Well, she needed that... desperately. Maybe, just maybe, she'd learn to like being by herself. Just when she found the battery-operated contraption Al bought her years ago as an anniversary gag gift—was it really meant to be a joke? Now she wasn't so sure—the doorbell rang.

It was, of all people, Sheriff Smith. She'd seen his picture in The Democrat many times. He was tall, and the brim of his hat cast a shadow on most of his face. All Hester could see was his mouth. He wasn't smiling.

"Mrs. Murphy?"

"My name's Randal now, well, not officially. Officially, it's Murphy, but I'd rather go by Randal." She hesitated as the man impatiently shift the manila envelope he was holding from one hand to the other.

"You live here, right?"

"Yes."

"I regret to inform you, Ms. Randal or Murphy, this condo is under foreclosure. You have to be out of here by noon. It's eleven o'clock. You have one hour to vacate the premises."

"What?" Hester wasn't sure she'd heard him correctly.

"I am really sorry about this, Ma'am."

"But, wait a minute. What are you saying? What do you mean?"

"It's all there in the papers, Ma'am," he shoved the envelope at Hester. Her hands flew up. She shook her head.

"No, no, I won't take it," she hollered, but he'd already forced the envelope on her and walked away.

Stunned, she stood there for several precious minutes.

One hour? What could she do in one hour? What could she save in one hour? There was too much, far too much. She couldn't think straight.

You, son-of-a-bitch, Al Murphy, mentally she cursed him.

But her frustration was past the boiling point.

"You son-of-a-bitch!" she screamed. The words echoed through the high-ceilinged hallway.

She began running from room to room snatching things off shelves, opening up drawers, rummaging through them. She threw things in a pile by the front door, all the while chanting, "You son-of-a-bitch! You son-of-a-bitch!"

It kept her going. She checked the clock on the stove as she stacked up her All-Clad chef's set and wrapped her Wusthoff Classics in dishtowels.

It was 11:48 a.m. She ran to her closet, ran her hands over the racks of her beautiful clothes: her coats, her suits, her slacks, shirts, scarves, snuggly robes. She stared at her shoes lined up like loyal soldiers, at her expensive handbags perched on high shelves like precious hens.

How could she leave them behind?

She ran to the kitchen for garbage bags, ran back, shoved armfuls of things into them, and lined them up in the hallway. She looked at the clock, 11:56 a.m. She needed a shower, needed to get out of her running clothes. There wasn't enough time. She hurried to the bathroom, raked all of her expensive cosmetics and creams into another garbage bag. Two minutes. She had to leave. She stood by the door and looked at all of the stuff in the hallway. Two minutes. How was she going to get it all downstairs, all in the minivan? It was already full.

One minute! No way. She fought against collapsing, against the descending doom.

Then someone was pounding on the door.

"Open-up," Sheriff Smith shouted. "I don't want to have to forcibly remove you from the premises, but I will if you don't open the door."

Hester didn't want the sheriff to touch her.

She unlocked the door and pulled it open. The man stepped aside, and Hester left.

Three

Hester drove around for hours too distraught to stop anywhere. She couldn't look for a job in her smelly exercise outfit. She was getting hungry, but she was too upset to eat. When she checked her wallet at a stop light in Trenton, she had one dollar and twenty-three cents. Between a rock and a hard place. It was an understatement.

Not knowing what else to do, she headed north again on River Road. The Delaware to the left was glistening in the slant sun, and the forest to the right was lush, the vegetation creeping onto the asphalt. At the bend about seventeen miles from the city, the Silver Nugget Flea Market stood on a couple of acres that use to be a quarry. The base of Goat Hill had been blasted away leaving a two level arena. At the north end of the lower level there was a stand of scraggly trees and two dilapidated barns, one of which housed the food stand. South of the barns along the road were drunken rows of rickety wooden tables. Behind them was an L-shaped, tin-roofed pavilion. More tables stretched out south of the pavilion and led to a non-descript, two story building that housed the indoor shops. Behind that on the upper level was the office and above the office, the manager's apartment. Up on Goat Hill, tucked into the dense woods were a motley assortment of barely visible bungalows.

Hester pulled in and parked beneath a tree at the north end. When the dust to settled, she unloaded several boxes and started putting her stuff out on one of the tables. No one was around. She was grateful to be alone, and busy, though the heat was intense, the oppressive air humming with insects.

One bat appeared at sunset and looped around near Hester's head. As she tried to follow the creature's erratic flight, frantic, ear-piercing cheeps filled the air. She looked west. Hundreds of the flying rodents rose up through the flaming sunset like ash. Then the great bobbing mobile of them moved over the river and swooped toward her.

She covered her hair, hunched against the fender of her minivan, and cursed the creepy mammals. She wasn't much into nature—except for the beach, the soothing rhythm of the waves, the pristine white sands of sunny Florida. Nothing about the beach bothered her; but there was much about the murky river, dense woods, and rugged hills that did. These creepy bats, for example, scared the hell out of her. Their wings, their little hand-like claws, the thought of those claws touching her made her gag. Their ravenous squeaks pinged and pinged. Even with her hands clamped over her ears, she could hear them. They flew east in a shadowy smudge beyond the Silver Nugget and up Goat Hill where darkness had already dropped and the night swallowed them.

Good riddance, she thought as she straightened up to unload the last box she needed to in order to be able to stretch out and sleep comfortably in the back of the Odyssey. She unfolded the tarp Al kept in the trunk for God-knows-what emergency and carefully covered her table. This stuff was all she had, and she needed every dime she could get for it.

She went to the back of the van, lifted the tailgate, and in the dim interior light looked at the narrow space where she would spend the night. As she stood there, the mosquitos discovered her. She felt them biting her ankles and calves, her thighs right through the Spandex of her running capris.

"Shit, get away from me you little bastards!" she scolded them as she climbed in as quickly as she could. For the second time in a day Hester cursed out loud. *That's not like me,* she thought as she lowered the hatch. But she had no patience left, no sympathy, not tonight, not even for some of God's smallest creatures who were simply trying to survive.

All afternoon she hadn't allowed herself to think about how hungry she was, about how she only had a dollar something in her wallet and not much more than fifty bucks in the bank, about the fact that she didn't have a stitch of clothes other than her smelly running outfit, and especially about how the back of this minivan was her only home now.

Four

Hester jolted awake. The face of a man in a baseball cap was pressed against the window of the van, his large nose smooshed to one side against the glass. Lights slashed the darkness behind him.

It's the dealers, Hester realized. She pushed the hatch of the van up, and scooted out into the dark.

"You're in my goddamn spot, Sister."

Hester couldn't see the person clearly yet, but the hoarse voice was definitely female.

The woman pulled a small flashlight out of her pocket, beamed it right into Hester's face forcing Hester to block the blinding light with her hand. Hester smelled cigarettes, mouthwash or booze, she couldn't be sure which. The woman rumbled up a wet cough. Her smelly breath was a hot assault on Hester's cheek, and Hester rubbed it as though she'd been slapped.

"I'm sorry, but the recording on the phone clearly said the tables were available on a first-come basis," Hester explained. "I thought that meant the first person to arrive can set-up wherever he or she wants. I know I'm new at this, but…"

"Listen, girly, I been comin' here for years; and I'm always in this spot, under this tree, so I don't give a damn what anybody told you on any damn phone. This is my spot, and you're gonna have to move."

Hester stared at the outline of the woman's head, the dome of a baseball cap, a wreath of frizzy hair sticking out on all sides. She looked beyond the headlights coming from the old lady's car. Black forms clomped around like zombies slowly unloading their wares.

If she moved now, where would she move to? The spaces all seemed to be occupied. The sun was about to rise. She could see the pale whiteness above the trees on the hill. No, she wasn't going to move. Her mind was made up. She wasn't going to give in. If it were last year or six months ago or maybe even the day before yesterday, she probably would have; but she'd spent most of her life giving in and where had that gotten her. No, she was going to try a different tactic now. No more Mrs. Door Mat, or rather Ms. Door Mat.

"I'm very sorry you got here so late; but I've been here since last night, and I'm almost completely set up so, no, I won't be moving anywhere."

"You kidding me? Didn't you hear me?" the woman raised the flashlight like it was knife she might use to stab Hester. "This is *my* spot."

"I heard you; but as I pointed out before, according to the manager, there is no such thing as anybody's spot. I am truly..."

"God damn you." The woman's voice grew loud and angry. "God damn you, you brazen little…. I'll teach you a thing or two about doin' what you're told to do." She was gesticulating wildly, the beam of the flashlight disappearing with the dawn.

The dealers nearby stopped what they were doing and stared. Hester nerves were frazzled. The last thing she wanted to do was draw attention. What if someone recognized her? Her face and her name had been plastered all over the local papers. If someone did recognize her, she might be run off the premises.

The angry woman hollered even louder, "Who do you think you are? Wait till the office opens up, and you'll find out just how fast you're going to have to move. Why I hope Jimmy tells you to get the hell out of here!"

A young man hurried down the aisle toward them shouting, "What's all the yelling for?"

When he was closer, it was clear to Hester he was young, only in his early to mid-twenties, maybe. His black T-shirt was faded, his blonde hair long and tangled, he needed a shave; but his face was surprisingly handsome and kind.

"Thank God, Jimmy," the woman screeched. "Tell this so and so to get out of my space." Her voice was like nails on a chalkboard.

The sun crested the hill and shone right in the woman's face, and Hester was surprised to recognize her. Years ago, Hester bought something from her. The Gaudy Welsh teapot. God, as Hester shelled out eighty-five bucks, the woman couldn't have been sweeter. And Hester didn't remember her looking so scruffy.

Is this what you turn into when you have no money? The thought sent a shiver up Hester's spine. *What you look like when you wind up on the wrong side of the table?*

The young guy named Jimmy was frowning down at the women, and Hester, despite being embarrassed, couldn't stop staring at him. *A young Brad Pitt*, she thought, which was nice.

She tried to remember if she'd seen him at the market before. As she gave him the twice over, her eyes met his, an incredible shade of violet, translucent as the violet Fostoria goblet she had on her table. His gaze was penetrating. She looked down at the dirt. She was filthy and probably looked as shabby as the crazy lady, maybe worse. Hester cringed. The older she got, the more young men seemed to look right through her. At fifty-two she registered with them about as much as a spindly tree in a thick forest registered on a young buck who need a good place to rub his antlers. So why was this golden-haired boy still staring at her?

She glanced up. Yes, his eyes were on her, and she watched in amazement as they slowly traveled down her body.

Hester steeled herself. Jimmy didn't look too happy. She couldn't crumble today. She had to stand up for herself, demand her rights. After all, she was there first, and rules were rules.

But this other woman was clearly a regular and Hester was nobody and this guy's eyes were boring a hole right through her confidence.

Jimmy's gaze shifted to the other woman, "Calm down, Joyce, would you? You're making a mountain out of mole hill, but what else is new?"

He looked around at the gawkers who had stopped what they were doing to observe the confrontation.

"Alright, everybody, show's over, go on about your business. I'll handle this."

The spectators dispersed. Joyce kept her beady eyes on Jimmy, one hand on her hip, and held the thin flashlight up like she planned to smoke it.

"Jimmy, how many years I been coming here? Almost as long as you been alive. Now this, this... interloper wants to take my spot. I got here, like I always do, just before dawn; and here she is already in *my* spot."

Jimmy plowed his hand through his hair, looked down at his clipboard. "Joyce, come on, you know what the rules are. The spots go in the order you arrive. This is nothing new. Look, I'll let you go under the pavilion for the same price as out here. If it rains, you'll make out a whole lot better than this lady."

"It ain't gonna rain, and you know it. I can't believe you are siding with a complete stranger. Have you ever seen her before? No, and I been selling here for as long as this place has been here, and this is how I get treated? I tell you, Jimmy, I want my spot! If your father were alive—God rest his soul—why he'd make her move and do right by me, his most loyal dealer."

"Joyce, my father's not dead. Remember, he moved to Florida."

"With that tramp, Theresa. Don't you think I know that? I just say 'dead' because he's dead to me. Where is he when a loyal customer like me needs him?"

Jimmy glanced down at Hester. In the brighter sunlight, the short stubble of his beard looked dusted with gold, and she saw his skin was pocked in a few places just enough to keep him from being too pretty.

He sighed, "Mrs.?"

Hester almost said Murphy, but caught herself.

"It's Randal, Ms. Randal."

"Look, Ms. Randal, Joyce has been coming here a long time, and she does always set up in this spot so would you consider moving? Please?" His voice sounded more patient, almost sweet.

24

Hester turned and looked at the tarp-covered table. All of that stuff would have to be moved, and then all of the stuff still in the van would have to be unpacked. Did she have the strength? Besides she had wanted to be in the shade. Her skin couldn't take the sun anymore. She didn't want to end up looking like a tomato or, worse yet, like the old crank, Joyce. She was tired and starting to feel pretty cranky herself. She wanted a cup of coffee, a croissant, a bagel, anything. She was hungrier than she ever remembered being before. She wanted a hot shower, a clean pair of clothes, and she didn't want to move.

She looked at this guy Jimmy and decided she owed it to herself to dig her heels in. She folded her arms across her chest.

He read her body language.

"Okay, so we have a stalemate. I can see that. So, Ms. Randal, I'm going to make you an offer-you-can't-refuse. I will personally help you move everything to not one, but two choice tables under the pavilion, and I'll only charge you for today, not for tomorrow. Sunday'll be free. That'll save you fifty bucks."

Fifty dollars! Don't give-in, and look what happens. Hester wanted to laugh and do a victory dance, but she didn't. She'd wait till the move was fully executed before she'd so much as crack a smile.

She nodded solemnly at the Jimmy. "You make it difficult for me to stick to my guns."

"Problem solved?"

"Yes," said Hester as Jimmy checked something off on his clipboard and looked at Joyce. "You owe me, old girl."

"Well, damn you, you didn't offer me a free day." Joyce stood on her toes and almost spit the words into Jimmy's face. "And cut out that 'old girl' stuff. It ain't nothing but a stupid oxymoron, you moron."

But Hester could tell by the glint in the woman's eyes she was teasing Jimmy. It was obvious she felt she'd won and was pretty satisfied about it.

Jimmy put his clipboard on top of Joyce's car and as soon as he helped Hester lift the tarp, the pickers descended. They were a mish mosh of dealers desperate to replenish their inventory, of middlemen hunting down anything they could flip to a more upscale operator, and of the delirious collector, which is what Hester had been. It was a food-chain, or the rings of hell, depending on the way you looked at it. These folks didn't get out of bed in the dark for nothing. They were a motley, cutthroat crew, jostling around each other, snatching up anything anybody else so much as looked at. Through jewelers' loops they examined potters marks, signatures, impressions trying to determine authenticity, detect repros. They ran fingers around rims feeling for chips. They held things up to the light and flicked them to check for cracks. It was a feeding-frenzy. Hyenas on a carcass couldn't have been more ruthless.

Hester recognized her past self in their hoary determination to get what they wanted. Had she really been this desperate? Back then she certainly didn't need to resell anything. No, back then it had been nothing but covetousness.

"How much on the platter, lady?"

"What'a you gotta get for the majolica?"

"Best price on that Fiesta gravy?"

Hester couldn't keep track. Everything was happening too fast. She hadn't planned on being rushed like this. She shouted out a number, unsure it was what she really should get for the item, or rather, needed to get for the item. Someone shoved a few bills in her hand and walked off with something that quickly disappeared into a backpack. What exactly? She wasn't sure. Every time she said a price, someone jumped down her throat about how she was crazy and asking too much.

"I'll give you half."

"No, I'm sorry I can't…"

"Here take half!" The crunched up bills were in her hand. The object was gone. There was no time to think or stop them from walking away with her things. Jimmy kept on packing, ignoring the impudent scavengers who were now coming behind the table to rummage through the bins he just finished filling. Hester had the sinking feeling she was getting ripped off.

Meanwhile, Joyce stood on the sidelines fuming. These were her vultures, and they should've been descending on her stuff.

It was getting out of hand. A big bald guy trying to reach a Limoges platter bumped into Jimmy and almost knocked him over.

"Look out, will you?" Jimmy snapped out of his stupor. "Would you just cool it, all of you? I've got to move all of this stuff over under the pavilion. Go get a fucking cup of coffee and come back when she's set up. She's got a lot more in the van that she hasn't even put out yet. So get a grip, you animals."

A few of them hurried to the van and shone their flashlights through the windows into the back.

"Hey, not now! Stop acting like a bunch of horny mutts who need a good hosing!" Jimmy growled. Hester watched as the pickers wandered off.

It took Jimmy and Hester another forty-five minutes to relocate her things. When they finished, Hester stood before the table and looked at it. How she wished she'd grabbed the camera from the shelf in the hall closet because the arrangement of her beautiful objects on her table was as good as any art installation she'd ever seen. A photograph of all that would soon be gone would've been a small something to have, but something nonetheless. So many hours of her life had been devoted to buying these things, and what a long, happy shopping spree it all had been. When Al was too busy, when it was Saturday and she couldn't read one more student essay, she went shopping. It was about that time Al started referring to her as a "junk collector" and what she bought as "trash." *Not trash, you...asshole, but treasure,* she thought now.

And already so much was gone, so fast she couldn't remember exactly what was missing, what the hungry hoard had stolen from her for a couple of bucks. She counted out seventy-two dollars. It seemed a small an amount. She handed thirty of it, the Saturday rent, to Jimmy and thanked him for cutting her a break. "I don't want to hold you up."

"You're not holding me up, Ms. Randal..."

"Call me..." Hester was afraid to say Hester. It was such an unusual name, and Jimmy might have read in the papers about the trouble concerning Alexander and *Hester* Murphy and a former student of theirs from Sourland High School, which was only a few miles from the Nugget.

Maybe she should say her name was Lucy. She liked that name, a saint's name, the Italian virgin who refused to marry the local prince so he had her breast ripped-off with pincers, or was it her eyes gouged-out with pincers? Hester couldn't recall the exact story, but the point was that Lucy was a great saint who stood her ground. If Hester used a fake name, she couldn't do better than Lucy.

But maybe the Lambertville papers didn't cover what happened at Sourland High. Maybe Jimmy didn't read the papers. Maybe she didn't have to lie. She didn't want to lie, and she didn't want to be lied to ever again. She was done with lies.

"Hester. Call me Hester." She felt brave saying it.

"I had fun helping you...Hester." Jimmy spoke her name carefully, like it was a cool pearl of a word that felt good in his mouth.

For some reason the sound of her name, the way he said it, made her shiver.

Five

Around three in the afternoon the wind kicked up. Dust swirled and covered the things left on the table. Hester was worried about what hadn't sold and how dirty it was all getting. The Imari service would've brought in big money. She was hoping around four hundred. It was worth three times that.

And there was the solid gold shaving kit she'd bought for Al on their first anniversary. It was in such pristine condition. By the end of the day, she would've taken an even hundred dollars for it if someone had so much as glanced at it. She lifted the lid of the case. There was the razor nestled in the black velvet. There was its blade. Something for a man who had the world by the balls. Maybe tomorrow one man would come by who would see it as she had and be willing to put up with inconvenience for a touch of class.

She closed the lid and put the case down again on the table.

Most of the dealers left hours ago. A few procrastinators, though, slugged along, wrapping, packing, lifting, loading. A bunch of weary bone-burners, like in Dickens, buying up horse bones and turning them into soap, this tribe of the self-reliant fringe tried like hell to turn trash into treasure. By this time of day, though, they'd run out of steam. A funeral procession would've been livelier.

The Silver Nugget doesn't look so silver now, Hester thought as she looked down the almost empty rows of tables and saw garbage spilling out of the cans and balled up newspapers rolling across the lot like tumbleweeds.

She had to sleep in her van again that night so she tucked her head down against the blowing dirt and picked up her pace. She was trying to straighten things up before she covered the table with the tarp.

Another night.

She had to admit she'd been half-expecting it. The possibility wasn't a cogent thought, more a persistent fluttering in her chest as though a nervous bird was trying to beat its way out. Those serious-looking envelopes shoved in the drawer. She ignored them, even the ones from the mortgage company and the condo association. Shame on her. As bad as ignoring a lump in a breast. You feel it, but don't panic right away. No, you keep palpitating, hoping you were wrong. Then you pretend not to feel it. Pretend it's gone. But in the end it is still there threatening to take the rest of your life away.

Not that being thrown out of her home was at all like getting breast cancer. It wasn't. It wasn't that bad. Nothing is that bad. Cancer could kill her. This wouldn't. This would make her stronger.

Repeat that affirmation.
This will make me stronger.
This will make me stronger.

She had her car, her stuff to sell. There were still unopened boxes in the van. Too bad, though, she hadn't gotten a single thing out of the condo. The year before they retired, Al had made numerous expensive purchases, including several George Nakashima pieces. He had a small fortune wrapped up in a table, bench, and two chairs. Al said they were an investment, and down the road, their value would sky-rocket. To Hester they seemed too primitive, made the way they were from rough-edged slabs of wood, but she had to admit the Nakashima touch did something to warm-up all the glass and steel.

Why think of that now? It was all gone.

She shook out the tarp alongside the table.

But what if she did find a lump in her breast? What if she got a fever or a broken bone or was struck with an attack of appendicitis? A sore throat, a toothache, even a cut that needed stitches would be a disaster. Along with her pension and Al being gone, all of her benefits were too. Ailments loomed in her imagination like the monsters that use to hide under her childhood bed. If she acknowledged them, they would come after her and gobble her up.

And her personal belongings were gone. As much as she liked antiques in her home, she was a modern woman when it came to clothes and accessories. She missed her Michael Kors silver sandals—she'd bought them last week when her credit card still worked. Her straight-legged Seven-for-Mankind jeans, her new black Polo shirt with the large pink logo, her Lily Pulitzer teal plaid sheath, her Bali bra with the racer back straps, her silk pajamas, her... She owned so many lovely things, or, rather, she had owned so many lovely things.

Who has them now? Where's my jewelry? Where's my Lancome mascara, my Chanel concealer, my Retin-A, my electric toothbrush? Who's sleeping in my bed? Who reached under the sink and found that vibrator?

Hester broke into a sweat and her legs wobbled beneath her. It was time to call it a day.

She turned her face away from the wind and the swirling dust, and saw Jimmy coming out of the office. He went to his pick-up, threw something into its bed, and headed in Hester's direction.

Please, don't make me leave. Please, don't make me leave.

The wind whipped his unbuttoned shirt back, and Hester could see the muscles of his torso through his thin white undershirt. She felt her hands go to her hair. It was grimy and knotted. She tried uselessly to rake it smooth with her fingers. She felt in her pocket for her lipstick, but it wasn't there. *Foolish, stupid lady,* she thought, *trying to be cute, look cute like one of those teenage girls you use to teach, like Nina.*

"What in the hell are you still doin' here?" Jimmy shouted loudly from several yards away.

Hester didn't know how to answer. He was in front of her. "Well?" He didn't sound that angry. Maybe she wouldn't have to leave and be forced to find some God-forsaken place like a back street in town or the food store lot to park for the night. If the police found her in one of those places, they'd arrest her?

What am I still doing here?

How should she answer?

31

Trying to keep myself out of jail?

It was the truth, but how could she explain it.

She couldn't.

The wind was tousling Jimmy's long hair and blowing hers in front of her face. She tried to gather it in her fist and pull it back.

"Uh, hi. I was just taking my time here. I hope you don't mind. I'm a little worn out from all the action today."

"How did you make out?"

"I haven't taken a final count, but I think I did alright." Damn, there she was lying again when she'd pledged not to. Hester knew exactly how much money she made, four hundred and sixty-eight dollars, but she didn't trust that this man wouldn't change his mind and make her pay for the table tomorrow, and surely he'd make her go rent a room somewhere. But she couldn't waste the money on a luxury like that. She needed to pay Lou the rent.

"For a virgin you probably did do alright. Those pickers this morning were brutal. I felt like kicking their butts for you."

Hester smiled. When was the last time she genuinely smiled? A year ago, before the hurricane, before she found Nina's dead body next to Al's naked one?

"Yes, in spite of those rude people," she agreed, "I'm pretty happy with how it all went."

"Want to celebrate?"

Jimmy was looking at her pleasantly, but she couldn't, for the life of her, imagine why. A man young enough to have been one of her more recent students, suggesting they celebrate? She turned and looked at the trees on the other side of the road and noticed how much their branches were moving in the wicked hot wind. She was a mess and ashamed. She could smell her own unpleasant body odor. Not knowing what to say, she kept watching the frenzied tree tops.

She was remembering something, something she'd thought she'd buried. It was a windy afternoon at Sourland High and so late that almost everyone had left but the janitors. She was sure Al had told her he'd be at the Board Office. She was out of computer paper so she headed to his office to get more. On her way she remembered watching the treetops dance in the wind through the windows of the main hall. The key went into the lock easily. Leave it to Al to see that the janitors kept his lock well-oiled. Hester didn't hear the heavy breathing until she had the door halfway open. She stopped in her tracks and peeked in.

Al was standing next to his desk facing the door, a girl was kneeling in front of him. Was this some kind of punishment? Making her kneel, her hair falling down between her narrow shoulders like a gleaming ebony waterfall?

Stop! Hester tried to holler. Nothing came out. Her hand was on the hard knob. Her secret hell. She'd known almost from the start what sort of monster Al was.

Jimmy was waiting. Hester looked at him. Why was he being so kind to her? Maybe all it was, was pity. He probably knew she'd been in his parking lot all night. He probably felt sorry for someone so old and so obviously desperate.

Hester blinked away the vision she'd dredged up.

Let go and let God... She'd read a story about a woman who was addicted to crack. When the woman was trying to stop using crack, she kept repeating to herself, let go and let God...let go and let God.

Hester dug deep and tried to find a reason to smile. This young man named Jimmy had taken the time to come over to talk to her, ask her how she made out, invite her to "celebrate;" and here she was reliving her shattered past and trying to figure out why someone, anyone, would be nice to her.

Maybe God sent him. A gift to help her let go.

Despite being exhausted and the sweltering dust-bowl-of-a-day and looking worse than she ever did, this thought made Hester feel light-hearted enough for a small smile to again transform her face.

Jimmy smiled back.

Six

Hester agreed to go with him for one drink. Jimmy helped her cover her table with the tarp and anchor the corners with rocks. She locked up her van. They walked to his truck, and he helped her in, even handed her the seat belt, pulling it out from next to the seat and passing it off to her.

How considerate, she thought.

But when he closed the car door and the wind stopped and it was still and quiet for a second, Hester had a sinking feeling. She knew nothing about Jimmy except that he seemed to own or run the flea market. He could be a weirdo, a rapist, a serial killer. Who knew?

On top of these misgivings, Hester felt dirtier than she had in her whole life. Dust clung to her running shirt and coated her sneaks. It was on her teeth and in her mouth. The polish on her nails was chipped. She tried to pick off the rest without the young man noticing. She didn't need a mirror to know she looked terrible: no make-up, no lipstick. This wasn't her.

Jimmy backed out of the space and turned on the radio.

Handel's Water Music? Hester snuck a look at Jimmy's profile. He was rolling his head around to the score, sort of conducting it in his mind. He appeared to be in his own little world—content, spellbound. The expression on his face was a shadow of what it had been when he was talking. He looked adolescent, weird, distant, and not that handsome. His nose had an odd bump in the middle, his ears were too small.

As the sun flickered through the thick foliage that lined the road, Hester sank into a lugubrious mood. If she wound up dead in a ditch, who would look for her? No one. She'd been estranged from her parents and her sister for decades. Friends? Former coworkers? They wanted nothing to do with her. She sighed audibly, but Jimmy had begun humming along with the Handel and didn't notice, had, perhaps, forgotten she was even there. He parked on Union Street across from Bull's Tavern, turned the ignition off, and the music died.

Inside, the bar was empty. Two waitresses were in the dining room folding napkins. When they sat down, the barmaid, a cute blonde woman who was probably as old as Hester but looked, at the moment, light-years younger, came out of the kitchen. Relieved Jimmy had actually taken her to a public place, Hester relaxed and watched the barmaid rinse her hands in the stainless steel sink. Hester envied her penciled-in eyebrows, her mascara-coated lashes, and pink glossy lips.

It was a little after four. A baseball game was playing on the flat screen. Hester ordered a glass of Chardonnay, and Jimmy, an Amstel draft.

Jimmy picked up his beer and tipped it toward Hester, "Cheers, virgin."

"Cheers." Hester clinked her glass against his bottle.

They sat there quietly and drank until Jimmy said, "I'm glad you made some money today. The first time selling is tough."

"Yes, it sure was especially since all of my things meant so much to me. But I have to let them go. I really have no choice." Only a few sips of wine in, and already Hester was opening up. She leaned back and held her glass up in front of her like she was at some cocktail party. Yeah, she felt pretty good all of a sudden.

"Most people in the flea market business don't have a choice. What's your story?" Jimmy asked.

"Long story short. I divorced my husband and he ran off with every dime we had."

"That's a damn shame, but, unfortunately, I've seen it happen over and over again. More now than even a few years ago. Times have gotten brutal. People have their heads in the sand. The economy's tanked. Don't get me wrong, though. For me it's great.

When everything else is going down the tubes, a place like the Nugget's golden," Jimmy said. "Look, everybody and their uncle wants a table just to get their hands on some cold, hard cash. And then there's the regulars, the dealers who make being a flea—that's what I call them—their fulltime job. In times like this they're the ones buying. In a down economy they stock up for when the prices go up. That's why they're all over you like flies on a carcass. You've got good stuff, the kind of stuff they hunt down. Just be aware of that. Don't let them harass you into a loss. Stand up for yourself. Don't be a pushover or they'll pick you clean and you won't have much to show for it."

Hester let the words wash over her a minute. *Stand up for yourself...*

"Good advice," she said and turned to face him. "You seem to know a lot for someone so young." Damn, if she didn't sound obtuse, empty praise from an empty-headed old woman.

"Hester, look, it's not how long you've been alive; it's what you've been through that teaches you things." Jimmy held her eyes in his violet gaze, and she thought, *if he only knew what I've been through and how recklessly stupid I've been in spite of it all.* But she didn't want to talk about herself. She wanted to sip her wine and pretend she could do this...she could start over again.

"So what exactly have *you* been through?" Hester's tone verged on being sardonic. There was no way this kid had a history that could top hers.

Jimmy downed the rest of his beer, pushed his mug forward to signal he wanted another one. "If I tell you what I've been through, promise you won't hold it against me?"

Hester laughed, a high-pitched giggle. She remembered what some of the lug-heads when she was teenager used to say to her, "If I tell you, you have a nice body, will you hold it against me?"

"No, Jimmy, I won't hold it against you." Hester, suddenly a bit dizzy and perspiring, fanned herself with the coaster.

How long had it been since she ate?

The barmaid put a basket of garlic bread in front of the guy next to Hester. How divine it smelled, that bread and the steak that came out next. Salivating, Hester considered ordering one, but would Jimmy think she expected him to pay for it? She didn't. But if she told him she'd pay, then she might get stuck with the whole check, and she'd rather starve then part with that much money. She could go without food, but she couldn't bear to lose what she had in storage. She blotted her face with her cocktail napkin.

"Alright then," Jimmy said. "Since you asked, I tell you *exactly* what I've been through."

Seven

By the time Jimmy's second beer came, he wasn't sure why he wanted to tell this almost complete stranger anything. He watched Hester take a sip of her wine. He wouldn't call her pretty. Once a woman got to a certain age the word "pretty" didn't apply, and neither did the word "sexy." "Over-the-hill" would've been the way his cocky father would have labeled her, but that was his father, mean. Some days just the thought of Harold Raymer made Jimmy want to jump in the river with his boots on, sink to the bottom like a slab of granite, and never come back up. That'd be fine by him. It'd be over. All the memories would stop. When his body got good and bloated, the swift current would carry it to the sea where some big shark might devour it. He'd become one with a great shark. It'd be better than he deserved.

Jimmy looked over at Hester thinking he should just keep his mouth shut about his poor-excuse-for-a-father. But Jimmy couldn't think about his mother and his sister, let alone tell someone about them, without his misanthropic progenitor popping into his mind. Poof! His old man, self-satisfied smirk on his face, doing a stupid little jig inside Jimmy's head.

No matter how long it had been since Jimmy saw him or how hard Jimmy tried to pretend his father was dead or, better yet, never existed, good old Harold was only a half-a-miserable thought away. Harold resented his only son, blamed all his problems on Jimmy. The nasty things Harold did, the drinking, the angry outbursts, he was driven to do by the "stupid" things his "little show-off" of a son did.

Jesus, how he wanted to shout it in his fuming, son-of-a-bitch-of-a-father's face, I'm trying to take care of the family because you

39

aren't! And he was, at least until he did do something "stupid," until he made that one horrendous mistake.

Yeah, he'd be better off not digging up any of it. He looked at Hester. There was something about her eyes that got to him. They looked brown now, but in the daylight he'd noticed they were amber and flecked with gold like his mother Agnes's had been. Damn if this woman Hester didn't remind him a whole lot of his Mom.

Hester pushed her tangled hair behind her ears. Her lowlights were fading, her roots growing in. Her greying center part was starting to look like the stripe down a blonde skunk's back; but Jimmy liked her heart-shaped face. It was more angular than his mother's and her nose longer, but her lips were plump and her top lip perfectly bowed like Agnes's, and even like his little sister Alice's. Hester was smiling at him, a small, sweet, closed-mouth smile. Suddenly, inexplicably, he had the urge to kiss her. Why? He couldn't say. All he knew was he wanted desperately to cover this woman's perfect mouth with his.

Eight

Jimmy shrugged off this insane impulse, took a sip of his beer, and started. "My father Harry was a self-centered bastard. A real commando type, though he'd never been anywhere near the service."

Jimmy ignored the frantic yelling of the commentator on the television above the bar. "And the Yankees do it again! And the Yankees..." He leaned over his mug, his eyes widened, and he shook his head slowly.

"When I was ten years old, and my Mom was about to have a baby, Harry sent me over to the only neighbor he ever talked to, Mr. Hansen, and drove Mom to the hospital. I'll never forget the date, March 21, 1990, the spring equinox. Mom said she couldn't have picked a better day to give birth.

But right off the bat the next morning, I got a bad feeling. Harry didn't have much to say when he came and got me at Mr. Hansen's. At home in the kitchen as he popped the cap off a bottle of beer, he told me the baby was a girl. Her name was Alice. He didn't sound at all happy about it, and I could see the beer in his paw wasn't going to be his last. I headed upstairs to my room.

When Mom came home from the hospital a few days later, she wasn't holding the baby. Harry was. That was my second clue that something wasn't fucking right, my father not being the type to be walking around holding a baby, even if it was his own. And my Mom, who hadn't seen me for days, walked right past me. No hug or kiss. Nothing. I followed her up to her room and stood in the doorway as she sat on her bed and started mumbling to herself.

Harry was pacing in the hallway like a madman with the crying baby in his arms. Finally, he burst into bedroom, put the infant on her back in the bassinet, and hollered at my mother, 'Get a grip on yourself, Agnes. Get a goddamn grip on yourself.' When he slammed the door shut behind him, the baby started howling and punching the air with her tiny fists.

'Mom,' I said, 'aren't you going to pick her up?'

My mother looked at me like she just realized I was there and who I was. She reached out, grabbed me, hugged me. 'You came out alright, Jimmy. Thank God, you came out alright.'

'Mom, you've got to pick her up,' I pleaded.

But my mother laid back, covered her face with her hands, and started balling like a baby herself.

I heard the refrigerator door slam. Harry getting into his beer. And Mom crying so hard the bed shook. And the baby screaming her fool head off. I didn't know what the hell to do.

I looked in the bassinet. The baby's face was beet red, her eyes closed, mouth open, snot from her nose running into it. I put one finger out to touch her hand and she grabbed it. I tried to pull away, but her grip was strong and by some miracle she stopped crying. Then Mom stopped crying and everything got quiet. I was afraid to move so I stood there and let the baby hold my finger. I could see her eyeballs ticking around beneath her lids. She had a pink blanket wrapped around her, but her bare arms were out. They were soft-looking like she didn't have any bones. Her mouth was closed now and her lips were a miniature version of Mom's. I just started thinking I might like having a sister, but then her little face scrunched up, and she started wailing again. I looked over at Mom. She rolled over and buried her head in a pillow.

'Mom?'

Alice was howling louder now than before. I shook the bassinet. 'Stop crying. Stop crying.' But the baby smacked her lips like she was trying to catch flies and shrieked even louder. I wheeled the bassinet into the hall and into the room across the way that was going to be hers. Maybe moving would make her stop crying. It didn't work. I'd never picked up a baby, never held a baby, never even held a doll before. I was pretty nervous, but I reached down, put my hands on her sides like she was a football and lifted her up. Her head snapped so far back I nearly shit myself. It was when I was trying to shift her into the crook of my arm, though, that I discovered something was wrong, terribly wrong. In a panic I put her back down and opened the blanket.

Now I really was going to shit myself, where her legs and feet should've been were short flaps of skin with something that looked like tiny toe nails on the ends. I stood there holding my breath staring at the spectacle of this deformity. Then I started screaming my fool head off. 'Mom! Dad! Mom! Something's wrong with Alice!'

No one came, no one even answered me. I was about to run to my mother and demand something be done to fix what was wrong with Alice when my sister suddenly stopped crying. She seemed to be looking up at me. Her flaps or whatever they were, were hideous, but her face was beautiful. I bent over her. She smelled sugary. Her big eyes were open all the way, and her lashes were all clumped together from crying so much. I felt so sorry for her. I kissed her cheek, and swore from that moment on I'd look out for my little sister. The hell with my parents.

But in the next minute, she started up again and was screaming like someone was killing her, and Harry, drunk as a skunk already—he must've downed a few shots—came storming up, snatched her up like she was sack of onions, marched into his bedroom, and put Alice on the bed next to my mother. 'I'll be damned if I'm going to listen to this fucking racket a second longer, Agnes. Unbutton your blouse and feed your daughter.'

I watched from the doorway. My mother obediently sat up and slipped Alice beneath her blouse.

For a few days, Harry hung around and brought Alice to Mom for her feedings and even changed her diapers, but after a week he called my school, told them we had a family emergency, and I would have to stay home for a while. Then he taught me how to change my sister's diapers and went back to work.

Mom stayed in her room, curtains closed and lights out. She fed Alice, barely ate what I brought her, and got out of bed to go to the bathroom. Then one morning, she asked me to get her a beer. I didn't want to. It was bad enough Harry was drinking all the time. But she insisted she needed it to help her make milk for Alice. How could I argue? Then she wanted a beer every time she fed the baby. By night time, she'd be plastered and moaning how the way Alice was, was her fault.

But I thought the way Alice was, was okay. If she was under a blanket or had her sleeper on, you'd of thought she was perfect. She was too little to walk anyway so she didn't really need legs.

I felt bad, though, for Mom. Every time Alice whined, I had the sinking feeling it really was the beginning of the end for all of us.

'Your mother has post-partum depression,' Harry told me. Not that I understood what that meant. All I knew was that it didn't matter what you called it, Mom was not the same as she'd been before Alice, and there wasn't anyone around to help. I had no grandparents, no aunts, uncles, cousins. It was like my mother and father stepped out of a space ship onto the shores of the Delaware River, hiked up the hill, bought a house, and made a family, in complete isolation from anyone who knew them.

So everything fell on me.

I figured out a way to put two diapers on Alice so nothing could seep out of the gaps where chubby legs should've been. I figured out how to turn on the washing machine, first time I put in too much detergent, suds all over the place. Good thing Harry wasn't home. The clothes line had snapped so I laid everything on the grass and flipped it so the sun would dry it.

When Alice cried and her diapers were clean, I took her to Mom. It wasn't pleasant for me to be in there, but Mom didn't hold her tight enough or look at her. All Mom did was stare out of the window while the baby poked around blindly for one of her nipples.

Then one day that summer, Harry came home and told me he'd bought the Silver Nugget Flea Market and gone into debt to do it.

'Look, boy, you can help your old man. Just take care of your sister and your mother, and we'll get by. I'm counting on you, son.'

The way he said this so nice and all, it made me want to help out. I thought he'd changed, but after a while, Harry stopped coming home. Thursday through Sunday he had to keep an eye on his investment. Dealers got there at the crack of dawn. Some even came the night before, and he didn't want any of them to think they had the run of the place. On Mondays through Thursdays, he had to work on fixing things up.

When Harry was home, he ignored Alice, but not me. We'd sit at the kitchen table at night just like Mom and him used to. Harry would drink and blab about his big plans. I have to admit, I was pretty impressed and began at some point to believe my father, especially when he told me, '...and I'm doing all of this for you and your mother and that little girl in there. That little baby is going to need a lot of help you know, a lot of help her whole life; and that's going to take a hell of a lot of money.'

By August, though, I began thinking about school. I wanted to go back. I wanted to see my friends. When September came, however, Harry told me that wasn't going to happen.

'We're going to home school you, son.'

'What's home school?'

'You'll see. It'll be easy. You just have to make time to do your assignments.'

'But who's going to teach me?'

'Your mother and me are going to teach you.'

That didn't make sense to me. Mom stayed upstairs and barely said a word. Harry was always gone. No, I couldn't see either one of them teaching me anything, but the following week Harry brought a stack of books home and put them on the kitchen table in front of me. I wanted to cry, but held back because I didn't want Harry, who, I could tell, thought he had my whole life figured out, to see me breakdown. I hated him more now than ever. I thought of running away. The farther, the better, but I knew I had to stay for Alice's sake. I couldn't help myself and started sniffling. Harry pushed the pile of books aside. A few tumbled to the floor with a bang.

'Cut the crap, son.'

Just as I was about to get walloped, Alice started crying. Harry opened a bottle of beer, flicked cigarette ashes on the floor, and tilted his head like he was listening to the wind. I went all sweaty worrying about getting hit and what was wrong with Alice. When my father put the bottle of beer to his lips, I got the hell out of the room and took care of my sister."

Nine

Jimmy stopped talking and stared straight ahead completely lost in thought until the barmaid tapped him on the hand. "Another?"

"Yeah, sure. Why not?" He looked at Hester. "How about you?"

"Yeah, sure. Why not?"

"You know imitation is the highest form of flattery," Jimmy said and winked at her.

Winked? What was that supposed to mean?

Geezus, the man just spilled his guts about his poor handicapped sister and then he goes and winks at her. Hester felt the heat rise in her face, either she was having a hot flash or she was blushing.

Her? Blushing? Well, it was probably back in the ice age the last time a man winked at her.

She remembered her father used to wink at her after he'd told her some silly joke.

Her father…she knew what it meant to fear one's father. Though, as a young girl she worshipped him and strove to make him happy, Dad had been the strict disciplinarian, the stern, dealer-out of punishments: no dessert, no television, no friends over. But the ultimate punishment had followed his swift judgment of her after her abortion. No sympathy for the devil she'd turned into. Rather, she had to be banished, perhaps not to taint her younger sister, or more likely because her parents firmly believed abortion was murder.

After the fact, she did too. She'd murdered her unborn child. How could she expect her family to look for her; and, even though forgiveness was also a tenet of the Church, how could she expect them to ever forgive her? Hester never thought her separation from her family would be permanent, but, turns out, it was. Decades passed, the ache in her heart for them, never did.

Yes, she felt sympathy for this young guy. A severely deformed baby sister, a withdrawn mother, an angry father, whose anger had not been provoked by anything his son had deliberately done. No, there was no denying, Jimmy'd been through worse than she had.

She took a sip of wine. Her hunger forgotten, the wine was dulling her senses, dulling the memory of her past iniquity, warming her up with tenderness for this man sitting beside her; and she found herself thinking, if only I were twenty-five years younger.

But she wasn't. The hands of time could not be turned back, so to stop herself from thinking anymore silly things, she asked Jimmy what happened next.

"What happened next?" he said. "Well, things went along badly like this for a few months," he said and was back staring into his beer. "Then one morning in October, I was on the floor in the kitchen playing with Alice when Mom, still in dirty pajamas, no slippers, hair all matted, walked into the room and went to the fridge. I thought, oh no, but instead of a beer, she came away with a carton of milk, poured two glasses of it, handed one to me, downed the other, and went back upstairs.

The next day around noon, I was trying to mash some potatoes when my mother's voice startled me. 'You want some help with that?'

'Mom, what are doing out of bed?'

'Taking care of you, that's what.' Her voice sounded hollow and shaky. She had on a pair of wrinkled white slacks and her old stretched out red sweater, but she'd combed her hair and washed her face. She walked over and hugged me hard and I could feel her heart pounding.

The next week I went back to school, fourth grade.

That first day I worried about Alice. Would she cry too much? Have a messy diaper? She was seven months old and starting to figure out how to pull herself around on the floor. She might get into the garbage, put something in her mouth and choke. When I got off the bus, I ran up to the house in a panic. Alice was on the floor on her belly with a pot lid in her hand. Mom was at the stove stirring soup. I was so relieved I threw my arms around Mom and damned near cried.

Two weeks later, Harry walked in while Mom and I were snacking on popcorn and watching the Sonny and Cher show. Mom had been laughing at a joke Cher made, but she stopped as soon as she saw my father.

'What are you doing here?' she asked. She didn't sound happy.

'What do you mean, what am I doing here, Mrs. Raymer?' Harry never called her Mrs. Raymer, not like that. It made me squirm in my seat. 'Don't I live here?' Harry asked, a fake-looking grin on his face.

'Well, let's see, Harry. I haven't laid eyes on you in three weeks and three days so I wasn't sure where you lived.'

'Agnes, don't start anything. I dropped off food. You're not starving. And I'm home now, aren't I? And finally you've snapped out of that zombie routine.' Harry laughed an empty laugh and went in the kitchen to stash his beer in the fridge. He came back in the living room with one, sat on the couch on the other side of Mom, propped his feet up, and took a swig. He reached behind Mom, tousled my hair, and said, 'Hey, son, did ya miss your old man?'

'Yeah,' I lied. I didn't want any trouble.

Sonny and Cher were singing their closing song, "I Got You, Babe." Why couldn't my parents be like them, singing love songs to each other? Geez, it was too good to be true.

I kissed Mom, good night, forced myself to hug Harry, and went upstairs to check on Alice. In the light that beamed in on her from the hallway I could see how big she was getting, and heavier. Soon she'd be too big to carry around. Then what? Her covers were off. The empty legs of her pajamas made me realize Harry was right. She'd need to be taken care of, and it wouldn't be an easy job.

I pulled the blanket up to her chin and tucked the sides in around her.

When I came downstairs the next day, empty beer bottles were lined up on the counter, and cigarette butts piled high on a dish. I grabbed a fistful of dry Cheerios and ran to make the bus. Harry's car was still in the driveway. I hated leaving Mom and Alice home alone with my father, but I didn't want to miss school. My teacher, Mrs. McKay was going to take the class outside for some games.

I'd never has such fun, egg-tossing contest, dodge ball, soft ball, even a scavenger hunt. After lunch back in the classroom, Mrs. McKay told me she'd found a nice high school girl to help me catch up. Another teacher came into the room to watch the other kids, and Mrs. McKay walked me down to the library to meet Cecilia Kurts.

Cecilia Kurts was beautiful, and I couldn't take my eyes off her. She had long hair, black as night. Her tan skin glowed. She had puffy lips and enormous dark brown eyes that were so dark brown they looked icy black.

I sat across from her and Mrs. McKay left.

'It's a shame you missed so much school,' she said, 'but I'll help you. You know one day I want to be a great teacher. Helping you will be like helping myself prepare for that. So, actually, we'll be helping each other. But, remember, Jimmy Raymer, you must do exactly as I say.'

She looked at me and smiled. My mouth went dry. Cecilia smiling at me was the biggest thrill I'd had in my entire life. That first hour seemed like a dream. She was going on and on about diagraming compound sentences and where adverbs were supposed to go and stuff like that, and I didn't get any of it because I just could not stop staring at her face. When I got up to leave and reached the door, I turned to check and make sure she hadn't been a mirage.

No, she was sitting there at that library table, watching me.

I couldn't stop thinking about her. When I got off the bus and up the hill, Harry's car was gone. Good, I thought and rushed into the house to tell Mom about my great day.

'Mom?' I hollered, but the house was quiet, too quiet. And where was Alice? She was usually done her nap by now. She should've been on the floor playing. I hurried upstairs. The bathroom door was closed. 'Mom, are you in there?' I said as I pushed the door open. Alice was in the tub on her back, the faucet dripping, the drops of water torpedoing her right between the eyes. Her face was white like a glowing moon under water.

I scooped her up. She was limp and cold.

'Somebody help me!' I screamed. I tried to shake her to get her breathing again, but her head wobbled on her neck like it'd been snapped.

'Breathe. Breathe.' I begged, but she didn't.

I sat on the closed toilet holding her, hoping the warmth of my touch would bring her back. I sang, 'La, la, le, la, la,' over and over because when I sang like that she always smiled. She didn't smile, didn't breath. I studied the ringlets of her hair, her open eyes, swollen tongue, her perfect arms, her baby belly, the crease of her private parts, and her flaps. There was nothing more I could do. She was gone.

I kissed the top of her head, wrapped her in a towel, and put her back in the crib.

I ran outside, down to the river, screaming for my mother. She had to be there. She loved that river. Before Alice was born, we went there every day, even in the snow. Mom would say, 'Those ice floes are as big as rafts. We could go all the way to the Atlantic Ocean on one of those. What an adventure we'd have, hey, Jimmy?'

I wasn't too keen on riding freezing ice floes, but in summer with the hot sun crystal-studding the river, getting on a real raft with my mother and drifting all the way to the ocean seemed like a wonderful plan.

At the river's edge I saw something red caught in the bare branches of a downed tree. I skittered down the bank, crawled out on the trunk, and grabbed it. It was my Mom's sweater. I'd seen it enough times to know. I was getting really worried now. I walked a bit further and found her Ked's.

In a panic I ran to Mr. Hansen's house and pounded on the door. Mr. Hansen called the police.

The police asked a lot of questions about my father, about the last time I'd seen him. Then they took me back to my house, and I showed them where Alice was. When one of the officers took the towel off her, I saw the shock on his face and it made me want to punch the guy. We all went down to the river, and I led them to where I'd dropped Mom's things. By the time we got back to the house, my father was there. His face white as a sheet, he patted me on the back and said, "Don't worry, son. I'll handle everything."

And he did, and pretty quickly at that. Like he'd had a plan all along. He put the house on the market the day after Alice's funeral— the same day he threw her ashes in the river. When the house sold, he used that money to pay off the mortgage on the flea market and moved me up there with him. Owning the Silver Nugget free and clear seemed to turn Harry into a different man, or maybe it was the fact that he didn't have Agnes and Alice to worry about any more. Either way Harry seemed happier than ever before.

I never got over suspecting my father did something that drove my mother to drown herself in that river. But I was only a boy, and afraid of Harry, so I had to go along with him. One lucky thing for me, Harry was, now, hell-bent on making sure I went to school every day. Even when I was sick as a dog, my father gave me medicine and said, "Get your ass on that bus, son."

So then I was spending three whole hours a week, alone with Cecilia in the library. Mrs. McKay was impressed with my progress. I forced myself to concentrate on more than just Cecilia. I had to do okay so I could keep getting tutored, but not so great that I wouldn't need Cecilia's help anymore because being with her was the only bright spot left in my life. All my friends had started ganging up on me and teasing me about what had happened.

'His crazy mother drowned her own deformed baby then jumped in the river.'

'Betcha he's crazy too.'

'You're as crazy as you're old lady, Jimmy Raymer!'

'Crazy boy, crazy boy, crazy boy…'

Yeah, if I couldn't go see Cecilia three times a week I probably would've thrown myself in the river too.

One day a while later, I was feeling pretty down, and Cecilia must've picked up on it. She put her hand on mine and said, "Jimmy, don't worry. Someday someone will love you as much as your mother did and you'll love that person back and together you'll have your own baby to love. Then you'll be happy again."

I sure as hell didn't want to start blubbering in front of Cecilia, but my hand was trembling under hers. I wanted to beg her, will you be that someone? Will you love me?

But, of course, if I did say that to her or even something like that, she would've thought I was crazy."

Ten

Hester pushed her glass forward and rubbed at the wet spot on the bar with her wadded-up napkin. What a hell of a story? She wanted to say something comforting. Jimmy's arms were crossed on the bar, his head resting on them. God, her heart went out to him, and she had to restrain herself from reaching over and petting his hair.

"I'm sorry I went on like that," he mumbled, "but don't say I didn't warn you." He picked his head up, took a deep breath, and leaned back. "Give me a few beers and a good listener, and I'm blabbing like an idiot. Really, I'm sorry." He pushed his mug forward. The barmaid filled it and set it back down. He took a sip. Hester drank more wine.

She was high now and knew it. She stared at Jimmy's profile. He was watching the television, the light flickering on his face as though he were running through a stand of trees at dawn. She'd been wrong when they were in the car, he was handsome. The ruffled feathers of his long hair at the back of his neck and his strong beak of a nose made him look imposing like an eagle.

"Sorry, I talked so damn much," he said. "Now, what about you?"

What about her? How to explain?

The voodoo doll popped into her mind. She could talk about the voodoo doll. If she'd grabbed it from the glove compartment of the minivan and brought it with her in her pocketbook, she could've whipped it out and shown it to Jimmy.

Show and tell. Here's where I did this to the doll because Al did such and such to me. Yes, I stuck the doll with lots of pins because Al cheated on me lots of times. You see the doll is Al, and I wanted, at one time, to make Al hurt, all over the place. I even pretended to drown little Al in the sink and run him over with the car. Can you believe it? No, I see you can't. Yes, I agree, it is totally unbelievable. Yes, I agree, I must be making it up.

After the divorce, on a whim, Hester bought the six inch, burlap doll at the Sojourner Gift Shop on Bridge Street. The eyes and mouth were embroidered in black thread, and its long hair was brown yarn. It was dressed in denim overalls so it kind of looked like a male doll. When Hester got home, she cut the yarn hair short and used a black magic marker to draw in a big nose. Now it resembled Al. She took a wire twisty out of the kitchen drawer and tightened it around the doll's left ankle, which had been Al's bad ankle. Then she dropped the doll on the marble kitchen floor and kicked him into a corner.

Hester slept through to morning for the first time in months. The next day she picked little Al up by his feet and slammed him onto the granite counter. Wham!

She'd have to fashion genitalia for the doll. It would be work, but satisfying work. She'd buy some fabric to fix up a little penis for him. Then she knew what she would do. For now, though, she threw the doll, temporarily, into the garbage can under the sink like it was a piece of trash.

In the beginning, at least, when the doll was out of sight, Hester was able for the most part to go about her business as usual. But as time passed, her urge to torture little Al became overwhelming. She began keeping him in the glove compartment of the minivan. If a need to vent came on her suddenly, she reached in and pinched him.

Whether the real Al ever felt so much as a twinge didn't matter. She'd never be able to find out anyway because she didn't have a clue where he was, and didn't care. If torturing his effigy made her feel better, and right now it did, then so be it.

But since her eviction, Hester hadn't even thought about doing anything vile to the doll. The eviction had been the last straw, had squelched even her lust for vengeance.

No, Hester wouldn't tell Jimmy about the voodoo doll, or about Al.

Yes, she would let it all go now. Tomorrow, she'd put the goddamn voodoo doll on her table, sell it to the first person who looked at it, and root out all thoughts of Al, the snake, forever.

"Maybe some other time, Jimmy. I'm kind of pooped now." Pooped? What in the hell was she saying? It was the wine talking.

Embarrassed, she started to excuse herself, "I've got to use the little girl's room." The little girl's room? That was worse.

"Be right back," she mumbled and slid off the barstool.

The Ladies Room was beautiful. The walls were pale green. Three miniature paintings of the Delaware were grouped attractively over the toilet. A rattan mat covered the floor. Liquid soap, lotion, a basket of paper hand towels, and a glowing lavender-scented candle were neatly arranged on a shelf next to the sink. Hester relieved herself leisurely breathing in the lovely air, listening to the soft, piped-in music. When she washed up, she pumped soap into her hands and lathered them up under the hot water. She cleaned beneath each nail, rinsed thoroughly, and dried them. As she rubbed the citrusy-smelling lotion into them, an idea came to her.

She checked the lock on the door; then quickly took off her clothes, layered several hand towels together, wet them, and pumped lots of soap on the wad of towels. She washed her face, her neck, beneath her breasts, her armpits, between her legs, around her backside. *Oh, hell.* She stopped up the sink, turned on the faucet, filled it and pumped soap into it. Then she lifted one foot into the sudsy water and scrubbed it. Next, the other.

How wonderful the water felt, the soap smelled. She'd been so dusty and dirty. She was about to stick her head under the faucet and rinse her hair when there was a knock on the door.

"Just a minute," she shouted.

She patted herself dry with more towels and pumped a handful of lotion into her hands and started messaging it all over her body. No way was she leaving without creaming herself up.

"Anybody in there?" the voice was impatient.

"Just a minute."

She finished rubbing the rest of the lotion between her toes, shook out her dirty clothes, and hurriedly redressed. She watched herself in the mirror as she pulled up her spandex capris. How greasy her hair was, greasier than it had ever been.

Rinse it out. Go ahead. Do it.

"What the hell are you doing in there?" An angry voice, a volley of loud knocks.

Hester reluctantly aborted her plan—she didn't need any irate woman complaining to the manager—and opened the door.

"Sorry. Really, I am. I was having a little problem." The woman pushed past her.

"You almost made me pee my pants," she shouted and slammed the door in Hester's face.

Eleven

At first Jimmy thought it was Hester coming back from the bathroom, brushing up against him by mistake; but that voice...he would never mistake that confident, rich voice. He turned quickly. Cecilia was so close her breath warmed his face.

"Jimmy, I can't believe it's you!" she said, and her voice sounded like the plucked strings of a harp.

"Cecilia!" Jimmy was in shock. Here she was standing in front of him. Five years! Five long years since she'd broken off their engagement and moved away with her "new love." Those were the last words she'd spoken to him. "Sorry, Jimmy, but I have a new love, now."

He hadn't seen her since, and here she was right in front of him, like his telling Hester about her, had conjured her up.

"Can we talk, Jimmy?" Cecilia smiled at him as though she'd never left, as though nothing between them had ever ended, and the look she gave Jimmy was brazen, and the glossy blackness of her big, almond-shaped eyes was as sexy as ever. His heart pounded. Her long-lashed eyes reminded him of the eyes on dolls he'd seen on T.V. adds. Sexy dolls in hideous, tight clothes. Not Barbies. No. Punky dolls with huge black-rimmed eyes and wild-colored hair.

What the hell's this world coming to? He thought when he first saw the commercial. *Little girls play with those things?*

Bratz, that's what they were called.

That's what Cecilia had, Bratz' eyes.

She threw her head back and laughed, and the five years of agony for Jimmy dissolved. Her gleaming teeth, her pink lips were like an invitation to the paradise that was Cecilia. Her eyes glistened like hammered silver. Her wild mane absorbed and shimmered with what little light there was. Jimmy took in the sight of her. He didn't just love her, he worshipped her.

But the shock of seeing Cecilia flustered him and for a minute his mind shot back to that night, the night of the day he'd first met her in his school library, the night of the day Alice died and his Mom killed herself. He had gone to his room. His father had shut off the television, and the house got quiet, too quiet.

Cecilia doesn't seem real when I'm not with her, he laid in his bed worrying that she might not be. Had he imagined going to the library and meeting her? Had he?

He rolled on his side, closed his eyes, and tried to picture Cecilia on the black screen of his mind; but he couldn't make her pink lips or her shiny eyes or her wild hair appear. But she had to be real, she just had to, or what he'd done had been for nothing. And what had he done? What terrible thing had he done? The roaring current of the river…the water dripping from the faucet…which had he heard first? It was getting all mixed up in his mind. It was a terrible accident. It wasn't an accident at all.

He could never ever tell anyone the truth. Cecilia would turn on him like the boys in his class, though he knew he deserved to be stoned with their cruel words. He could absorb that pain, but the pain of not being able to see Cecilia again? That would've killed him.

That afternoon he did what he did so nothing would ever stop him from being able to see Cecilia.

Nothing.

Not even his beloved little sister.

Twelve

Hester had been in the restroom a long time. Jimmy knew he should stay right where he was and wait until she came back before he went anywhere with Cecilia, but there Cecilia was, right in front of him, finally. He'd felt nothing for so long, her nearness was enough to drive him mad with desire. She laughed again, "Let's go out and have a cigarette."

"Since when did you start smoking?" he said without thinking and knew immediately he sounded too judgmental. What did he care if she smoked? What did he care if she murdered somebody? He'd still love her, and still do anything she wanted him to do.

Cecilia shot him a glance that went right through him, and her voice had an uneasy edge to it. "Since nobody's business," she said firmly.

He stood up without taking his eyes off her. She was as tall as he was with shoulders nearly as broad. She wore no lipstick, but her lips were wet-looking.

To kiss those lips, that was what he needed.

He scanned the bar and looked into the dining room where the restrooms were. He didn't see Hester. Maybe, the woman had left without telling him. Anyway, he'd be right back. How long would it take for Cecilia to smoke a cigarette?

Cecilia took his hand— the feeling was electric—and led him in the direction of the door. He was so wrapped up in the moment, in the sensation of her hand in his, he didn't notice Hester's open pocketbook still hooked over the back of the bar stool. Cecilia was pushing her way through the crowd. Jimmy was holding his breath and felt like he was swimming upstream, pulling himself out of the muddy river, up onto a boulder, and into the sunlight.

He felt exactly the way he'd felt the first time he'd seen Cecilia outside of school. It was during the darkest days of his life, the days after Alice died, and his mother went missing.

It all came back to him now in a flash, Jimmy and his father waiting in a drab office while the cremation took place. Jimmy asking his father what cremation was.

"They burn up the body until it's nothin' but ashes." Harry was succinct if nothing else. Well, this information just tore Jimmy up inside. His sister would end up a pile of ashes.

After the cremation they drove to the house in silence. Harry pulled into the driveway, got out, and headed down to the river with the canister that held Alice's ashes. Jimmy followed and watched through the barren limbs of the trees. Harry crossed the road, the footbridge, the towpath, and went down the bank and out onto the rocks. As Harry was dumping the ashes into the muddy water, the wind kicked up and blew some back in his face and onto the front of his shirt. He put the canister down and furiously brushed his face and chest as though the ashes were alive and might singe him. Then he picked-up the canister and threw the whole thing in. He walked back past Jimmy without saying a word, got in his car, and waited for Jimmy to get in the other side.

At the apartment Harry parked himself in front of the T.V. with a beer. Jimmy went to his new room, threw himself on his bed, and put his pillow over his head so his father wouldn't hear him cry.

A month later, this lady friend of Harry's, Mrs. Theresa Marino, moved in and things took a turn for the worse.

Mrs. Marino was this dealer who came to the market every weekend to sell crappy old jewelry. Her display cases were full of piles of jumbled necklaces, bracelets, earrings, but because she always rented three tables, Harry considered her a valuable customer and even started helping her pack up her junk and chatting it up with her. Finally, one day he invited her up to the apartment for a drink. She kicked her dusty shoes off at the door, sat on the sofa, and put her feet up on the coffee table, the same one Jimmy's mother used to put her feet up on.

Then Harry said to Jimmy, "Take your stupid comics and go to your room. Theresa and me want privacy."

After that, she was always dropping in, fat rear end squeezed into stretch pants, gaudy earrings dangling from her big ears, fuchsia lipstick smeared on her fat lips. She bossed Harry around terribly and got away with it. Jimmy's mother was always the one who jumped up every time his father needed a beer or his plate was empty. Now it made Jimmy sick the way Harry catered to that whale, Theresa.

'Honey, how about I pick up a pizza and a couple of six packs for later?' or 'Hey, Theresa, sweetie pie, let me get that for you.' Sweetie pie? It stung Jimmy's ears to hear it.

He watched Harry hold the car door open for Theresa one night when he was taking her to the ice skating rink north of Stockton. The goddamn door. The goddamn ice skating rink. He never took Jimmy. Hell, Jimmy didn't even know there was an ice skating rink within a hundred miles of Titusville. It made Jimmy want to get a gun and shoot them both. Theresa with her fake-looking hair piled up on her head, her painted-on eyebrows making her look like a witch. God, he hated that woman, hated his father looking at her, which was a lot. Harry would yank his jeans up, unbuckle his belt, and tighten it the minute he saw Theresa's burgundy Explorer pull in. Harry had bought a brown leather jacket and gone to some hairdresser named Craig in New Hope and gotten what was left of his hair styled.

"Makes me look younger. Right, son?"

Jimmy wanted to tell him, makes you look like an idiot, Dad, but he wasn't old enough not to get slapped.

Right after Harry spruced himself up, he convinced Theresa to move in with him. She would, but she had to have her own room. "I gotta have my own space, Harry. A woman like me needs to spread out."

So Harry and Jimmy took his bed apart and carried it downstairs into the closet off the office. Jimmy was angry as hell at first, but then he got used to being by himself and was happy he was this far away from Mrs. Marino. He read a lot and spent hours dreaming about Cecilia, how one day he was going to marry her. He figured out the age difference. He was ten; she was sixteen. He'd wait to ask her until he was twenty-three, and she was twenty-nine. At least they'd both be in their twenties at the same time.

Jimmy's life downstairs was tolerable, but upstairs was a different story. Theresa was tough, always standing around with her hands on her hips complaining.

"Don't expect me to clean up this mess. Not on your life, Harry and Son-of-a-Harry. Not on your goddamn life. I'm no doormat!"

Her eyes narrowed into slits, her lips clamped shut into a mean, thin line.

Jimmy soon realized Theresa said "not on your life" a lot. There were a million things she'd never do, "not on your life," for Harry, or, as she took to calling Jimmy, Son-of-a-Harry. Jimmy knew she wanted to say son-of-a-bitch. He felt like shouting, just say it, say what you really mean. You think I'm a son-of-a-bitch, my mother was a dog. You hate me and my mother. And Theresa wasn't going to do "one goddamn thing" for little Jimmy because, as she put it, "Goddamn it, I am not your mother."

Well, he didn't want her for a mother. He didn't even want to be anywhere near her. He hated when she sat at the office desk painting her nails with that disgusting smelling polish or picking at a scab or smoking one of her Newport Menthols or humming some stupid song or telling his father what to do and exactly how to do it. The nastier she was, the better his father seemed to like her.

Young Jimmy couldn't help but conclude, Harry was getting what he deserved. Theresa was as bossy and self-centered with Harry as he used to be with Agnes. Jimmy loved his mother, but he could see now she'd been a "doormat." Theresa had planted this distressing thought, and it grew in his mind like a weed.

God, he tried to keep his distance and ignore her, but Mrs. Marino made him sick, her big mouth, her tight shirts, her big breasts, the furrow in her forehead that looked like a cut about to bleed. Jimmy wanted to hurt her. She made him feel like a-not-so-nice boy, like she knew bad things about him she had no way of knowing.

Before the old house had been sold, Harry put all of Alice's baby things in the trash, but packed every last one of Agnes's belongings and hauled them up to the market. At least, he told Jimmy, he'd get something back for all he'd spent. In the evenings, with Theresa's beady eyes boring a hole in the back of his skull, Jimmy was forced to help his father sort through his mother's things. Each item had to be priced, and each item pricked the thin skin of Jimmy's grief. Then Theresa spied something she liked and reached over Jimmy and snatched it, it was too much for him. It was the bracelet with two heart-shaped charms. One charm was engraved, James 3/19/1979, the other, Alice 3/21/1989.

"No!" he yelled, "you can't take that."

"You're not hollering at me, are you?" Theresa yelled back. "Harry, did you hear that? Did you hear your little brat?"

"My Dad gave that to my Mom. It has our names and birthdays on it. It isn't yours! You can't have it!" Jimmy's gut was on fire.

"And it isn't yours either," shouted back Theresa. "Your mother is dead. Get it, dead. That means she isn't coming back so I might as well wear it if I like it. Right, Harry?" She didn't even look up to see Harry nod, yes. She was too busy trying to force the tiny clasp of the bracelet to close around her fat wrist.

On the weekends, Harry opened the barn doors and made Jimmy sit on a stool and take the money when somebody bought something. In a notebook Theresa gave him, he had to write down what the item was and next to it the amount he got for it. Then he had to take the sticker off the item and stick it next to the notation. Theresa told him about twenty times exactly how she wanted it done.

After the first day of sitting there and watching as strangers tried on his mother's coats, twisted-up tubes of his mother's lipstick, sat at his mother's vanity, and stared at themselves in his mother's mirror, Jimmy had had enough. He got up his nerve just in time to snatch the old Beacon blanket his mother wrapped around herself on chilly nights out of the hands of a woman who was admiring it.

The next day in the office he begged his father, "Please, don't make me do it again, Dad."

"Don't make you do what again?"

"Sit there. Sell Mom's things." He kept his eyes on a spot on the floor in front of his father's boots.

"Are you kidding me, boy? What do you think? You're going to get a free ride? Money don't grow on trees so stop acting like the spoiled brat your mother turned you into. Now get out there, make some money, and don't come back in here till you do."

Jimmy's expression turned dark. Before he could leave, Harry grabbed him. "Grow up, son, and stop looking at me like that. I know you think I had something to do with what happened to your mother and your sister. Well, I didn't, so don't ever look at me like that again."

A few choice curse words crossed Jimmy's mind, but he kept his eyes down and left.

An hour later, who comes walking toward the barn but Cecilia, more striking in daylight than in the school library. Skin glowing, eyes bright, her lashes fluttering like moth wings, her lips, covered in fiery red lipstick, plump like ripe strawberries. Wisps of her long hair, freed from her ponytail, rode the breeze like seaweed caught in a wave. It was the first time he'd ever seen Cecilia outside of school. She was with an older woman, probably her mother, Jimmy thought. She held the woman's hand and seemed to be pulling her in his direction. The older woman frowned and shook her head as though she didn't want to go where Cecilia was leading her. Cecilia persisted, though, and soon they were close enough for Jimmy to hear Cecilia's voice. "Let me just say hello to him, Mom. Really, he's nice."

Nice. Jimmy couldn't believe it. Cecilia thought he was "nice." He stared at her mouth, at the lips that had formed the word, "nice." He wanted his lips to touch hers. He'd never kissed anyone

66

but Alice and his mother. They were gone, but here was beautiful Cecilia, and he wanted to kiss her.

Cecilia introduced her mother and chatted about the weather and the flea market. He was too shy to say much of anything, let alone get off his stool and kiss her; and now she was leaving. Cecilia had his back to her and was walking away when she turned and shouted over her shoulder, "See ya later, kid," like she was a hundred years older than him.

Kid? He almost hollered after her, I'm not that much younger than you; but Theresa was watching from her tables, and out of the corner of his eye, he saw her coming quickly toward him.

"Son-of-a-Harry," she shouted at him. "Why are you talking to a girl like that? I saw you staring at her with big puppy eyes. Your father isn't working his ass off to have you going after a girl like that. Can't you see she doesn't have a pot to piss in? Are you that blind?"

Theresa was such a loud mouth, and Jimmy saw Cecilia turn around and look at Theresa and then at him. Her eyes narrowed.

She'd heard.

That night Jimmy tried not to think about going upstairs and stuffing a pillow down Theresa's throat, but it was hard not to want to kill her after what she'd done. He despised her more now than ever. Who was she to say mean things about Cecilia?

When he stopped thinking about Theresa, he started thinking about how Cecilia had called him a kid.

There was some hope, though. What she said to her mother when she didn't know he could hear her, "…he's nice."

Nice. He turned the word gently over in his mind. It would be something for him to hang onto when he couldn't stop remembering Alice, under the water, the water scummy from urine and mucous, from her baby-life leaking out of her; when all he could think about was how the water fell away, the sound of it splashing back into the tub. He picked her up, shook her, the water running out of her nostrils, her mouth. He shook and shook her. Her head and arms flopped back and forth, back and forth. How heavy she was, how impossibly heavy.

His mother's body must have been even heavier. She must've sunk like a rock.

That night Jimmy had the same dream he'd been having for a while. He's on the bank of the river when he sees his mother pop up from the churning current and pull herself onto a boulder, shedding water like she's emerging from liquid glass, her wet blouse clinging to her like a second layer of pale skin, the sun glinting off the gold buttons. He tries to run to her, but his feet are gone, his legs are gone. He tries to holler to her but his tongue is gone too.

Yes, he would need that word that had come out of Cecilia Kurts' mouth so easily, because what he'd done was wrong, very wrong, and not one bit…nice.

All of this haunting memories passed through Jimmy's mind in the time it took him to follow Cecilia out of Bull's and around the corner of Union and Elm where they stood facing each other beneath the spotlight on the front of Nieces Hardware Store. Jimmy took a deep breath. He was close enough to smell Cecilia, coconut and tobacco. He watched as she pulled a Newport Menthol out of the box with her teeth and lit it.

Now that he saw her smoking, he didn't like the way it looked, and it wasn't good for her. He tried to ignore the way she sucked so hard on the cigarette. With her head in profile, thrown back, her thick hair falling away from her face, and the smoke streaming out her nostrils, she looked more dragon than human. Jimmy watched, at once disgusted and fascinated by the spectacle of his Cecilia smoking. He tried not to be turned off by it.

We all have bad habits, he told himself; but he couldn't help blaming Cecilia's "friend," that bitch Lola, for this, for a lot of things.

Cecilia inhaled again and her chest rose. His eyes dropped from her face to her breasts.

They're so huge they must be engorged, he thought. If he had the nerve to reach under her tight polo and squeeze them, he was sure milk would squirt out of their nipples. Her shirt was unbuttoned enough for him to see the tops of those mounds and the deep cleft between them.

Now that was the place he wanted to be!

He had all he could do not to reach out, pull her close, and rub his body against those goddamn perfect breasts. He would have if he thought for one minute she would let him.

Damn, it had been so long since he'd seen her, since he'd touched her.

Goddamn, if he didn't love every last fucking inch of her—so much it hurt.

Years ago, when Jimmy was only sixteen and Cecilia a senior in college, he rode his bike to Trenton State College, and they had their first sexual encounter in her dorm room. He'd come so fast he'd barely had time to suck on one of her huge tits. Just watching her take off her bra had been enough, and he struggled to get his thing in her before he ejaculated. After, lying next to her naked body, holding her hand in his, so grateful to her for letting him touch her, wanting to touch her again, he told her the same, long, sad story he just told Hester Randal. Maybe, Cecilia would feel pity, maybe Cecilia would understand how lonely he'd been. She had known his mother and sister were both gone, but she didn't know about cruel Harry, about Agnes' post-partum depression, about how everything had fallen on Jimmy, and how he'd risen to the occasion…well, for as long as he could.

When he stopped talking, Cecilia held him tightly and rubbed his back, and whispered, "I'm so sorry," in his ear. In a second he was hard again, and this time he did a little better. He got one of her breast in his mouth and did suck on it until he heard her breathing get heavy. He knew she was watching him and that made him feel like an idiot because he really didn't know what in the hell he was doing, so he rolled her over and took her from behind and was able to get in a few hard thrusts before it was over again.

Every chance Jimmy got he showed up at the dorm, and they did it again and again until Cecilia had to stop to study or go to a class. After a few months, Jimmy was so crazed with love for her, he got up the balls to beg Cecilia to marry him when she finished getting her masters. He knew she had plans to get her advanced degree in English Education. To his surprise—he was well aware of the fact that Cecilia Kurts was way out of his league—she said, yes, right after she became a teacher. And so the future spread out in front of the young couple like a verdant pasture.

But that was before Lola Giordano latched onto Cecilia. Cecilia had introduced herself to Lola, a renowned author, educator and guest speaker, at a professional development conference. Eager to advance, Cecilia wanted to get into this superstars inner circle. Maybe some of Ms. Giordano's shine would rub off on her.

"She's a genius. There's nothing she doesn't know," Cecilia gushed when she came home from that first encounter. "Jimmy, what can I say, I just love her!"

Lola was all Cecilia could talk about for days. And when Lola called and asked Cecilia to lunch, it was the beginning of the end, even though Jimmy didn't have a clue then that it was.

Thirteen

Bull's was crowded and noisy now. Hester was grateful. No one would've heard the commotion outside the Ladies Room. She worked her way through the dining room and into the bar. She felt so much better. How smart she'd been to think of freshening up like that.

She came around the end of the bar and excused her way back to where her seat had been. Someone else was in it. Jimmy was gone. Her open pocketbook dangled on the back of the stool behind the stranger. *Damn,* she thought, *thank God, nobody stole it.* She zipped it up, slung it over her shoulder, and left.

Hester stood in front of Bull's and looked around. The streetlights were on. She walked toward the corner but stopped when she saw Jimmy talking to a tall, young woman who was smoking and gesticulating wildly with the hand that held her cigarette.

Hester had been enough of a bother to the flea market manager for one day so instead of interrupting them, she crossed the street to the pick-up and sat on the curb to wait.

Her mind drifted back over the last twelve hours as she tried to remember exactly what she'd sold. She should've written it all down. The vaseline glass compote? Twenty-five dollars? Twenty-eight dollars? She couldn't remember exactly, but she knew it was worth ten times whatever she got. The guy with the toupee who bought it, knew it. After he'd haggled her down as low as she would go, and she wouldn't budge on her price, he put the compote down disgustedly and began to walk away. She had no choice but to call him back and let him have his way. It was the old bird-in-the-hand quandary.

The Redwing Stoneware, a fifty gallon crock. She'd only gotten fifteen dollars? She'd never find another one, not in that condition, not for hundreds of dollars.

The Millersburg carnival glass, the de Gourney crane, the French enameled La Toilette plaque. Things she thought she'd always have, sold off for a pittance.

The child's chair? Thirty measly dollars? How she loved the dark patina, worn seat, spindle legs, *Clyde* inscribed across the center support. She'd spent a small fortune on it when she thought Al and she were pregnant, when her life was on track, when she was sure she'd have a boy and Al would agree to name him Clyde…agree to anything she wanted.

Good the chair's gone, let the memories go too.

At least she'd made some money. Four hundred and sixty-eight dollars. She'd put it in an old envelope and shoved it in the bottom of her bag. It was a start, something to slip through the slot in Lou's door and rescue what was left in her storage unit.

Hester put her palms on the still-hot concrete, leaned back, and looked up at the wedge of sky between the houses. A cloud traversed the full moon. Jimmy's voice traveled down the deserted street. Hester couldn't make out what he was saying. Then he laughed. The woman laughed.

Hester turned. They were walking in her direction, their voices advancing.

Jimmy's body was close to the woman's.

Someone he knows well, Hester thought, and she felt a little pathetic sitting on the curb waiting around like some reject. She scrambled to her feet, hurried down the side street, and disappeared on the towpath.

She did have some pride left.

Fourteen

Cecilia tossed her cigarette butt into the gutter and watched its smoke trail. When she looked up, she spotted an unkempt-looking woman sitting on the curb by Jimmy's pick-up. Obviously another of his charity-cases.

How exasperating, Cecilia thought, *the way he's always catering to losers. His father being the number one example.* This lack of a backbone was the main thing, probably the only real thing, Cecilia didn't like about Jimmy.

She looked up at him. He was damn handsome, and there was so much they used to do that she did like…but Lola was waiting.

"Sorry, baby." It was what Cecilia used to call him when they were engaged. "Glad I ran into you, but you know how it is. Have to get to Dina's Trattoria. Can't disappoint my meal ticket," Cecilia said and then laughed at her own mean, little joke. She shouldn't tease Jimmy like that. She knew damn well Jimmy was no fan of her partner's. He blamed Lola for their break-up. Lola had money, fame. Jimmy had nothing, was nothing, compared to Lola. No, Lola hadn't been to blame. Lola hadn't seduced Cecilia. It had been, admittedly, the other way around.

After Cecilia got her first teaching job and moved into his apartment at the Silver Nugget, she assumed they'd buy Jimmy's father out. However, Jimmy was perfectly content to keep sending hefty checks to Harry in Florida, without any agreement to eventually take the business over. As long as his father and Theresa stayed there, Jimmy confessed to Cecilia, he didn't care if he owned the Nugget or not.

"Your father is a real whip-cracker, using you and abusing you; but that's not the worst part, baby. The worst part is, you let him. You refuse to stand-up to him." Cecilia was trying to nicely light a fire under Jimmy's ass, when what she really wanted to say was, where the hell are your balls?

She kept at Jimmy, though, and finally got through to him. He sent the next check with a note attached: Dad, want to buy the market. Name your price. Jimmy

No response, and Jimmy actually seemed relieved.

Cecilia saw the dead end sign at the crossroads and made a sharp turn in order to save herself from a life of too-modest means. When she met Lola and began to work for her, it didn't take her long to hitch her wagon to Lola's star. She didn't look back. She'd hurt Jimmy and felt awful about it, but she'd been raised poor and staying that way was not in her stars.

The sound of Cecilia's laughter echoed along the narrow street. She pulled the collar of her shirt up and flipped her hair from under it. She jammed her hands into the tight rear pockets of her jeans and looked up at Jimmy. She sighed, shrugged her shoulders, and kissed him, softly at first, but then harder. She held his face, pressed her lips against his, and forced her hot tongue into his mouth. She swirled it around and jabbed it deeper until he responded and his tongue was whirling around in her mouth. When he put his hand on her back and tried to draw her close, when her breasts touched his body for a split second, she pulled away.

"You know I love you, kid. Always did. Always will," she said as she ran two fingers over her lips, wiping away Jimmy's saliva.

And she was gone, walking down the street, running her fingers through her hair, shaking her head, shaking off their kiss.

Fifteen

The moonlight unraveled down the center of the Delaware & Raritan Canal in a wide white ribbon. No one was around. Hester picked up her pace. Everything would be fine as long as the moon was out. She could see the towpath clearly, the canal, the opposite bank, and the wide river beyond.

She had always lived close to the Delaware, and it'd always been a part of her life. She swam in it, fished in it, rode her bike along it, ran beside it, and drove thousands of miles of road in view of it. Exciting things took place on the river. There was the Shad Fest in spring, fireworks at Lambertville Station in summer, antique and quilt markets in the fall up in Tinicum, but her favorite event took place in winter on Christmas Day. The reenactment of George Washington crossing the Delaware was a big deal in the small town of Washington Crossings, eleven miles south of Lambertville. Her parents had taken her every year when she was a kid, and she took Al when they were married, even in snow and freezing temperatures. After all, the weather had been intolerable the day the General and his men made the trip. The only time there was a cancelation was if the river was so frozen the boats couldn't launch from the Pennsylvania side. That didn't happen often, so she had seen many George Washington's cross the Delaware.

Hester was grateful she was making her dark journey in late summer, at least she didn't have to worry about dying of frostbite. She was already approaching the Bridge Street underpass and thought about going up the ramp and to St. John's. Maybe the church would be unlocked, and she could light a candle, pray for a good day at the flea market tomorrow. But she was pretty sure she'd read somewhere that pastors didn't leave their churches unlocked anymore to due to the threat of vandalism. Too bad. Many nights when she was a young girl, her parents took her to church to light candles mostly for someone who was sick or who had died.

Hester kept going and passed the Lambertville Station and the backyards of the houses in the south end of town. Then the light of the moon reflected off the windows of her condo complex. So already she was this far. There was her unit! Her things! Her bed, her television, her cell phone, her stash of Tandy Cakes, her unread New Yorker!

She ran her thumbs over the tips of her fingernails. She could feel the ragged edges of her last manicure, the chipped polish. Her emery board? In the drawer of her vanity. She could see herself sitting at the vanity filing her nails, stopping a second to glance in the mirror, to admire her large amber eyes, straight nose, still-firm jawline, and perfectly high-lighted hair. On a Saturday night in the world of before, her sometime very attentive husband Al would have poured her a glass of Pinot, put on some smooth jazz, and admired her as she applied her lip gloss.

Snap out of it, she told herself. She had to stop thinking about Al like he was in any way, shape, or form a desirable human being. She'd been blind, but now could see what a low-life he'd been. He'd left her penniless and homeless, high and dry. Hester lowered her head, put one foot in front of the other, and trudge past the condo.

Soon she was in the wilderness, only trees, the canal, the path, the river. And as luck would have it, the moon disappeared.

Hester stopped. Two more miles to the Silver Nugget, and it was so dark she couldn't see her hand in front of her face. Should she go back? Take Bridge Street to River Road? But once you got out of town there were no streetlights on River Road either. And no shoulder. Some nut case could pull over and force her into his car, rape her, strangle her, dump her body where it would never be found. Or a drunkard driving home from some bar could run her over, turn her into road-kill.

She'd stay on the path.

As her eyes adjusted to the darkness, and she moved on, she thought of Henry David Thoreau hiking back from the village of Concord to his cabin in the woods by the pond. Did he ever make the journey at night? If it was in *Walden*, she didn't recall reading it.

The sound of the river thundering over the sluice grew louder. She put her hands over her ears, but the deafening noise reverberated inside her head. Her bag was heavy. She flung it over her other shoulder, across her chest, and settled it on her hip. Now she might've been able to jog the rest of the way if she wasn't terrified of tripping and falling.

She thought of humming, but dismissed the idea because in her estimation people who hummed struck her as odd. Going around humming a happy tune? Come on? Hester found it annoying. Why not just sing the song? Whistling was just as bad. Hester couldn't whistle worth a darn, but Al sure could. It was one of the few things he did when she first met him that she honestly hated. He liked to whistle that song from "The King and I," or was it "The Sound of Music"? The one about whistling a happy tune so no one will suspect you're afraid.   It was a silly song. How the hell was whistling going to help with anything?

She bet Thoreau whistled all the way from the village back to the pond, but not because he was afraid. No, a man alone never had to be afraid. Not like a woman did.

Sixteen

Lola Giordano was in a booth back by the bar. Cecilia knew that the woman had ordered the pumpkin squash ravioli for her and the farfalle bolognaise for herself. It had been a while since they'd been to Dina's; but when they'd been regulars, they'd always ordered the ravioli and the farfalle. And Cecilia was sure by now that Lola would be on her second or third glass of the Ruffino Select. And Cecilia was also sure by now that Lola would be extremely mad at her.

As C slid into the seat across from Lola, the older woman glanced at her watch.

"You don't have to check your damn watch, Lola. I know how late I am." Cecilia placed her napkin on her lap.

"Late? If I were a piece of wood, I'd be petrified by now." Lola's annoyance was palpable.

Cecilia widened her eyes and mumbled, "Sorry."

"Not a very convincing apology, C. So where were you for the last hour and half, and who put that glow in your cheeks?"

"Glow in my cheeks? Are you kidding? What the fuck, Lola, where I've been is none of your business. What do you want? Us joined at the hip?" Cecilia's lips quivered. She was sick of Lola keeping tabs on her, but she didn't want to start a fight right here and now, so she controlled her tongue and changed the subject.

"How's the wine?"

"Bene. The Select is always multo bene. But you know that. Right, C? It's all you ever drink. Only the best for my girl," Lola said, her voice dripping with sarcasm.

"Just trying to make conversation, but I can see you are in a mood."

"A mood, Cecilia? Why, what would put me in a mood? Let's see. Maybe sitting here sprouting moss while you're off somewhere with someone else?"

Cecilia knew Lola wanted an explanation and an effusive, royal pain-in-the-ass apology. Okay, so she dropped Lola off at Dina's to get a table and said she was going to run to the deli for cigarettes. So she didn't come back for an hour. Regardless, she hated when Lola got on her high horse.

Cecilia took a deep breath and poured herself a glass of the Ruffino. She'd apologize, but not right away. She'd wait until Lola was about to reach her boiling point then she'd be syrupy-sweet to her, and the old broad would fall like a sack of potatoes for it.

Like a pro, Cecilia sniffed the wine and swirled the ruby liquid, examining the disc in the candlelight. She took a small sip and let the Chianti sit on her tongue as she breathed in through her slightly open mouth.

"Mmmmm." She closed her eyes and swallowed. "Yes, perfecto. Gracie, Lolo, for always managing to make me happy even when I don't deserve it."

"Please, don't call me that."

Cecilia knew Lola hated when she used this nickname in public, hated any sort of informalities or public displays of affection. The older woman thought it disrespectful, unprofessional, and downright dangerous. "You never know who's listening," she'd say. And in the Professional Development business reputation was everything. Broadcasting your intimacies and relationships wasn't a good idea. If people got wind of the fact that you were some wild and crazy lesbian, well, it could ruin your empire.

Lola ran her hands over her fat stomach and tried to smooth her bunched up silk top. Cecilia could tell by the frown on Lola's face she was probably once again agonizing over her short barrel of a body, her small breasts, and that bulging stomach. Lola in one of her private, more drunken rants had admitted that she hated everything about the way she looked; but she hadn't let self-scrutiny hold her back. No, she overcame the obstacles God had given her.

She put on her Spanks and her wedge heels, made the most of her sharp mind and big mouth, and built herself an Education empire. The way she looked didn't matter because all anyone cared about was what she thought.

Lola had been only twenty-five when she was driven beyond the brink of boredom by having to sit through a professional development seminar by someone named Greg Waggons. How many tortuous, worthless seminars like this could she sit through for the next two or three decades of her life? If this man at the front of the room shifted his weight and waggled his finger at her one more time, she feared she might leap out of her seat and stab him in the jugular with her Bic.

Convinced she could do better, Lola went back to school, got her Masters in Supervision, wrote an enormously popular book entitled "Professional Development for the Soul," and set out on a lecture tour of her own.

Turned out she could tell a good joke and adlib. Word spread through the Education world that Lola Giordano could be downright entertaining, while also making some good points about teaching. One thing led to another, and after she appeared on a segment of the Today Show, her second book, "The Power of Positive Thinking in the Classroom" took off. In subsequent years she published seven more books and was inundated with so many requests to speak at all sorts of gatherings that she could command almost as much money as Bill Clinton.

At the peak of Lola's success, young Cecilia Kurts was about to crash and burn as a first year English teacher.

"Read this," her supervisor said and plopped down a copy of "The Power of Positive Thinking in the Classroom." Not wanting to lose her job, Cecilia volunteered to attend one of Lola's seminars at Trenton State College. Cecilia was impressed. The small, ungainly woman had fire in that fat belly of hers. After the lecture, Cecilia introduced herself and confessed, "I feel a little foolish saying this, but I think you just changed my life."

Ms. Giordano looked her in the eyes.

Is she seeing something in me that I can't see? Cecilia thought as the older woman pressed her business card into Cecilia's hand.

"Please, let me know how you make out when you actually try some of my techniques," Lola said and gave her hug.

Cecilia's teaching improved. The first email she fired off to Lola was out of gratitude, but soon they were in constant communication. And then Lola invited Cecilia to lunch. Cecilia was engaged to Jimmy at the time and living with him at the Nugget. She put on her best dress, one Jimmy had taken her shopping for and had bought for her, and twirled around in front of him to show off.

"You haven't worn that since forever? What's the deal?"

"The deal is this woman was a measly teacher, and now she's a big deal, worth a fortune, and she's invited me to lunch. All I want to know is how she did it."

"Oh, so it's her money you're after." Jimmy sounded like he was joking, but Cecilia knew Jimmy was well aware of how much money meant to her, well aware of how poverty-stricken she'd always been so he shouldn't have been joking with her like that.

Cecilia was in front of the mirror by the steps putting on pink gloss. "When I was growing up, all my clothes were second-hand. It was embarrassing. I will never go into a thrift store again. I don't care what it takes, but I'm going to make money somehow, someday; and I'm going to have the best of everything. You mark my words." She smirked at him from across the room and left.

Now Cecilia, full of internal upheaval, sat across the candlelit table and studied Lola's long, flabby, wrinkled face. Her eyebrows were carefully drawn in with light brown pencil and the lashes of her small eyes were thick with brown mascara. Her very thin lips were tainted purple from the wine, and her double chin made it look as though she had no neck. At times like this when she was confronted with Lola's imperfections, Cecilia regretted all of the secret, dirty things they'd done together.

It was true, Cecilia had to get filthy drunk, close her eyes, and pretend to be into what was happening not to disappoint the old lady. At first, she tried to believe that sex is sex. It doesn't matter if you're doing it with a man or a woman. But after numerous attempts, she knew she was just kidding herself. But there was the money, the fame, the power. Cecilia wanted it all so she hung in there. On the first anniversary of their first night together Lola bought her a charm bracelet; and Cecilia giddy with the possibility of making what was Lola's hers, told her she wished it was a ring.

Lola had laughed. "In good time, C. All in good time." It made Cecilia want to spit nails.

God, she prayed that one day she would find a way to love this old lady. Then it would all be so much easier. Then they could go somewhere where they could marry and make it official. The way it was now, Cecilia owned nothing, not even a car. She got a small salary and as Lola put it, "big benefits." Yes, she was living the high life, but all of the accoutrements belonged to Lola: the beach house on Long Beach Island, the condo in Manhattan, the Escalade, etc.

"Good evening, strangers." Dina, herself, had brought out the steaming plates of ravioli and farfalle. "Long time no see."

"It has been a while, hasn't it?" Lola said brusquely.

"A while? More like years, Lola. Maybe like five years?"

"You could be right, Dina. Tempus fugit. We'll catch up later. Okay? My assistant and I are in the middle of something right now," Lola said dismissively.

"Well, buono appetito. Let me know if you need more vino." Dina went back into the kitchen.

Lola didn't look down at the food. She stared stonily at Cecilia, and Cecilia saw the displeasure in the older woman's eyes and could read her mind. Lola was too old to tolerate such insolence as Cecilia had just dished out, letting the genius herself sit like a bump on a log for over an hour. If Cecilia had gone to see her old fiancé, well, that would be the icing on the cake.

Lola had met Jimmy Raymer once when she hired a moving company to get the few things Cecilia owned out of that ramshackle apartment in that godforsaken flea market. Jimmy stood in the parking lot glaring at Lola and Cecilia and the two workers.

"Sorry about this, Jimmy," Cecilia said for the hundredth time.

Later, Lola told Cecilia she felt bad for Jimmy Raymer. She'd seen the hurt in the young man's eyes, how hard he was trying not to burst into tears or beat somebody up; but C would have a much better life with her. If Jimmy truly loved Cecilia he would let her go. And the best thing for Cecilia would be to never get in touch with him again.

Lola made it sound like she really cared about Jimmy Raymer's feelings, but Cecilia knew Lola was trying to control her, keep her all to herself, keep her as far away from her first love as she could. Lola had confessed that she'd been hurt too many times in the past to have her heart broken one more time. Lola had confessed, again when she'd had too much to drink, she would just die if she lost her C.

"Lolo," Cecilia leaned forward and whispered as quietly as she could, "you're food is getting cold. Why aren't you eating?"

"You know why, Cecilia." The older woman's face hardened even more.

"Come on, now, Lolo?"

"Don't call me that."

"Are we going to get into a fight over this, Lolo?"

"No, but we are going to get into a fight over you not apologizing to me for making me wait. It was rude, Cecilia. Extremely rude. Remember, young lady, I am not a doormat."

"Look, I ran into an old friend so I talked to him for a couple minutes."

"An hour is not a couple minutes. It does not take a normal person one hour to buy cigarettes and say hello to an old friend, not unless that old friend is someone who was more than an old friend."

"What are you implying?"

"That you, as you say, you 'ran into,' not an old friend, but an old fiancé."

Cecilia knew the shit was going to hit the fan, but she didn't back down, "So what if it was Jimmy. Why should you care?"

"Because you are mine."

"I don't see a ring on my finger, Lola."

"Why you ungrateful little…" Lola almost at a loss for words, sighed and whispered. "After all I've done for you."

It was true Lola had done much for her, but that didn't give Lola the right to take Cecilia for granted. And Cecilia hated the way Lola treated her like a child. Okay, the woman was a shitload of years older than she was, but that didn't mean that Lola and she couldn't be equals. Cecilia had worked her ass off for Lola. After that first lunch, Cecilia gave up her teaching job and became Lola's assistant. For the past five years, every waking minute she was working for Ms. Giordano. Christ, she was practically writing Lola's books for her. The research, the outline, the preliminary edit, the corrections. What was left?

The fact that she'd become Lola's lover didn't give Lola the right to boss Cecilia around. If anything, it should've leveled the playing field. But no, Lola seemed obsessed with acting out some warped boss-employee slash mother-daughter scenario.

Nothing irked Cecilia more because Cecilia had an odd and troubled mother, for whom she had little affection. The slug of a woman's neediness and inability to accomplish much of anything had driven Cecilia nearly mad. And Cecilia could not remember a time when she hadn't been responsible for her mother. This year, even, she'd found an efficiency in Lawrenceville for her that was much nicer than any place her mother had ever lived, and Cecilia was paying all of the bills, which was getting tougher to do since Lola was so damn tight-fisted.

"After all you've done for me? Are you kidding? How about all I've done for you?" Cecilia retorted. "I should have half of what you have, not some pathetic salary. I'd have done better being a teacher and marrying…"

"C, darling." Lola's voice was trembling. "Now you've gone and let your temper get the best of you. And the truth has come out. You do love that poverty-stricken loser, don't you?"

Cecilia said nothing, but shrugged her shoulders.

"I knew it all along. Your body language is more damning than anything that could come out of your lying little mouth. Well, Ms. Kurts, I have my pride, and to prove it to you I'm calling my lawyer in the morning and instructing him take your name out of my will. Too bad, because I know how much you love *my* beach house."

"The beach house?" Cecilia was incredulous. The oceanfront beach house was worth a million dollars. Now what in Hades had Cecilia gone and done?

Seventeen

The sound of the river pounding over the sluice receded. Some old song took its place inside Hester's head. Something about Saturday night…*ain't got nobody, got some money 'cause I…got paid…wish I had someone to talk to, I'm in an awful way…*

"In an awful way," was exactly what she was in, but, damn it, she'd pull herself together come hell or high water.

She was trying to remember the rest of the words when she spied the white railing of the canal footbridge. Across that bridge was River Road and the unlit, deserted Silver Nugget, the limits of which Hester could barely discern from the wilderness that surrounded it.

So this was her new home. *The place God put me.*

There was an old Oprah episode on this exact topic. Wherever you are is where you are supposed to be. If you're standing in line at the grocery store and you have a million things to do, don't be impatient because you are there instead of, perhaps, getting hit by a car or mugged or contracting the West Nile Virus. *So I'm living in the back of my minivan and that's keeping me safe from? Being gored by a bull?*

Ah, the moon reappeared. Hester's spirits lifted. The double yellow lines of the road caught the light. She crossed and entered the driveway at the north end of the acreage. The pavilion was about a hundred yards south and set back about forty yards from the road. Beyond the pavilion was a dried up creek bed, then a stretch of six rows of tables running parallel to the road for another two hundred yards. A second level was up on the hill with one more row of tables, parking, and the office, above which was Jimmy's apartment.

Hester's car was a lonely sight, the rear reflectors catching the moonlight like devil eyes, but it was better than nothing.

She rummaged in her bag for her keys, opened the door, and stood in the dim light of the overhead lamp. Tired as she was, she had to go. She'd held it as long as she could. She shoved her handbag under the front seat, climbed in, and flipped on the headlights. She checked her bag and the glove compartment for tissues and came up empty.

The thick woods at the base of Goat Hill were impenetrable. She'd be forced to go at the edge, in the open. Hester pulled her capris and panties down, backed into the foliage as far as she could, squatted, and relieved herself. It was a novel experience she wasn't thrilled about. She felt like a dog or cat peeing wherever, whenever. She wasn't good at it either. She dribbled on her panties and with nothing to wipe herself with she was forced to take them off and use them. After which she threw them as far as she could into the woods.

When she was done, she pulled up her capris and got back in the front seat. The van smelled musty. Hester gagged. When they lived in the old Victorian, she made her own potpourri from the lavender that grew around the patio, the scent soothing, intoxicating. In winter when the lavender faded, she lit scented candles. Hester had lived mostly in a world of olfactory pleasure, until now.

She clicked off the headlights, pulled the keys from the ignition, and tossed them in the catchall between the seats. She got out and went to the back and lifted the rear hatch. Even though she'd sold lots of stuff, the back of the van was still packed with containers shoved up against the front seats and stacked along one side. She pushed them as far forward and to the left as she could and shook out the dirty towel she used to clean her windshields. It would be her blanket. Something was better than nothing.

She thought again of Thoreau. At least he'd had a proper bed and a proper blanket. Several years ago she begged Al to take her to Concord, Mass. That first afternoon, they went to the village cemetery. Al took pictures of Hester leaning on the top of Thoreau's headstone, crouching next to Hawthorne's tombstone, sitting on the ground next to the Alcott family plot, that kind of thing. That afternoon they drove a little out of town in the opposite direction of Walden to tour Emerson's house where Thoreau often visited, and Hawthorne and his wife Sophia had lived. Hawthorne had etched on a window pane in their bedroom, "Man's accidents are God's purposes." The tour guide said Sophia composed it and asked Nathaniel to etch it where she could see it each morning at sunrise.

Man's accidents are God's purposes. Really? As Hester crawled in between the bins and wall of the minivan, she hoped "God's purposes" would be revealed to her, and soon! She rolled on her back and pulled the rank-smelling towel over her. This was smaller and more pathetic than the make-believe house she made when she was just a kid. She and her younger sister lugged blankets and stuffed animals into the closet beneath the stairs, and pretended it was their secret cottage. But she could stand in that closet, turn around, and spread her arms wide because it was a fairly large closet and she was only a small child. Here she was much too big for this space.

But, hopefully, living out of her minivan was only temporary. She thought of the money she'd made. In a few hours it would be Sunday morning, and she'd make more.

Be a little smarter, she told herself. *Don't let those dealers take advantage of you.*

God, she couldn't stop thinking about that ugly man with the stupid-looking toupee. She wanted her vaseline glass back. She'd kept the compote on the top shelf of her Eastlake cabinet in the Victorian dining room. She'd hired Dave Leftowicz, the electrician, to install a black light above the shelf. It cost almost $500 but was worth it. In the evening, she lit the cabinet and watched the compote glow neon green, and light dance across the cuts in her other pieces of crystal and transform her other treasures into magical things. Hester couldn't stop staring, couldn't stop admiring all the beauty that was hers.

Hester closed her eyes. Blackness. Tomorrow would come soon. Better lock herself in and get some shut-eye. She felt around for her keys and couldn't remember where she put them. She wasn't sure, without the keys, if she could lock herself in. She tried to reach over the bins to the front door to hit the lock button, but there was too much stuff in the way. The hell with it. She gave up and instead started praying the Hail Mary. The Blessed Mother'd keep the creeps out, but when she got to the "fruit of your womb" part, she thought of Nina— that girl was the closest thing she ever had to a child of her own. She'd never get over Nina's death, never get over the fact that her womb never bore any fruit.

Hester tried to calm her breathing, but her heart was pounding. How alone she was in this flea market parking lot, miles from town and an insurmountable distance from anything that resembled a decent life.

She couldn't even say a simple prayer without it making her crumble inside. She held her hand up in front of her face. She strained to see it, but couldn't. No moonlight, no starlight, no nothing, but blackness; and, oh, how she feared it would swallow her up.

Eighteen

Jimmy hated himself for being so easily taken in by Cecilia, again, and after all that time. Maybe if he hadn't had so many beers, he wouldn't have been. He stood there, dejected, for several minutes before he returned to Bull's. Time to once again drown his sorrows. Another beer. That's what he needed. And he'd buy his new acquaintance, Ms. Randal, another glass of wine.

But Ms. Randal was gone.

Oh hell, he thought. He paid the bill, put a generous tip on the bar, and pushed it toward the barmaid.

Honestly, he intended to immediately drive around looking for Hester, but once he got in his truck, he couldn't stop himself from pulling up outside Dina's to, maybe, catch one more glimpse of Cecilia.

Cecilia, Jimmy whispered her name to himself. He'd been so shocked to see her he couldn't think straight and followed her outside like he was her goddamn puppy dog. All she had to say was, "Can we talk, Jimmy?"

And he didn't have the balls to say no, as much as he knew that was exactly what he should've said, given the way she'd dumped him, the way she'd infuriated him by leaving him, and for a freaking woman.

It broke his heart. For five long years now he'd been sleep-walking his way through life, in pain every time he thought of her, and he thought of Cecilia all the time. Yes, she'd left him with a bitter taste in his mouth and with no taste for any other woman. He hadn't had a single date since Cecilia left him.

Then there was that kiss. She initiated it, she made it long and soulful. Then he'd watched her walk to her black Escalade, get in, and drive away.

He sat in his pick-up for God-knows how long, his lips on fire, the inside of his mouth tingling, thinking about his former fiancé and wanting her more than ever. But Jimmy wasn't hopeful, not really. He had the sinking feeling that Cecilia's show of affection was a one-shot deal, like a fucking meteorite blazing through his sky before disintegrating.

No, he'd be better off finding the woman named Hester and apologizing. Let his mixed-up ex go back to her lesbian lover. He'd go home and get some sleep before the dealers lined up at five in the morning waiting for tables.

But as he drove down Union Street, he knew if he made the left on Church it would lead him to Dina's. Before he could think better of it, he flipped on his turn signal, made the left, pulled up just shy of the front entrance, and parked.

You stupid son-of-bitch, he told himself, but he didn't pull away. He turned off the truck and sat there in silence and thought about the woman he loved sitting inside that restaurant across from Lola Giordano, smiling at her, laughing at one of her sarcastic observations, her stupid jokes. They'd be sharing a bottle of something red and expensive, and in the candlelight Lola's wrinkled face would look younger than it was; and Cecilia's beautiful face would glow with its youthful and perfect beauty.

Jimmy tortured himself by sitting there for close to an hour listening to country music. All the lyrics were about him, about how much he wanted the woman who didn't want him. He wasn't proud of himself, wallowing in loneliness, but he felt defeated and angry with Cecilia for finding him and kissing him and making him hurt all over again. Even the stupid romantic candles in the windows of the small, intimate restaurant made him want to puke, but he couldn't stop himself from getting out of the truck and peeking through the window of the bar door.

There they were in a booth along the back wall. He could see them. There were so many plates of food, water glasses, wine glasses that he couldn't be sure, but he thought they were holding hands.

Disgusted, heart-broken, he went back to the truck, got in, jabbed the key in the ignition, revved the engine loudly, and sped away.

He drove up and down River Road twice looking for Hester and even went back to Bull's. It was ten o'clock and they were closing up. No one had seen her. He cruised every street in town before heading south again. If she wasn't in her car, he'd have to head up the towpath. It was the only other place she could be.

If something bad happens to her, it's my goddamn fault.

By the time he pulled into the Nugget, he was unnerved that he hadn't found her. He parked by the office out of habit and ran all the way to the van, and peered into the side window. He couldn't see a thing. He went to the back and tried to lift the tailgate. To his surprise it opened.

There she was sound asleep, pale and ghostly-looking in the dim interior light, her mouth open, her snoring like the sound of dry rustling leaves. She had no pillow and her blonde-streaked hair fanned out into a halo on the grey carpet. Her skin was unblemished, smooth except for wrinkles on her forehead and at the corners of her eyes. Her thin, slightly hooked nose seemed carved from wax. Her chin was small and square. She looked to Jimmy like one of those female saints on those holy cards his mother had kept in every purse.

Hester? Jimmy thought of her name and how it came from a famous book he'd never read. He'd seen the movie, though, the one with Demi Moore in it. Demi Moore reminded him of Cecilia, especially the way she looked in that movie, so he watched it many times. The Hester in the movie was an adulterer, a sinner; the town leaders, the men primarily, made her wear a big scarlet A on her chest. God, he felt sorry for poor Hester.

What an odd name for parents to give a child? But Jimmy had to admit he did like the sound of it when he said it over and over inside his head. *Hester... Hester... River water rushing over rock.*

The old girl had somehow made it back safely. *She's got freaking balls...*Jimmy thought with relief. He leaned forward to wake her, but was repulsed by a bad odor emanating from the packed belly of the vehicle.

Though the night air was stagnant and the temperature still in the eighties, a chill ran through him. He knew he should close the hatch, go home, and go to sleep. The dealers would arrive before the crack of dawn, and he'd feel like shit if he didn't rest. But he seemed rooted where he was, standing in the sweltering heat staring at the sleeping woman.

He watched as she exhaled, her mouth rounding, quivering like the mouth of a fish out of water. His eyes moved to her chest. It rose slightly, collapsed slightly with each breath. But her mouth fascinated him more so he looked at it again.

A small mouth. Easy to cover. Easy to hold a hand over...

For a split second he visualized how he, or rather, some bad man could've snuffed her life out on that lonely towpath, before she knew what hit her.

Hell, he shivered at the thought and saw it in his head. Hester on the ground, in the dirt screaming for her life. Some nutcase clamping his hand over her mouth, his other hand groping to find her pants and pull them down.

It would've been his fault, all his fault.

Or would it?

She should've waited for him, should've known better. Damn, she didn't even lock her car.

Jimmy Raymer's head buzzed from all the beer he drank. The pressure behind his eyeballs was on the verge of turning into one bitch of a headache. He tried to shake off his dizziness and straighten up a bit, but his ears started ringing, making things worse. He began thinking about his mother and how much Hester truly resembled her.

He did the math. If his mother were alive, she'd be turning fifty. Hester had to be around that age. And Hester was probably the same height as his mother. Five feet three or four? And their hair was the almost the same length. And the shape of her lips. And her chin. Goddamn. How different his life would be if his mother…

What good did it do him to dwell on what had happened fifteen years ago?

No good.

He was about to step back, shut the tailgate, and leave when a strange and appalling urge overtook him; and instead of getting the hell out of there, he climbed into the back of the van and crouched by the sleeping woman's feet.

Now they were alone together in a sweltering world of their own. Sweat streamed down Jimmy's temples. He wiped it back into his hair. His armpits and crotch were soaked with perspiration. Yes, it was ungodly hot with oppressive humidity, not a single breeze to scatter the zillion, eager, blood-sucking mosquitos, some of which had come into the back of the van with him. He listened to them buzzing about and swatted blindly at them as the air grew more redolent. His body odor, Hester's, the neoprene stink of used sneakers, the pong of dampness all melded into one heady mixture.

"Hester?" Jimmy whispered.

She didn't wake up.

Jimmy reached back and pulled the tailgate down. He maneuvered as quietly as he could into a kneeling position closer to the sleeping Hester. She wore a tight pink running shirt with a giant Nike swoosh over her flat-as-a-board chest. Her body looked, Jimmy thought, a little like a boy's, perhaps, even like his might have looked when he was a boy. She had on a pair of black stretch capris that clung like a second skin. He looked again at her chest. He'd always been attracted to women with big knockers. Cecilia's were perfect breasts, perfect ripe melons. How many times had he cupped them and kissed them? How many times had he imagined cupping them and kissing them? Even tonight her breasts strained against the fabric of her shirt and looked much larger than he remembered.

He shook his head. Thinking about Cecilia drained his last ounce of resolve. He shifted his weight from one throbbing knee to the other. His legs were numb, and he feared he might get cramps. That was another thing that happened to him when he drank too much—he got Charley horses in his calves, sometimes in both calves at once. They hurt like hell and he had to pound on his muscles with his fists to stop the pain.

Right now, as a matter of fact, Jimmy still felt high, though it had been hours since he left the bar. It was one of those highs that might make it impossible to sleep. If he put his head down on a pillow, the room might start spinning.

Tired of dwelling on the past, Jimmy inexplicably leaned forward and touched Hester's leg. It wasn't like him to do crazy things, but kneeling here like an acolyte at the feet of a woman he barely knew and then actually touching her *was* crazy. It was like something his father would do, not him. He wasn't like his father, and he would never be.

He took after his mother, whom he loved more than life itself, more even than he loved Baby Alice, more than he loved Cecilia. He'd always taken after his mother. She'd always said so. And even though he knew she wouldn't like what he was doing, he was unable to stop.

Imperceptibly, slowly, Jimmy leaned over the sleeping woman and planted one hand near her ribcage. His arms strong from lifting weights, he supported himself by pressing his other hand against the side of the van. All that working out since Cecilia left, wearing himself out so he didn't have an ounce of strength left to find her and beg her to come back, had paid off.

He hovered over Hester's body waiting for the right moment to scoop up her small frame and slip in beneath her.

He'd done that with Cecilia many time and she was a much larger woman. And once he'd gotten Cecilia on top, he'd reach under her shirt and massage her breasts through her bra. It was how the foreplay began, though if he were in it only for himself, he'd have ripped her shirt and bra in two and swallowed one of her huge breasts whole. But he controlled himself, and one at a time he carefully took her clothes off and kissed or licked whatever part of her he just exposed, licked even her underarms and the soles of her feet. He wanted her wet, perspiring, and panting before penetration. Once he was in, it would be over fast.

He loved the surprised look on her face as though she, once again, couldn't believe how big he was. When they were moving together, sometimes he grabbed her hair and clung to it like it was a horse's mane and he the upside down, wild rider. Sometimes she screamed nasty words, "Fuck me, goddamn it, fucker, fuck me hard." He'd let go of her hair, hold her ass, and hump up into her as hard as he could. She was young and strong, and took what he dished out.

How damn excited he'd be. He tried not to come too fast; but, damn, it thrilled him so much to see wild Cecilia, he couldn't help himself. No matter what, though, Cecilia always smiled at him; and after a few minutes, her voice soft and happy, she'd murmur, "Nice, Jimmy, that was so nice."

Nineteen

Cecilia sat across from the much smaller woman watching her devour the farfalle, and in between bites she saw a smug expression fill Lola's face. Lola was still furious. Lola had made up her mind, and it'd be hell to get her to change it. If Cecilia wanted to keep her name in that will, she'd have to patch things up, and fast.

Cecilia put her wine glass down. "Look, Lola, alright, I went to see Jimmy, but only because I was angry. I'm tired of waiting for you to come around and do what I want for a change, and what I want is to be your wife. I want us to be a family. Please?"

"I'm too old for that," Lola said derisively and put another forkful of pasta in her mouth.

Bullshit, thought Cecilia. She pushed her ravioli around with the tip of her knife. She'd remind Lola of how valuable she was to her operation.

"Look, old girl." Cecilia called Lola "old girl" when they were doing it. "I'll apologize for being late when you apologize for what happened with our last book."

Lola choked. "Our last book? Are you trying to say you had anything important to do with "English in Motion"?"

"Anything important? Are you kidding, Lola? Remember, it was my idea from the start. Look at you. You wouldn't know the first thing about physical fitness. I'm the one who came up with the idea of putting physical activity into the English curriculum, of planning lessons that would get students and teachers on their feet. Admit it, Lola, it was my idea, and you said, 'Run with it.' And I did, but then you put your name on it and made another goddamn fortune when it turned out to be your biggest seller yet."

"Cecilia, be careful. You are crossing a line."

Cecilia took another sip of wine. She was getting off on a tangent. "Come on, Lola, all I'm saying is that you need me. And why can't we be partners, truly equal in every way?"

"What you seem to be forgetting, Cecilia, is that you will never be equal to me. I've busted my hump for decades to establish myself in a cut-throat world as a writer, an expert, an icon. What do you know compared to me? What connections do you have besides mine? You'd get chewed up and spit out by the competition in a hot minute. I don't need you, Cecilia Kurts. You need me!"

"I do need you. I want you. I want to be your wife. I want us to start a family and do all the things normal couples do." Cecilia was desperate to end the argument, but then the exact thing that would further infuriate Lola leapt out of her mouth. "But most of all, Lola, I want my name on the next edition of *Math in Motion*."

She could tell by the sourpuss on her face that Lola was through with her.

"I didn't mean that. I take it back, Lola. I don't care about my name being on anything. Really, I don't. Let's just get out of here and go back to the hotel and get naked. Forget about all this talk about whose name is on what." The back-pedaling wasn't working.

"Okay, okay, I am very sorry I made you wait."

Lola pursed her lips and said nothing.

Damn if Cecilia wasn't just so sick of it all, and on top of everything, she couldn't stop thinking about kissing Jimmy. It was a nice kiss. She could tell how excited he was and that excited her. How goddamn nice it was to kiss someone other than Lola.

Oh, what an *effing* charade. Here she was ranting about wanting to spend the rest of her life with this stingy, domineering woman and she didn't even like to kiss her. In fact she couldn't figure out how she ever had the nerve to do so in the first place. Drunk as she was, how had she ever followed through?

Lola had invited Cecilia to Loveladies on Long Beach Island. They sat on the top deck of Lola's oceanfront beach house drinking and watching the whitecaps sparkle in what was left of the sun. They talked about Lola's next lecture tour. Cecilia had some good ideas for marketing the concept of "backward teaching" Lola had stolen from the Waggons' model by reframing the concept as "behavioral objectives." It grew dark. Lola lit candles, opened more wine. Cecilia drank too much and Lola insisted she stay. Around midnight when Cecilia started slurring her words. Lola took her hand, led her to the master bedroom, and helped her out of her clothes. Lola undid Cecilia's bra and let it drop to the floor. Cecilia closed her eyes and it felt just like a man was touching her, just like a man was kissing her. That first night in the dark hadn't been all that bad, Cecilia now concluded; but subsequently, in the light of day Cecilia had had to put on quite a performance to convince Lola of her affections.

"Cecilia," Lola said, interrupting Cecilia's thought. "Call Dina over and get our check. I'm going to drop you off at your new home, better known as that dump of a flea market. Silver Nugget, my eye."

Twenty

Hester's first thought was, *it's Al sneaking up on me.*

Like in the old days, when she'd be waiting in the car for him to get out of a late night meeting about teacher contracts or something like that. Who would they hire? Who would they fire? The debate was lengthy, sometimes ugly, but always these meetings got Vice-Principal Al Murphy pumped up. He had strong opinions. He knew who had potential and who he had decided—day one—didn't.

"That's what I get the big bucks for." He'd tell Hester. "To know when to hold'em and know when to fold'em."

For Al it was his way or the highway, even though he was still only just the vice principal, still...only...just. How it aggravated him to have to give in to the "pompous principal," the "supercilious superintendent." Al had a thing for alliteration when he was pissed-off. He hated when someone disagreed with him, and with his brain so inelastic, his hatred never wore off quickly. By the time he got to the car, he'd still be pretty wound up. He'd take his ring finger with the ring on it and tap loudly on the window right by Hester's head and scare the living daylights out of her. I'm fired up now, look out, wife, look the hell out. It was a warning. Only sex—sometimes rough sex—made him feel better.

If he didn't take her right there in the car, Hester drove him home. All the way he'd go on and on about which "asshole" said what, about how once again he hadn't completely gotten his way on anything. He was, after-all, still, only the vice principal. He couldn't wait, he kept telling Hester, until he was in charge of the whole goddamn place.

At home, Scotch straight-up for him, a glass of Chardonnay for the wife, no shower, no shave, he'd come up behind her while she was trying to make him a sandwich. Hungry, he was always hungry. One time he ripped the whole front of her blouse apart, and ping, ping, ping, like shots from a pistol, the buttons hit the Italian tile

Most of the time he fucked Hester from behind, pushing her skirt up or pulling her slacks down, ripping her silk underpants if he had to. He grabbed her hair and held her up with his other arm around her waist so she would be right where he wanted her, right where she needed to be to make him come.

But other times on nights when things did go his way, he could be entirely tender, embrace her from behind, and gently kiss her on the neck and guide her to the floor. He'd lean over her and knead her breast through her shirt, then lie down next to her, kissing her, touching her face. When she was naked, he carefully lifted her on top of him so she could squat; and he could bang her from below, but without hardly moving.

Al, she hoped, would be like that now, gentle. She hated when he was rough, even though she came, she hated it. It was hard to explain how she could hate and love and hate the same thing. She was thinking this in her dreamlike state when she suddenly realized, someone was on top of her, and it wasn't Al.

It was *Jimmy*.

How Hester knew in the pitch black, she couldn't say; but she was instantly sure and instantly frightened. She tried to scream and push him off.

"Hester, it's alright. I'm not going to hurt you."

"Then what the hell are you doing here? Get off me! Get off me!" Her voice was full of alarm.

"I was worried about you. Why did you leave Bull's and not tell me?" His voice was calm and sincere.

Hester said in a shaky voice, "Please, let me go?"

"Please, don't be upset. I wanted to tell you I'm sorry." His hot breath reached her face and smelled of beer. "Hester, I'm so sorry. Don't be angry. I just want you to hold me."

He lowered his body on top of her, and she felt his chest against her breasts. His head was by her shoulder, and he kissed her skin gently. "I won't hurt you."

Hester's heart was beating so fast she felt faint. Her throat constricted, but his lips were soft and warm on her neck. Hester remembered how handsome he was, how nice he'd been to her, all the heartbreaking things he'd been through.

She stopped resisting. Why?

The sensation of his body touching hers, of being this close to this man was…? She stopped thinking about why, wrapped her arms around Jimmy, and pulled him closer. They lay motionless, sweating, poised for what might come next. The tight space filled with the odor of their perspiration, their offensive breath, but it seemed to spur them on, making them hot, unbearably hot.

Suddenly, Jimmy pushed himself up, knelt between Hester's legs, and helped her out of her exercise shirt and bra. One leg at a time, he peeled off her capris. He pulled off his shirt, unbuttoned his jeans, and got them down around his ankles. He maneuvered Hester on top of him, and she rested her hands on his bare chest before she lay on him and found his mouth. His lips covered hers and his tongue went deep into her throat. His grabbed the cheeks of her ass, pressed them together, and lifted her onto his penis. He was as big as a club or bat, and Hester feared for a moment all of him wouldn't fit in her. Then it did. He moved beneath her and she took up his rhythm. Time turned into music and this dance they were doing…love? Kunitz had written something like that. God, she loved everything that old poet had ever come up with.

Had all else happened for this moment to be?

The memories of thirty years with Al, and only Al, floated from Hester's consciousness like falling feathers as this moment with Jimmy Raymer went on and on.

When it was over, the moonlight came through the minivan window and illuminated the young man's stunning face.

All around the clouds are breaking...of all things the lines from a hymn came to Hester...*soon the storms of time shall cease; in God's likeness we, awaking, know the everlasting peace.*

Jimmy's eyes were closed, his still-rigid penis beneath her thigh, she rising and falling on the waves of his heavy breathing. Outside the world was astoundingly still, but in her head the hymn went on...*death and sorrow, earth's dark story, to the former days belong.*

Jimmy stirred, lifted her off, laid her back down, and kissed her on the forehead. He gathered his clothes, whispered, "Sweet dreams," and left.

As Hester listened to the hatch click, something clicked inside her; but unlike back in college with Arty when sex precipitated her shameful abortion, and unlike in her marriage to Al, that homage to dysfunction, when sex was usually the white flag signaling the end of another skirmish, she surprisingly felt no regret. Many would judge her action as incredibly stupid, she knew, but they weren't her, and they weren't inside her, feeling the divine feeling of someone's healing touch on her lonely skin. All of her past guilt had risen up and not deadened her, not made her sodden, not made her withdraw, but instead had helped her come frantically alive and grab for something she'd missed too many times before.

She lay there for a while contentment overtaking her. She breathed in slowly, exhaled slowly. She was floating in the night sky, a cirrus cloud, the lace through which the moonlight passed and she thought of a poem by Yeats, something about a young man's lament. Part of a line came to her, "love is a crooked thing...like when shadows eat the moon..." Then like she was the shadow eating the moon, she devoured, one by one, her dazzling past sins. Slowly, she came back to herself, and gently, she touched herself down there. She was sore and very wet.

She hoped she wasn't bleeding. She felt around for the towel but only found the filthy rag Al used to change the oil. It disgusted her to press it between her legs, but she did. There was no air, only oppressive heat, but still the sex had been hot. She pulled the rag from between her legs, wiped the sweat off her naked body, and tossed the rag down by her feet. She was exhausted, on the verge of tumbling into sleep, but some creature squealed, maybe a raccoon or skunk. Then she heard bats cheeping and frogs croaking. Next the cicadas started to chirp. There was such a racket that she couldn't shut the world out so she pictured Jimmy, his golden hair, his violet eyes, and the pleasing arrangement of his features. So damn-near perfect on the outside, but how terribly scarred on the inside he must be. Losing his mother and baby sister in one day? What a dreadful thing for a ten year old boy to live through.

Yes, she'd liked Jimmy immediately when she met him only yesterday morning. My God, all that could happen in just hours. But it wasn't until they were alone in the dark, and he kissed her shoulder, that she desired him. She let her mind drift over their lovemaking. The way he sucked on her small breasts made her yearn for him, and she was wet again. As raw as she was, she wanted him. If he came back to her, she'd be more than…

So what if she swore she wasn't going to ever get involved with a man again?

This time no one could get hurt. She couldn't get pregnant because of the adhesions from the abortion, but even if she didn't have adhesions, this time she was far too old to conceive. So why not give into the wild and savage instinct that had come upon her? Why not believe that this night was meant to be?

Twenty-One

As Jimmy headed to his apartment shaking his head in disbelief of what he'd just done, a black Escalade pulled into the parking lot. Lola Giordano hurried from the driver's side to the passenger side and opened the door. No one emerged, but Jimmy was pretty sure Cecilia was sitting there.

He was close enough to hear Lola's indignant voice. "Get out of my car!"

"No," yelled Cecilia. "It's my car. You gave it to me."

"Well, have you checked the title? You aren't getting this car. You aren't getting anything. As soon as my lawyer's office opens up…no, tonight I'll leave him a message, tell him to get your name off everything, and then I'm calling my agent and telling her to get me a new assistant."

"Please, Lola, don't do this?" Cecilia begged.

"You cooked your goose with me, young lady. So get the hell out of my car before I call the police." Lola reached in. She had Cecilia by the arm. Jimmy ran up to them and grabbed Lola's shoulders.

"Get your hands off me!" Lola turned and screamed in Jimmy's face.

If he had a gun, he'd have shot the old hag.

"It's my car," whined Cecilia. She was sobbing.

Jimmy let go of Lola, but tried to reach around her and help Cecilia out of the car.

"Leave me alone," screamed Cecilia at Lola.

Lola grabbed Cecilia's arm again. "You better get out and go with him because you are dead to me, Cecilia Kurts. Dead." But Cecilia, larger and stronger, was immovable.

Lola dropped her arms to her sides. "Fine. Sit in the car all night, but when the cops come in the morning and arrest you for theft, don't be surprised."

"And when I tell them what kind of predatory dike you are and that gets out to the press, what's going to happen then? Huh, Lolo, what's going to happen then?" Cecilia said, her voice exploding like a bomb.

In the moonlight, Jimmy could see Cecilia's red, contorted face.

Lola walked to the driver's side of the car, grabbed her purse, and whispered to Cecilia, "Keep the goddamn car because it is all you are ever going to get from me."

And Cecilia, weeping, replied, "It doesn't have to end like this, Lolo."

"Oh yes, it does." Lola put her purse on her shoulder, pulled her too-tight top down, turned, and headed toward the pavilion and River Road.

Cecilia leaned forward on the dashboard. Jimmy stood listening to her sniveling. He didn't know what the hell to do. What if something happened to the old goat? He couldn't just let her walk all the way back to town, could he?

"Wait," he hollered after the fading figure. "I'll drive you to wherever you're staying."

Lola turned and yelled, "Thanks, but no thanks, asshole!" She was almost to the pavilion and becoming one with the night.

Jimmy suppressed the urge to run after and choke the life out of the old woman. Instead, he looked at his ex-fiancé and said, "You better go after her, Cecilia."

"She can drop off the face of the earth for all I care. I'm sick of her, of everything."

"Then do want me to go after her? It is late and a hell of a long way to town. What do you want me to do?"

"Nothing, not a damn thing. She's plenty old enough to take care of herself. She deserves whatever she gets for...Oh, I can't even think about it. I've ruined everything."

"You've ruined what, Cecilia?"

"I can't talk about it tonight. I can't talk about anything. I'm so over all of this."

"Well, get out of the car and come upstairs. You can sleep in the guest room."

"No way am I leaving this car alone. Be just like her to come back with the extra set of keys and get it."

"Then I'll stay with you."

"No, for Christ sakes, please, Jimmy, just leave me the hell alone." Cecilia was crying now, and Jimmy could hear the anger in her voice. He prayed it wasn't aimed at him. Then she added, "You understand. Don't you?"

Not really, he thought dejectedly. Whose wounds would he rather lick than Cecilia Kurts'? But he knew how stubborn Cecilia was once she made up her mind, so he closed the door and said, "You better lock yourself in."

When he heard the click, he went up to his apartment in a daze over the incident, in a daze over the whole crazy night.

Twenty-Two

Dead to the world, Hester was startled awake by the sound of a car pulling into the gravel lot. Headlights swept over her. She hadn't a clue as to the time and couldn't check her phone because she'd left the damn thing plugged in on the condo's kitchen counter. More cars pulled in, doors slammed, she heard muffled voices. The dealers were here. Early-bird pickers wouldn't be far behind.

An owl hooted. The sky turned one notch from black to grey.

Hester rubbed her eyes and looked through the dirty minivan window. In the shadows the heavy tarp she'd pulled over her table last night looked wet with condensation, and there was a large puddle on the ground as though it'd rained.

She struggled into her damp, smelly clothes, combed her fingers through her tangled hair, and rubbed her face with both hands, exasperated by the fact that she couldn't wash it. Already the heat was oppressive, already she was sweating. She pushed the hatch open, crawled out, went to the driver's side door, and grabbed her sneakers. Jammed down in between the seats she found one of Al's old baseball caps. She hated to touch it, but, hell, she had to hide her hair under something. Her teeth were scummy. If only she could brush them, but that wasn't going to happen. Too bad she'd taken so many small things for granted.

She slammed the car door shut and walked to her table. Sunday mornings were always the best for the dealers at the Nugget— so she'd been told.

No time for a pity-party. Time to make money. Time to get back at least one shred of dignity.

When she went to pick up one end of the tarp, she noticed the rocks that had been holding it down had been kicked aside. *How'd that happen?* she thought but didn't dwell on it because she was trying to lift the tarp and get it off the table without knocking anything over. She had to stop because some things were already clunking into others. Clearly it was a two man job.

"Wait, I'll help you." She turned toward Jimmy's voice.

In the twilight she saw his shadowy bulk approaching and wanted to crawl in the van, slam the hatch shut, and curl up in a ball so she wouldn't have to face him.

"You'll knock something over doing it yourself." He jogged past her to the other end of the table and took hold of the tarp. "Well, come on, lady, help me."

Lady? Hester was stung, though she didn't want to be so sensitive. She'd never had a one night stand, but she guessed by the way Jimmy was acting, last night had been her first.

"Ready?" he said.

The sun popped up over Goat Hill. Hester could see Jimmy's wrinkled shirt and shorts, disheveled hair, unshaven face. He looked a mess, but the cresting sun gilded his wild locks and whiskers, and made his cheeks rosy. Only his brooding eyebrows belied his angelic glow.

Jimmy grinned at Hester, and for the first time she noticed his crooked teeth. His left front tooth crossed over the right. One eye tooth was so high into his gum it looked like it was missing. His bottom teeth were small jagged squares that looked fragile enough to break if he bit into anything too hard. He should've had braces, she thought.

He was still looking at Hester. His eyes on her made her blush and want to slither under a rock somewhere. She shrugged off the threatening shame.

Enough acting like a scorned, love-crazy teenager. Love had nothing to do with what she did with Jimmy last night. Lust did. And was that a crime? Was it a crime she took pleasure in having sex with a man half her age? If she were a man, she'd be cock-a-

114

doodle-doing all over the place about such a conquest and begging for more. But she wasn't a man, and being any further interested in Jimmy wouldn't do her any good.

She squared her shoulders. *A one night stand. A damn good one night stand.* She was going to concentrate on moving forward with her life, only doing things that would improve her lot. No libidinal backsliding anymore. Skepticism, and restraint, full steam ahead.

The only thing unfortunate about the encounter with Jimmy, Hester concluded was that while she derived an immense sense of wellbeing from it, it probably wasn't all that exciting for him. Most likely he had hundreds of much more exciting experiences.

Good for him. Hester thought as she smiled at Jimmy and they lifted the tarp.

When they stepped to the side to clear it from the table and fold it, what was on the table beneath stopped them in their fucking tracks.

There, on top of Hester's precious things, was the body of a woman Hester thought she vaguely recognized. Hester dropped her end of the tarp and rushed toward the woman.

"Don't touch her!" Jimmy put his arm out to block Hester's forward motion.

"Stop!" Hester screamed and struggled to get past Jimmy. "Maybe she's still alive. We've got to do something!"

But Jimmy held her back. Hester struggled against the grip he had on her and reached toward the woman with her free hand.

"She's dead. Can't you see that?" Jimmy's voice was strained.

"But…"

Jimmy took his cell phone out with his other hand, flipped it open, and punched 911.

Hester gasped, "No! She can't be dead!" Her hands flew to her face. "How do you know she's dead?"

Jimmy was listening to someone on the cell. He spoke into the phone. "Yeah, dead. Get here as fast as you can," he paused. "Yeah, she's dead. I'm sure."

Hester yanked her arm out of Jimmy's grip and sunk to her knees.

"How awful," she mumbled. "How terribly awful."

Jimmy put his phone back in his pocket, reached down, and took Hester's arm again. He tried to pull her up, but she was dead weight.

Dealers crowded around.

"Stay back! The police are on their way," Jimmy hollered at the people who were pressing in to get a better look. He shouted again, "Get the hell away from her. Don't touch anything!"

It was too late. A man Jimmy didn't know had his hand on the woman's neck. "I don't feel a pulse. At least I don't think so. Shit, I think she really is dead."

Another man rushed forward and put his palm on her chest. "No heartbeat. Dead as a fucking door nail."

"Get the hell away from her!" Jimmy pushed through the crowd, stood between them and the corpse, and corralled them backward. "I said get the fuck away from her. You heard me."

When he was sure they knew he meant business and they started to move, he went back to Hester, squatted next to her, and whispered, "I know this woman. She was not a nice person."

His breath smelled of beer, the same as last night only stale. "I know you're upset, but don't be."

In the bright sunlight, Hester looked at him askance. He turned away. She followed his eyes to the body of the woman sprawled on top of Hester's things.

The woman was on her back. Her face drained of color, her mouth and eyes open. Her floral top was scrunched up exposing her big stomach. If it weren't for her grey hair and wrinkles, one might have concluded she was pregnant. Her legs were splayed, the crotch of her slacks soaking wet. Her naked arms, hanging off the sides of the table looked like parboiled pork loins. On her wrists were gapping mouth-like wounds drooling blood. Her hands flapped back unnaturally, baring gnarled fangs of sliced tendons. The puddle Hester had thought made by rain, was blood.

"The poor thing," Hester lamented. "Who is she?"

Jimmy put his arm around Hester and whispered in her ear, "I'll tell you later."

As distracted as she was by the ghastly spectacle in front of her, at the sound of Jimmy's voice, something inside Hester quickened. His breath was hot on her ear, his arm heavy on her shoulder. The fierce spotlight of the sun beamed on them. Hester glanced up and followed the dense foliage of the woods to the treetops that bore down on the dusty market like the curl of a giant green wave. Hester, against all resolve, wanted to kiss Jimmy, lead him back to the minivan, forget about this horror, and get lost in the pleasure his body promised, and she knew, could deliver. Yes, she wanted him inside her again, and she might have tried to make it happen, but there was no escape from what was in front of her.

It was too much and too horrible. She put her head down. She did feel bad for this woman, her unattractive body, her messy death, people hovering around her corpse whispering wild speculations to one another.

Nice or not nice? What did it matter now? The woman, whoever she was, was good for nothing now but fodder for gossip. In a matter of minutes, hours, or days, she'd be history.

Hester's eyes welled up with tears.

She's in a better place now... Hester tried to comfort herself with the kind of thing her mother or father or sister would've said, but it had been decades since she'd seen them or heard their voices. She didn't believe much of what they believed anymore. She was as dead to them as this woman was to the world.

Jesus Christ, she didn't want to, but she couldn't help feeling sorry for herself.

Look at all that'd gone wrong. And she had only herself to blame. Her overpowering desire to be loved, her fear of failure, her stupid delusions, and her utter denial of reality had reduced her life to its present pathetic state. What a coward she'd been!

Look at last night, drawn to that young man like a moth to a flame. It had felt good and satisfied her in a way that reminded her of the first time with Arty, back in college in that ancient Airstream, the black light making it seem the whites of his eyes were boring through her very soul. Or even that time with Al in her place in Trenton. She didn't want to remember anything good about Al, but that was one of the best times ever for her.

She hadn't regretted either of those encounters initially, but she had lived to regret both, deeply. So would she end up regretting what she did with Jimmy?

Last night she was sure she wouldn't, but in the light of day she knew, of course, she would. Does a bird have wings? A camel a hump? Sure as hell, it would come back, as Al would've put it, "to bite her in the ass."

So be it. But for now, she must do better and rise above her own crass urges.

Hester looked again at the dead woman. It was obvious now that the woman had slit her own wrists.

Unlike this poor old girl, I'm still alive to straighten my life out, and I will. Hester promised. But as she stared at the body, she started crying, her nose started running. She wiped it with the bottom of her shirt and was disgusted with the smear it left. When would be the next time she'd be able to wash her clothes? Would she have to go and rinse them off in the muddy river? When would she have enough money to go to the Laundromat? Enough to buy some decent clothes?

The corpse, Hester could see, had broken many of the precious things she needed to sell in order to get enough money to get her life back. The corpse had turned beautiful things into a pile of trash.

Hester stood up, moved toward the dead body, and looked into its open eyes. They'd rolled up into the sockets and were now milky white moons that made the woman appear to be oblivious to everything, but most of all to Hester's grave disappointment.

Twenty-Three

Jimmy Raymer struggled to contain the—would the right word be—joy he was feeling.

Lola, goddamn Lola Giordano is gone. Good riddance.

The blood, the fatal wounds, the obvious pain she'd suffered, the woman deserved it. Jimmy didn't give a damn if she had a penis or not, Lola had seduced Cecilia and stolen her from him. He hated Ms. Giordano; but now the old bitch was out of his life. Finally, he could stop thinking about her, period.

Already, those in the crowd who knew how much Jimmy adored raven-haired Cecilia were watching him, trying to size-up his reaction to this unbelievable turn of events. He stood his ground defiantly, legs spread wide, arms crossed over his chest, his face expressionless.

Along with the relief, he was feeling a barrage of memories exploded on the blank slate of his brain.

Last night, crawling into the back of that woman's van, having sex with her, when he barely knew her, was reckless, something his father would've done, and he did not want to be like his father. Never! On the verge of breaking down, though, Jimmy didn't back out of the minivan and leave. No, he leaned forward and touch Hester's leg and…

He'd been thinking of his mother, longing for her, remembering that day, the red sweater tangled in the branches of the fallen tree. Seven years after it happened, the day he got his driver's license, Jimmy made up some big lie so Harry would let him take his car. He drove south, followed the Delaware to Trenton, pulled into the marina lot, and walked along the river bank as far as he could go. He searched through brambles and waded into the shallows. He walked almost to Bordentown until the brush got too thick and the bank of the river too steep. He was looking for his mother's bones, one bone, any small part of his Mom.

He remembered the time before his sister was born. His father and mother would sit at the kitchen table drinking beer, smoking cigarettes, and watching moths careen into the screen door. They got along okay as long they stuck to talking about the heat and the moths. Jimmy stayed in the corner, reading his comic books. If he was quiet and didn't pester them for anything, they let him stay up.

Every once in a while Harry, his curly hair glistening with sweat, sweat ringing the pits of his sleeveless T-shirt, would push his hot body back from the table, stand up, and pace around the small kitchen. Built like a wrestler, thick neck, broad shoulders, huge biceps, Harry talked as he walked, "I'll take a second mortgage on the house, Agnes. I can make that dilapidated flea market into something. And it's close to home. Only three goddamn miles from here. I can go back and forth no trouble. I'll be around so much you'll be sick of me."

Jimmy's mother's face had grown plump like a full moon. She smoothed her thinning hair with her hands and pulled it up into a ponytail. Her belly was huge, and under her old red sweater her belly button stuck out like a small thumb. Jimmy hated looking at what seemed like one of his mother's private parts. He was short for his age, just above eye-level of the thumb thing. He didn't want to, but when she was standing anywhere near him, he couldn't stop staring at it.

Agnes shifted her weight and propped her feet up on a chair in front of her. Her swollen toes resembled cocktail wieners. She stared at them, lit another cigarette, and looked at Harry.

It was Harry's dream, not hers. Jimmy could tell by the crooked expression on her face, the way her voice cracked a little when she said, "Well, Harry, it is up to you what you do; but, if you want my opinion, I think you got a pretty good job right now with the county water department. Maybe it's better not to look a gift horse in the mouth."

"A gift horse in the mouth?" His father stopped in his tracks. "A gift horse? I'll tell you about the gift horse of a county job I have. You get up every morning and spend the whole day digging ditches and see how you like it, Agnes. You slave away out there in ninety degrees for eight, ten hours diggin' a hole till your back's nearly broke, and you're so hot you think your head's gonna to burst into flames. Or how about when it's ten degrees and the wind's howlin', and you're so cold you're afraid your face is gonna fall off, and you still have to keep digging cause the pipes are frozen and half the town doesn't have water? No, Agnes Raymer, you're the one who got the goddamn gift horse. You lounge around all day regulating the thermostat and seeing that Junior doesn't kill himself or starve to death. Now that's what I call a gift horse of a life, Mrs. Raymer. So, no, if that's your opinion, then I don't want it!"

He started circling the table. He was a shark again like he was the other day when his Mom didn't feel good and was still in bed. Jimmy was in the kitchen eating a bowl of cereal. Harry came in the door, circled the table, and slapped him so hard on the back of the head he fell off the chair. Harry bent over him and whispered, "That's for trying to show me up, you little asshole."

Jimmy didn't know then—hell, he didn't know now—what his father meant; but that was the first time Harry hit him. After that Harry started roughing him up every time his mother wasn't around. He never told her. What could she do about it? Harry wasn't nice to her anymore either.

"Goddamn it." Harry stopped circling the table, stood in front of Agnes, and slammed his empty beer bottle down. "Why can't you just go along with me? Look, Agnes, I don't want to spend the rest of my life living in a little bungalow in Titusville. It might be alright for you, but I got aspirations." Harry was at that point where he couldn't shut up or sit still, at least not until all the beer in the house was gone. Then he'd stagger upstairs and pass out.

Jimmy snuck out of the kitchen and up to his room, closed the door, and put a chair in front of it. From the window he watched clouds move across the nearly full moon. He heard Harry's heavy footsteps on the stairs, in the hallway; the door slamming; Harry's body flopping onto the bed.

Outside, his Mom walked through a shaft of moonlight just before it disappeared. All Jimmy could see of her now was the tip of her cigarette. It swung back and forth then upward. When she inhaled, her face glowed in its light for a second, and Jimmy felt like he was down there, inside her like the baby was.

The fickle clouds kept making Agnes disappear and reappear. The cicadas were so loud Jimmy's heart raced. He wanted to run to his mother and her to hold him and say what she used to. "Our moon is always full to the brim, Jimmy. We have a good life compared to a lot of people."

But if Harry woke up, he might find Jimmy and dig his thick fingers into the soft spots on the back of his neck.

The clouds passed and Jimmy saw his Mom twirl in a slow circle, her head back, her face a small luminous planet. Despite the fact that she didn't want Harry to buy the flea market and despite Harry's angry words to her about it, Jimmy knew she was probably thinking, "God, I am so lucky."

Maybe it was because she was having another baby. Or maybe it was because she was always such a goddamn optimist. Well, at least she was until Alice was born.

Twenty-Four

In a matter of minutes three police cars descended on the flea market. Jimmy was still trying to keep the crowd back. An officer with a blood hound approached the corpse, let the dog get a good sniff, and waited until it got wind of something. In a few seconds the hound was sniffing Hester's legs, nosing her hand, and her pubic area. Hester stood still, barely tolerating the invasion, thinking, why do they have a dog here? Can't they see it was a suicide?

She wished the dog would leave her alone. Running out of patience, she almost hollered at the young officer to, please, get the beast away from her.

Then the dog sat down next to her, his head swiveling back and forth between the officer and Hester. Meanwhile other police personnel examined the body. Hester watched a woman place her stethoscope on the dead woman's neck. She shook her head, no. A man put his head to the dead woman's chest. He shook his head, no. The examination was senseless. By now you didn't need to be a coroner to know the woman on the table was dead: hands dangling, cuts like bloody vaginas, severed cartilage glinting in the sun.

It reminded Hester of the cat dissection she'd done in high school. The thought of cutting open a dead animal made her sick, but the ritual was necessary to pass the class. She begged Mrs. Johnston to make an exception. She loved cats, and it would make her sick to cut one open. Mrs. Johnston said she was being immature, told her to rise to the occasion. Learning what lies beneath the skin of any creature was an invaluable experience. She should be grateful for the opportunity, not all students got to do a cat.

Okay, the cat had given up its life so she could learn something. In gratitude to the cat, she'd do it. The smell was off-putting enough; but when she cut through the skin, pulled it back, and saw the internal organs, she almost threw-up.

"This your table?" the officer holding the hound's leash said to Hester. She nodded dumbly.

"This your car?" Again she nodded.

"Can we ask you a few questions?"

"I guess so," she said weakly and immediately hated how she sounded, how like a little girl instead of a person old enough to be a lot of people's mother.

"What is your name?"

"Hester Murph...I mean Randal. Hester Randal." God, she sounded like she didn't even know her own name. She'd hesitated because she wasn't married to Al anymore, but she hadn't taken her maiden back when she signed off on the divorce. So, technically, she was still a Murphy.

"Is it Randal or is it something else, Ma'am?" An older policeman who'd been standing nearby listening, stepped forward and took up the questioning. A small crowd gathered behind them. Hester felt penned in.

"Murphy." She hated to say it, but could see this was official business.

"Okay, Mrs. Murphy, where..."

"It's Ms. Murphy actually," she corrected the man.

"Sorry, Ms. Murphy, okay? Do you know the dead woman?"

"No."

"Have you ever seen her before?"

Hester glanced at the body on the table. "Well, she does look vaguely familiar."

"Now where were you last night?"

"Last night?" What could Hester say, in the back of her vehicle having sex with Jimmy, a man young enough to be her son? No, she couldn't. But she didn't want to lie. She'd promised she never would again.

"I went to a restaurant in Lambertville for a drink."

"What restaurant?"

"Bull's."

"What time?"

"Around four, after the market closed."

"Wasn't that a little early for a drink?"

"I…I guess it was a little early," Hester stammered.

"Were you alone?" the officer asked.

"No." Please, she silently prayed, don't ask me anymore…

"Who were you with?"

"Jimmy…" God, she couldn't remember Jimmy's last name. Had he even told her? "I'm sorry," she continued, "I don't know his last name."

The officer shifted his weight, looked around until he found Jimmy in the crowd, and pointed. "Is that the Jimmy you're talking about?"

"Yes."

"Raymer. The last name is Raymer. Hey, Jimmy," the officer hollered. "Get over here."

Jimmy hurried over and shook the officer hand. "Hey, Steve, how goes it?"

My God, Jimmy and the cop are on a first name basis. Relief washed over Hester. Obviously, this whole process would be expedited. The truth was simple. The woman had slit her wrists. Jimmy would clear the whole thing up. Was it her lucky day or what when she met this young man?

"You took this lady to Bull's last night?"

"Yeah, Steve, I asked Ms. Randal…"

"The lady told me her name was Ms. Murphy," Steve interrupted.

Hester clarified, "Randal is my maiden name. Murphy was my married name. Officially, I'm still Murphy because I neglected to get my name changed when the divorce went through, but I prefer to be called Randal."

"You should just say Ms. Randal-Murphy and keep it simple,

Ma'am," said Steve.

"Anyway," continued Jimmy, "I asked her to join me for a beer. It was her first time selling. I felt a little sorry for her when she didn't have the greatest day. You know how it is, just divorced, got screwed over by the old man."

At this Steve said to Hester, "Do you realize what a great guy Jimmy Raymer is? There's not a nicer guy in the whole town, lady. Do you realize that? I've been looking after this kid for years now, ever since I realized his old man was no good."

"Yes, Officer," said Hester. "I guess I do. He's been really kind to me. He's really gone above and beyond helping me to..." She meant to say, set up, but almost slipped and said, come.

Was she losing her mind?

"So what time did the two of you get back here?" Steve was looking at Jimmy.

"About six."

About six? Hester kept her eyes down, flinching inside at the lie.

"What did you do after that?"

"She..." Jimmy looked down at Hester. "...got into the back of her van to catch some sleep before today's market. After I knew she was locked in, I went to my apartment, watched some T.V. until I heard a car pull in. Nothing exciting."

Nothing exciting? Another lie? But hadn't Hester thought exactly that. Jimmy would not have found what they did exciting. And obviously he had his reasons for not admitting that he climbed in the back of the minivan and ravished her body. Jimmy was leaving a whole lot out, but, maybe, he was trying to protect her reputation. Lambertville was a small town, and Hester Randal Murphy was already carrying enough baggage. Besides their encounter had nothing to do with this dead woman's bizarre suicide.

"Whose car pulled up?" asked Steve.

"Lola Giordano's..."

"You mean," interrupted Steve, "the dead woman is *the* Lola Giordano?"

"Yep," said Jimmy, "makes you wonder, doesn't it, why somebody as rich and famous as she was, would do something like this to herself?"

Hester was in shock. That's why this woman looked so familiar. Hester knew Lola Giordano's work and what a powerhouse the woman was in the world of Professional Development. *And she killed herself?* Hester was confounded. That woman had the whole world in her hands.

"Anyway," Jimmy continued, "Cecilia was with her. I guess they had a fight or something. By the time I got downstairs, Lola had stormed off and Cecilia was sitting in the car crying. She told me, she'd broken up with Lola. She begged Lola not to try to walk back to town, but Lola just kept going. Cecilia finally took off in the car to go look for her. I went back up to my place. When Cecilia didn't come back, I figured they'd made up. Can't say I wasn't disappointed, but I managed to fall asleep anyway. So, I guess that's why Ms. Giordano did herself in. She couldn't stand losing Cecilia."

"Sure does make you wonder, but you never know with suicides. Maybe she did, maybe she didn't. Maybe somebody just made it look like she did. But, let's get some facts straight first. What time did all this happen?"

"Probably around ten or eleven," said Jimmy.

"Where's Cecilia now?"

"I don't have a clue. I imagine they were staying somewhere in Lambertville."

"Lambertville's a small town. Won't take long to track her down." Steve stuck his hands in his pockets. "Kind of bothers me, though, how Ms. Giordano's on top of this table and all of Ms. Murphy's stuff. And how in the hell did she get the tarp back over herself. What a hell of a place to kill yourself? We'll have to see if she left a note and what Forensics makes of it."

"I agree it's odd; but the woman was odd." Jimmy corrected himself. "I mean, she was a genius and eccentric. You know how crazy somebody who's too smart for their own good can be. She was like that, I think. Too damn smart for her own good. Well, Steve, I hope you guys can figure it out. Let me know if I can help?"

"Will do, Jimmy. Market's closed for today, though. Going to take a while to process the body and search the area."

"No problem. Do what you have to do. I'll let the dealers know it's time to pack up." Jimmy shook Steve's hand and left.

Hester was in a quandary. She wanted to leave too. She wanted to get in her van and drive as far away from all this as she could, but she couldn't afford to leave her belongings behind. She had to salvage what she could. The thought of waiting, though, of looking at Lola Giordano's body a minute longer was too much.

She hurried to her vehicle and pulled her handbag from under the seat. She'd take the money she made yesterday, fill her gas tank, and head up to Lou's to pay him something so he wouldn't lock her out of her unit. After, she'd get a nice room at the Stockton Inn. She could feel the hot water, the fluffy towels, the soft bed. She'd even treat herself to dinner. Salmon, a glass of Malbec...she'd worry about what was going on at the Nugget later.

She closed the door and leaned against it rummaging through the cavernous pit of her handbag for the envelope.

A few drops of blood from Lola Giordano's fatal wounds were still plopping onto the dirt.

Jimmy, clipboard in hand, was all business as he systematically checked off those dealers who would get a refund and those who wouldn't because they'd paid discounted rent by the month, rain or shine...or death.

It wasn't there! The envelope full of money wasn't in her bag!

Hester opened the car door, dumped the contents of her pocketbook on the driver's seat: wallet, keys, a pen, tissues, check book, old grocery list, useless tampon.

What the ...? Hester was in a panic. Where in the hell could her money be?

She had to find that money. She knelt outside the van, put her head on the floor. Nothing under the seats. She pulled everything out of the glove compartment and went through it paper by paper.

She went to the back, lifted the hatch, and proceeded to take out the remaining boxes, the towel, the rag, old food wrappers, the tire iron, the pump, the jack, a golf umbrella, one quarter and three pennies that must have fallen out of Jimmy's pocket when he'd wriggled out of his pants.

No envelope. No money. Her heart was pounding. She wanted to scream and slam things around. How had this happened?

"Mrs. Murphy, what do you think you are doing? This entire market including your vehicle is a crime scene." Steve was behind her.

She turned to face him, "Not my car." It was to her a fact, plain and simple. Not my car. Not me, I have nothing to do with this. She ignored him, turned away, crawled into the van, and lay down to check under the seats from the rear.

"Mrs. Murphy, your car *is* part of this crime scene."

Hester heard the exasperation in his voice. He might as well have said, what the fuck, lady?

"Look, Ma'am, your car was here. You were here. We're not through with you or your car yet."

"But I don't know anything about any of this. I've never seen that woman before. Well, that's not true exactly. I mean I do know who Lola Giordano is. Who doesn't? But, I don't know any of these people really. None of them. I just want to find my money and leave." Hester was on all fours again shouting over her shoulder. The fact that Officer Steve was more or less forced to stare at her behind didn't register with her at all. She stretched forward to reach under the passenger seat and feel around.

"Okay, that's enough," Steve said emphatically. "Get out of the vehicle. Move away from it and don't touch another thing until we tell you."

Hester froze, shimmied out of the back of the van, and stood in front of the man. He pointed at a spot several yards away. Trembling, Hester moved to the spot.

Where in the hell is my money?

She wanted to grab the sides of her head and scream. Too stunned to remain on her feet, Hester sat down on the dirt and put her face in her hands.

She must've been robbed.

Mentally, she retraced her steps from Saturday, when she'd made the money and put it in the envelope, to now, when she couldn't find it anywhere.

She remembered leaving her handbag hanging on the back of the chair at Bull's, unzipped.

Jimmy left with that woman, left the handbag where it was without giving it a second thought; or, for that matter, me a second thought. Oh, hell. Somebody walked by, reached in, and took it.

How could she have been that careless?

She had enough gas in her car to get up to Lou's, but what good would it do her? She had the twenty-eight cents she'd just found, and that probably belonged to Jimmy, and the one dollar and twenty-three cents in her wallet. That was it. She wrung her hands together and tried not to come undone.

The wind kicked up and shoveled the clouds into a dark pile over the river.

One of the investigators was feeling around with his gloved hand in the puddle of blood that had just about turned to mud. He stood up. Another investigator opened a baggy, and the man dropped something in it. They whispered together for a minute, huddled with Steve, retreated to their vehicles, and drove away.

Now the only people left beside Hester were Steve, the EMTs, and dead woman lying there with her mouth open, her eyes open, and her fat legs spread irreverently apart. Hester wanted to go and push her legs together, but she'd already been told to keep her distance once.

Around noon, a hearse pulled up, and two guys from the funeral parlor lifted the body and moved it onto a stretcher. Lola Giordano's hands flapped up and down, the wounds like two mouths trying to form words. Slowly, the men lowered her into a plastic bag and zipped it up. More of Hester's precious things got knocked onto the ground in the process. Neither man seemed to notice.

Steve picked through the broken items on the table and carefully checked under each thing that had toppled over, then he filled a vile with mud from the puddle and used Q-tips to swab samples from the splatter that was everywhere. He spent quite a bit of time rummaging through the stuff Hester had taken from her van and inspecting the empty inside with his flashlight even though there was plenty of natural light.

Around three o'clock, he signaled thumbs up to Hester, went to his vehicle, and drove off in a cloud of dust. She guessed his gesture meant she was off the hook for…what? Being in the wrong place at the wrong time. Surely, he didn't think she had anything to do with the dead woman. Then it struck her that they had her in their computer. Officer Steve probably already knew she was *the* Hester Randal Murphy, former wife of that perverted high school vice-principal, already knew she was the Hester who buried the dead body of a young woman instead of reporting the death to the authorities.

Oh no, thought Hester as she planted her hands on the ground and tried to help herself to her feet. She was numb inside. Her knees were stiff, her back ached. It took her a few minutes to stand up straight and take a couple of steps. She brushed the dirt off the seat of her pants and started to put her stuff back in the van. It took her awhile to organize it so there'd be room for her to sleep.

She went over to the tables, stared at the mess, and took an inventory. Anything metal or wood was okay. Lola's body hadn't made a dent in the silver footed tray or the pewter tankards or the hand-carved American eagle, but her turn-of-the-century German doll was a mess, its golden hair matted with dried mucous, its blue satin dress black with blood. Hester dragged the trash bin next to the table and threw the doll in. How she hated to do it. She looked in. The doll was staring up at her. It was how she imagined her own baby after the abortion, the quack throwing her golden-haired girl in that big galvanized trash can. This terrible deed she'd done, she tried to keep the memory of it caged in a far corner of her brain, but, here, it had escaped again.

Think only of the doll…how charming the guest room, the doll in it doll's chair in the corner by the window, the sun reddening the maple leaves.

Everything about her old Victorian was charming. If only she could go there, climb the mahogany stairs, sit by the window, the leaves beckoning in the breeze.

Hester almost snatched the doll out of the trash, but how would she ever get the gunk from its hair, the blood from its dress? She went back to picking up the broken pieces of her fragile things and was about to throw a handful in the bin when she saw what looked like her shaving kit beneath the doll. She put the broken fragments back on the table and retrieve the kit.

When she opened it, it was empty.

What the…? Did she get ripped off again? She couldn't remember seeing anyone look at it yesterday, although most of what happened yesterday was a blur. But the razor was 14 karat gold!

Hester sighed. What else could go wrong? Then she thought of the investigator with his hand in the mud. What had he found?

If the dead woman used the blade from Hester's razor, then where was the razor?

Oh hell, if Hester went to the police and told them she'd had the razor and the blade on her table, they might think she had something to do with the lady's death. She couldn't risk getting involved. Besides, out of the blue, anyone could've walked by and stolen the case, dropped the blade, taken the valuable razor, and thrown the case away. Hester stared at the empty case. *Nothing but trouble*, she thought and tossed it back in the trash.

She turned to the table, gathered up the broken pieces of things, and threw them in on top of the case. She wiped off a set of six ornate brass Arabian skewers and worked her way down the table cleaning things up as best she could. Her other dolls, all celluloid, the cowboy, the cowgirl, and the one with the blonde hair and red dress had survived unscathed. Thank goodness for small favors, she really liked those three little dolls, especially the blonde one.

It would be dark soon. She should have been famished, but burdened by the proximity of death, by the shock of it, Hester's aching heart trumped her gnawing hunger. This stranger's suicide brought back all of Hester's despair. She knew once she crawled into the back of the minivan, she would not be alone. No, Lola Giordano would be right there with her all night long.

Of all the luck...

Twenty-Five

Cecilia was awakened by someone pounding on the hotel room door. She'd been almost at the end of the familiar nightmare. Her mother holding her, her mother's arm tight around her small waist, her mother's lips on the nape of her neck. She was so little and at first she liked the sensation of her mother kissing her there, but as the dream went on the kissing became urgent, the snakelike arm constricting. She could feel her mother's breasts rubbing against her back. What was her mother doing? Where was her other hand? Why was she breathing so heavily? Her tongue licking, finding little Cecilia's ear? Her mother moaning with... The pounding on the door persisted.

"Hold your horses, Lola, I'm coming," she yelled as loud as she could as she hunted for something to put on.

More pounding.

Cecilia ripped the sheet off the bed, wrapped it around her naked body, and opened the door saying, "What the hell, Lola....Oh, Officer Steve. It's you. What are you doing here? I thought you were my partner Lola. I've been waiting all..."

"Look, Ms. Kurts, Cecilia, you better sit down. I've got bad news. I came myself out of respect for Jimmy. You know he's like a son to me, and, well, since the two of you were engaged and all, I figured it best to tell you myself."

"Tell me what?"

"I'm going to get right to the point. Lola Giordano is dead."

"Dead?" Cecilia's big cat eyes glistened with tears. She lowered her head; her black hair veiled her face for a minute. She slunk back, sat on the bed, and looked up forlornly. "What happened, Steve?"

"Appears to be a suicide. Jimmy found her on top of a table full of stuff at the Silver Nugget. She was under a tarp, her wrists slashed."

Cecilia's uttered the word, no, several times before she burst out crying. "Oh my God! It's all my fault. We had a terrible fight! I never should've broken up with her. She loved me so much. Oh my God, I will never forgive myself."

"Look, I talked to Jimmy. I know about the argument. I hate to ask you at a time like this, but it's my job. Was Ms. Giordano having any other problems? Any money problems? Any depression?"

"Money problems? Absolutely not. She was making money hand-over-fist. New books in the works all the time. No, money was no object. But, lately, she had been getting more sensitive, more jealous of me actually. See, Steve, I want a baby. I want to start a family, but Lola didn't want any part of it. Last night at Dina's I told her I was thinking about getting back with Jimmy. I only said it to make Lola jealous, to make her give in to me about the baby. But she must've taken me seriously." Cecilia's hands were shaking. She pressed them against her lips to make them stop. The sheet around her was loosening, her cleavage almost entirely revealed. She did nothing to hide it. She could feel the eyes of the officer, Jimmy's dear friend, on her.

"Don't take this the wrong way," Steve said, "but I have to ask. Did Lola Giordano leave you anything? I mean, are you going to profit from her death?"

"Steve!" Cecilia's voice was indignant. She straightened up; the sheet slipped even more, more of her huge breasts became visible. "How would I know? Lola was good to me. She was generous and loving. We never talked about money or wills or anything like that. She paid me well for the work I did for her. She was a wonderful person. I never asked her for one thing, but a baby. And that's the truth."

"I believe you, Cecilia. Have no reason not to," Steve said, "and I am very sorry for your loss."

"Can I see her now? I mean, can I see the body?"

"I'd wait until they get her to the morgue. Are you the executor?"

"I told you, I don't even know if there's a will," Cecilia said defensively, but quickly softened her voice. "I'll call her lawyer as soon as I get dressed, Steve, to see if she left a directive."

"I have a few more loose ends to tie up and have to wait for the autopsy before I can make the suicide official, but it looks like that's the direction we're headed," Steve said as he backed up and put his hand on the door knob. "Just two more things, Cecilia. One, do you know Hester Murphy? And two, if your friend Lola did kill herself why crawl under a tarp on a flea market table to do it? And on top of all that lady's stuff? I mean, think about it. Why climb up on a table full of antiques to slit your wrists? Why not sit in your car or go down by the river or into the woods? It's just too random, doesn't make sense; and according to everybody we interviewed, she wasn't a stupid person by a long shot. I'm sure you know that, Cecilia."

"One, I never heard of Hester Murphy; and two is simple. Lola, as I told you, was a jealous person when it came to me. She probably would've done anything to hurt poor Jimmy if she believed I was going back with him. Getting under that tarp would make people think Jimmy finally got back at Lola for taking me away from him. Yes, Lola was smart alright. Smart enough to figure out a way to take Jimmy down with her." Cecilia stood up and caught the falling sheet, but not before she knew Steve had glimpsed one of her rosy nipples.

She heard him catch his breath as he pulled the door closed behind him and mumbled, "Thanks, that does shed light on precisely what was bothering me."

Twenty-Six

A week later on the last dog day of August, Officer Steve drove down to the Silver Nugget to personally let Jimmy know before it hit the news—Lola Giordano's death was ruled a suicide. The woman slit her wrists and bled to death.

Cecilia, who in the intervening days had moved her things from the hotel to Theresa's old room in Jimmy's apartment, stood next to Jimmy listening.

"She used a double-edged blade," said Steve. "The kind from one of those old metal razors. The ones nobody in their right mind uses anymore. Blade in left hand sliced right wrist, victim quickly switched blade to right hand and sliced left wrist. We found the weapon in the puddle of blood beneath the table. Ms. Giordano must've brought it with her to the market."

"I never saw a razor like that in Lola's house," Cecilia offered. "But then again, Ms. Giordano had so many possessions, I couldn't be sure whether she had an antique razor or not."

"Well, they still sell those blades in some drug stores today," said Steve. "She could've gotten her hands on one lots of places."

Cecilia nodded, her face as blank as a sheep's.

"You want a beer, Steve," Jimmy asked.

"Been on the wagon, but thanks, kid. Just wanted to let you know since you two can vouch for each other, and the only other person on the property was Ms. Randal-Murphy, and we can't tie her to Ms. Giordano beyond the fact that they both were educators, I'm ruling it a suicide. Coroner, county prosecutor, all agree."

"Good, because Hester Whatever-Her-Name-Is, is harmless. Trust me."

"I do, Jimmy. Case closed. But I can't help wondering why somebody who had life by the balls like that woman did, would do herself in?"

At that Cecilia started to cry.

"Look, stop wondering, Steve. All I know, is neither Cecilia nor I meant for this to happen. Right, Cecilia?" Jimmy said as he put his arm around Cecilia's shoulder. "Who really knows what goes on inside a person?"

"You got a point there," said Steve shaking his head. "Oh yeah, and find that poor lady friend of yours a place to stay. It's illegal to sleep in your vehicle in the fine State of New Jersey."

"Not to worry, Steve. I moved her into my old room downstairs, temporarily."

"You mean your old closet. Well, good. It's better than breaking the law."

When Jimmy went to show Steve out, he saw Cecilia sink into the couch. God, he felt sorry for her, but he didn't feel one bit sorry for that sicko Lola.

That old bitch... he thought as he came back up the stairs. She was gone for good, and Cecilia could be his again, if he was careful, and patient. Yes, he could win Cecilia back. He knew he could. He had to.

Cecilia was still slumped in the sofa. She swiped one weary palm over her forehead, over her long wild hair, and gathered it in her fist. "What am I going to do? What in the hell am I going to do without Lola?"

Jimmy looked down at Cecilia, at her bronzed skin, thick eyebrows, grey eyes. Her mouth was open, the small, sexy gap between her bottom front teeth visible. She was almost perfect, but not completely. He loved her even more for that, and he was grateful to her for kissing him that night outside Bull's. She'd made it a soul kiss right away. Let his tongue in her mouth, and he'd moved it around like it deserved to be there. He'd had to suppress the ugly thought of Lola's tongue inside her mouth too, maybe more times than his; and focus on how good it felt, how it was just like old times, just like before Lola.

Jimmy wanted to sit next to Cecilia, reach under her shirt, and touch her breasts. Instead, he started pacing back and forth. Periodically he'd pause and glance down at the top of her head as she stared down at her hands.

He wanted to fuck her brains out so badly he could barely continue putting one foot in front of the other; but she seemed, for the first time since he met her, fragile. If he sat down and touched her or said the wrong thing, she might sense his neediness and the enormity of it might scare her off.

Cecilia picked her head up, and Jimmy saw her tears.

He'd never seen her cry before, not even when she'd fallen down on the ice one winter and had nearly broken her arm. Her sadness pained him. He wanted to shout at Cecilia, Lola was no good! But he knew never to say that or anything bad about Lola Giordano.

"Look, C." He'd never called her that before, but with her crying and all he was trying to be as gentle as he could. "I'll do anything I can to help you. You know you can count on me."

"Yes. You're there for me. I get that. I appreciate it," she said without sounding too convincing. "Really, I do, but I can't help feeling that if I hadn't seen you the other night, then none of this would've happened."

"What? You think Lola killed herself because you saw me at Bull's?"

"I don't know. If I hadn't told her you kissed me…"

Cecilia had kissed him, not the other way around. But Jimmy wasn't about to point that out at the moment.

"So what if we kissed?" he said. "What's the big deal? We were engaged to be married at one time. We were close for crying out loud, C."

"Please, stop calling me C. That's what Lola called me. It was her pet name for me. God, I should never have said anything. We were having dinner, and we got into a fight over something stupid so I told her you kissed me." Cecilia looked down at her hands again. Her voice was a whisper like she was talking to herself, and Jimmy just happened to be there. "I told her how I didn't mean to, but I kissed you back. I didn't think she'd care. You're a man; and she thinks, thought, I wasn't into men anymore. But you should've seen the look on her face. It was like I slapped her. She was so hurt she started to cry, and I felt like a piece of crap for hurting her. I should've never told her anything." She stood up and looked into Jimmy's eyes. "Damn you, it was all your fault."

That word "fault" was like a bullet ripping through Jimmy's flesh. He felt like a piece of shit. He wanted to grab Cecilia and shake her. If she blamed him for what happened to her dyke girlfriend, well…. "Cecilia, don't give me so much credit. I don't think someone as smart as Lola Giordano would kill herself just because of one little kiss."

"It wasn't a little kiss, though, huh?" Cecilia taunted Jimmy.

He knew he was on thin ice here, but, God, he had to stick up for himself and nip this craziness in the bud. He had to get her to see him, and herself, and their kiss in the right light.

"Calm down, and let's think about this for a minute before you start blaming me. We had a past together, and, as I recall, a damn good one. I loved you and thought you loved me. We were friends for a long time, then lovers. You couldn't have forgotten all that." She pressed her lips together.

"And do you remember how we good we were at kissing? We can't help it if old habits die hard."

Just talking about kissing her made him want to kiss her. His body ached to have her. He turned away and pretended to look out the window, not sure if he'd won his point or made things worse.

Cecilia flopped back on the sofa. "I know you're right, but I just never should've mentioned it to her. She was a little crazy you know."

No kidding, he thought, and someday, maybe, he'd like to hear about just how crazy the old bitch was. But now wasn't the time. Now was the time for him to sit down next to Cecilia and take her gently in his arms, not to kiss her, but to hold her like he would if he were her brother, and she were his sister. That is, if she'd let him.

Twenty-Seven

Hester slept in the van the Sunday and Monday after Lola Giordano's death. Jimmy wasn't happy about it. He told her on Tuesday she couldn't camp out there forever.

"I'd have left by now, but all of the money I made on Saturday was stolen. I think somebody took it out of my bag when we were at the bar." Hester tried not to make it sound like an excuse or an accusation, tried not to sound angry about it; but she was. "And now I don't have a dime to pay for my storage unit up at Lou's in Frenchtown. He's probably already locked me out. All of my things are his now. Imagine that? I can't."

"Geez, the money you made is gone? Wow, Hester, I'm really sorry, but I don't know how long you can sleep in your car out there. There are laws against it. Look, I'll try to think of something and in the meanwhile, how about I call that guy Lou and see what I can do?"

"Thanks, that would be great, Jimmy." Hester lowered her head, studied the small damp clumps of clay peppered with dust. She thought about sticking one in her mouth, about the gritty feel of the earth on her teeth, the soil clinging to the back of her throat. She was hungry, hungrier than she'd ever been before in her whole life. Was this what starving felt like? Was this what made people do crazy things like eat dirt?

"You barely know me, and you've done so much to me. I mean, for me." *A Freudian slip if ever there was one.*

"Well, I like you." He smiled and folded his arms across his chest. "You remind me of my mother."

Your mother? Really? Hester wanted to say something. Maybe, shut-up, I'm not your mother, or remember me, the woman whose brains you fucked out a few nights ago. She wanted to yank herself back to the surface, get a breath of air, and make everything clear between them.

But thoughts pushed their way into her head, thoughts she'd been trying to avoid for days like how attracted she was to this man, how the thought of him touching her excited her, how the last thing she wanted to be to him was a mother.

Why, she wanted to say, did you come to me in the middle of the night? Why did you do what you did to me? Why, for a few seconds, was I the center of everything for you? And now I am nothing.

Hester knew she'd live to regret not stopping him that night, and here it was, the remorse. And she was too old now to bear it. She'd allowed him to consume the last of her beating softness. Now all that was left was her bones.

To go on she must mortar the chinks in her walls.

But with him so close to her, her own body started working against her. Inside, she ached for him. She stood silent, steeling herself against herself, while Jimmy surveyed the landscape of dust and wooden tables, turned, and left.

On Wednesday, the next flea market day, Hester had to talk to Jimmy. She could not set up in the spot where the dead woman was found. Alright, yes, she was superstitious. Yes, she was being silly.

"But, please, Jimmy," she begged him, "it really was bad luck in that spot. Look at all that I lost." He talked Joyce into switching, and Hester set up under the tree.

She sold one piece of majolica, a six inch platter shaped like a leaf, for sixty dollars. That was it, but to Hester, at that moment, it seemed a fortune. She told the man, ninety, he said fifty. She broke out in a sweat. She had to sell something, but she'd spent almost two hundred dollars for the platter in a fancy shop in Boston.

"How about sixty?" she blurted out.

The short, bald man licked his thumb and peeled three twenties off a fat roll of bills and slapped them into her open palm. Hester clutched them tightly; and when he walked away, she counted them over and over till it sunk in that she had hard cash in her hands. She pulled the collar of her shirt open and stuck the three bills into her sports bra. No one would steal her money ever again.

She asked Irwin, the guy selling next to her, to watch her stuff and hurried to the cafe in the front section of the barn and ordered bacon, eggs, whole wheat toast and a large coffee. She sat on the back of the van, her first inclination to shovel the food down her throat as quickly as she could. How many days had it been since she'd eaten anything? Since she'd found a half rotten baggy of prunes underneath the front seat. Since she'd found five stale peanuts in the bottom of the glove compartment. She forced herself to slow down. Relax. Enjoy the way the food looked, the way it smelled. Small bites of egg, toast, bacon. A sip of coffee. God, she tried not to gobble it down; but she couldn't stop herself, and in a few minutes her stomach ached from the onslaught.

And she'd hated to break that twenty, but she had to eat. And she wished she'd gotten the ninety dollars for the platter. She started mulling over her disappointment. The platter was worth ninety, worth much more than ninety.

Oh, stop it, now, she admonished herself, *more would have been better; but for Christ's sake, be grateful your stomach is full. Focus on what you did get, not on what you didn't.*

And her luck really was turning around because right after she finished her food, Jimmy came along with his clipboard and told her she could sleep in his old room off the office if she didn't have any place else to go, at least for a while until she got some money up.

"Thank you so much." Hester tried to steady her voice. She was dying of embarrassment that her life had come to this, having to accept charity from a man half her age. "Oh and thanks for calling Lou and getting me a reprieve on the rent. It must have been a real pain having to…"

"Whoa, wait a minute, I said I'd call, but unfortunately, it was too late. The jerk had already slapped a new lock on your unit; and no matter how much I argued with him, there was no way he was going to take it off. Sorry, Hester, God knows, I tried."

Well, she should've seen it coming, but it was a blow. Everything in her unit, all of her books! Everything she was counting on for money was gone! Just like that. And what was left?

She shrugged her shoulders. Not much.

"Well…" her voice cracked as though what she was about to say was going to hurt her too much to say, but she swallowed hard and went on, "…thank you for your kindness and consideration and for letting me stay in your old room."

"You're welcome. And don't hesitate to ask if there's anything you need. Cecilia and I will be right upstairs." He turned and left.

Of course, Hester would never bothered them. Why would she? She didn't know this Cecilia, had only glimpsed her on the street outside Bull's and in the doorway of the apartment. Hester tried not to think about who she was and what she and Jimmy did up in his apartment. And she fought with herself not to be jealous of Hester the younger, beautiful woman.

There were no windows in the six by eight closet, and the once white paint was a dingy yellow. A single bed was jammed up against the wall furthest from the door and next to it was a rusty two drawer file cabinet. An old wooden ship's wheel lamp with a faded blue shade sat on top of it. On the other wall a couple of wire hooks had been screwed into the sheetrock at chest level. Hester had to admit it wasn't much, but she was growing accustomed to small spaces, and the closet felt much less claustrophobic than the back of her van. Besides, who was she to complain?

Jimmy told her this was where he'd slept for years after his mother died, before Theresa convinced his father to move to Florida. Theresa whined about how the upstairs apartment wasn't even large enough for his father and her, but Jimmy knew they slept together in the big bedroom and that all Theresa used the spare room for was her stuff. The big bedroom was right over Jimmy's closet, and he could hear all of the disgusting noise they made. He wasn't an idiot.

"But, believe me in the end I was glad to be down here even if it was only a closet," Jimmy told her. He wasn't a complainer when it came to living in pathetically cramped quarters. "If I had to live upstairs with that Theresa, God knows what I would've done? I blame her for what my Mom did. She kept my father from coming home to my Mom. I know she did. I saw right away how selfish she was, and my father tiptoed around her like she was some sort of prize he couldn't bear to lose. I really do hate to call anybody a bad name; but hell, Hester, she was a real bitch."

The glory of Hester's first night in the closet was the office restroom. She spent a lot of time in there washing her hair in the small sink with the thin bar of soap. She used paper towels to clean herself and dry herself. Instead of cupping her hands together to get a drink, she drank the sulfurous water directly from the spout.

She fell asleep quickly and slept soundly under an old blanket that probably belonged to Jimmy. The next morning was the room was freezing cold, and it was only the first week in September. She went into the office. The big silver radiator was cold and the Formica floor like walking on ice. She went back into the closet and put on her only clothes and headed outside where it was actually warmer. She crossed River Road, crossed the bridge over the canal, and stood on the bank of the Delaware facing west waiting for dawn to rise up behind her. She watched the hillsides and the tops of the trees on the opposite side of the river turn rosy.

There is still beauty in my world, she thought as the sun warmed her back. Then a chill wind came at her from the river and chased her back to the office.

When Hester opened the door to the closet, she saw a thin towel and washcloth had been laid out for her on the bed. It almost made her cry. Instead of being grateful, she was wounded—he, or they, don't want me upstairs, ever, even for a bath. Hester tried not to feel bitter. Beggars can't be choosers. No, they can't. She was surely finding this out.

During the days when the market was closed, Hester laid low in the room reading whatever newspapers or magazines or books she'd found in the trash bins. The things people threw away amazed her: lamp shades, old photographs, paintings, a soup bowl, a crystal vase with one small chip, faded pillowcases, a whole half of a turkey sandwich, and books, all kinds of books. Some she knew were not worth much, but others, though ragged and stained, were leather-bound or hand-printed or first editions or signed by the author, or some combination of the above. Regardless of worth, Hester salvaged every book. Even if the poor book's cover was smeared with ketchup or wet and sticky from soda dripping all over it, Hester took the book and cleaned it as best she could and dried it in the sun or on the radiator, when it was on. Then she'd put it under a pile of other heavy books to press the pages flat again.

Saturdays, Sundays, and Wednesdays she made her rounds as soon as the last dealer pulled out of the market. She checked each bin, took anything she thought she could get money for. She wasn't too proud now to pass up anything she might be able to get even a quarter for. Any book she found she took to the room and stacked on top of the others under the bed.

In a short time she built up quite a library. Many of the books she'd already read, but there were a fair amount she hadn't: cookbooks, books on hot water heaters and instamatic cameras, paperback romances, histories of places like Constantinople and Burma, a biography of Caravaggio, odd things like that. So that would be her goal, to read every book she found that she hadn't already read.

Having a goal immediately made her feel better, gave her something to think about other than the drastic downturn her life had taken, or that sexual encounter with Jimmy, which seemed to hang on in her memory like the last petal on a rose.

The first book she chose to read was journalist Joshua Schwartz's autobiography, "Between the Lines." He began with a story about the time he went to a small town in Israel to interview a world-renowned rabbi. Schwartz was stunned to discover the holy man lived in a one room shack with only a bed, a chair, a desk, and a lamp.

"Rabbi," he said, "you're so famous, and your books are bestsellers. Why do you live like this? Where are all of your things?"

The rabbi answered, "Well, Mr. Schwartz, where are all of your things?"

"My things?" Schwartz was puzzled. "Why all my belongings are in my home in the United States where I live. I don't need anything here, Rabbi, because I'm only passing through, but you, you live here."

"That's where you're wrong, Mr. Schwartz. I may live here, but I, too, am only passing through."

Hester read it over a couple of times and let it sink in. She'd lost so much so fast. Her job, her money, her home, her clothes, her cosmetics, her hair brush, her tooth brush (her brand new Oral-B supersonic electric tooth brush). She could see it sitting on the marble double sink vanity. My how she'd grown accustomed to abundance, to owning, to having. It was difficult for her to wrap her brain around the idea of scarcity. She tried to picture herself in a bare-boned efficiency in a borderline neighborhood. A bed, a chair, a desk, a lamp. She would have little, so little that a list of everything wouldn't fill one side of a sheet of paper.

And soon the back of the van would be empty. She would be left with the discarded books piled under her bed, and the chipped and damaged things she salvaged from the trash. Everything else she'd ever owned would be gone, and she, like the Rabbi, would be passing through unencumbered.

But for tonight she had a roof over her head, and she wasn't sick. For that she should be grateful. For the setting sun and the moon and the stars and the big black bats that flew up from the river at dusk she should be grateful, but it was difficult not to dream of what she used to have, where she used to live and not be bitter about traipsing around the market rummaging through the trash and sleeping in the same clothes for a couple of weeks now.

What would happen when winter set in? All eight of her coats, including her mink from Flemington Furs, were hanging in plastic protectors in the condo's walk-in closet. She'd be cold, maybe freeze to death if she didn't save enough money to buy a coat. She'd have to count every penny. Walk the three and half miles to CVS instead of taking the van and buy generic soap, shampoo, deodorant, toothpaste, and a toothbrush. Skip the moisturizer and the conditioner. She'd have to keep an eye out on the dollar tables at the Nugget for fingernail scissors, a file, a comb. The tampons, well, she only had that one in the bottom of her handbag. Even though they cost a king's ransom, she decided she better buy more. Her period had been so erratic, which was par for the course at her age; but she couldn't be sure it wouldn't come back any minute with a vengeance, and then what would she do?

And damn it, if someone hadn't pilfered that razor and blade, she would've figured out a way to use it without mutilating herself. Even though she'd grown up in the sixties, she still couldn't fathom not shaving her legs and her armpits. And now, since it'd been weeks and the hair had gotten so long it had started to curl, she stopped looking at herself, even touching herself.

Passing through unencumbered? Now that Hester thought about it, it seemed too lofty an ideal for any woman. A woman had needs. A woman had to have things. Maybe it was easier if you were a man to sit there and be satisfied with yourself in a small room with nothing in it. Maybe a rabbi or a nun could do it, but what self-respecting woman of the world could? Maybe she wouldn't keep Schwartz's book. Maybe she'd throw that book in the river and let the current take it as far from her as it could.

Hester had been sitting on the edge of the bed. She turned off the lamp and lay down. The pile of books beneath her had grown so high they were firm against her back. She felt them through the thin mattress and imagined they were all that was supporting her, all that was lifting her sagging spirit.

Okay, she'd keep the Schwartz book and finish it.

Twenty-Eight

Jimmy flipped the switch on the coffee maker and listened to the gurgle and hiss of the coffee. He pulled the curtains aside and looked out of the kitchen window. The morning sunlight laced the treetops on the Pennsy side of the river with pink, but in the distance to the west thunderheads were gathering.

We will be married, he silently resolved as he closed the curtains and poured one cup of black for himself and a cup with skim milk for Cecilia.

He rapped gently on the door and said, "Honey, it's me," before he walked in.

She was facing away from him and balled-up under the covers, her luxurious black hair was all he could see of her. He put the coffees down on the night table and waited.

He hadn't touched her, and she'd been living with him on and off, mostly on, for close to a month now. She left the apartment only to go to the beach house which, as Lola had promised, was now hers. Everything in it—the place was packed to the rafters—was hers. She wanted to redo Jimmy's place with some of the pieces from that place. It was all she talked about.

Jimmy was mesmerized by the profusion of Cecilia's hair. He took a few steps along the side of the bed, reached down and boldly touched it. She moaned and rolled over.

"I smelled the coffee," she said and yawned. Slowly she emerged from under the covers and sat up. She had on a black thong and half her breasts hung out of her low-cut camisole. Her skin had lost its tan, but glowed white now like mother-of-pearl. She stretched her arms over her head and her legs straight out in a wide V. Jimmy felt himself starting to get a boner.

Shit, he had the urge to push her down, grab her ankles, and open her up so he could crawl inside her, die inside her. He had to turn away.

"Where are you going, babe?" she asked as she rolled across the bed and took a noisy sip of the steaming coffee.

Jimmy turned and faced her, hard on and all.

"I love you," he said. He hadn't wanted to come right out with something so serious, but his brain and body were about to explode, and he couldn't think straight. "You do know, Cecilia, how damn much I love you."

"I love you too, babe," she said and sat up and looked at him, a childlike expression in her eyes.

Jimmy sat next to her and said what he hadn't wanted to say, "Then why can't we be together?" Begging was such a turn-off.

"Because I'm just not ready yet."

"Will you ever be?"

"It hasn't been easy for me losing Lola."

"But she is gone, Cecilia. You have to accept it."

"Accept what? That she killed herself. Do you know how hard it is to accept that somebody you love doesn't love you enough to stay alive?"

"Do I know? Have you forgotten what my mother did?" Jimmy said. Hell, it sort of aggravated him that Cecilia didn't seem to remember something so important to him. Was she really that upset about Lola? She couldn't have loved Lola as much as he loved his own mother. Lola had been one big opportunity for Cecilia, for little Cecilia who didn't have *a pot-to-piss in*. Theresa's words rang in his head.

But there was no way Jimmy could say these things to Cecilia. If he did, she might get in her Escalade and drive off into the sunset so instead he said, "I understand completely, Cecilia. You've been through an awful time, and all I really want to do is help."

"You can help me by just being my friend, by giving me some time to grieve for my loss." She took another sip of her coffee, and smiled at him.

The smile was honey, thick sweet honey. Jimmy saw himself licking the honey of her, pulling aside the thong, putting his tongue in her, moving it around inside her, in, out, in her as far as it would go. He'd pull the camisole down, grab her breasts, bite her nipples till her insides hummed, till she screamed for him to stop.

Too bad he didn't have the balls to try.

Twenty-Nine

On a blustery Sunday afternoon in late October, Hester made her rounds checking the trash bins for anything of value. Rooting through the one by the food stand, she found a filthy dirty copy of *Walden*. Its cover was smeared with mustard, the spine was cracked, the edges worn, and it looked like half the book had been saturated in coffee. Hester was about to toss it back, but it looked really old so she turned to the first page, and there was a lovely engraving of Thoreau's cabin. Beneath it was the inscription: *"I do not propose to write an ode to dejection, but to brag as lustily as chanticleer in the morning, standing on his roost, if only to wake my neighbors up."*

An ode to dejection? Hester could write that, no problem. Hadn't gloom become her constant companion? The one bright light of her existence for the past year now had been that one night with Jimmy. So, yeah, she could write one hell of an ode to dejection.

Hester closed the book. She was supposed to have read *Walden* in college; but found it, from her admittedly immature point of view, boring, so she skimmed, scanned, and read a boat load of criticism to get the themes down. That's all her professor really cared about anyway.

It wasn't until she was teaching high school seniors back in the eighties and got assigned a section of 19th Century American Lit that she sat down and read the book in its entirety.

Well, she definitely wouldn't call it a page-turner. No, it was more a font of knowledge if you gave a rat's ass about simplifying your life or compound complex sentences. How would she get her bad-ass Punks and Goths to read, much less appreciate, bean-planting Henry David's excruciatingly detailed record of his alone-time on the edge of an isolated pond? And his delirium about the change of seasons, a wood chuck, or a hole in the ice? Come on, they'd think it was ridiculous. And, let's face it, the whole transcendental philosophy thing was going to be a hard sell. She could see them now, rolling their transparent eyeballs at her.

But the book was optimistic and full of clever sayings. What kid wouldn't want to "suck out all the marrow of life" or wasn't in need of "the tonic of wildness"? Yeah, there was a hell of a lot in the book to make a person stop and think. "My greatest skill in life has been to want but little," or "There are a thousand hacking at the branches of evil to one who is striking at the root," or "Not till we have lost the world, do we begin to find ourselves."

And Hester really liked how methodical Thoreau was. He kept track of what he bought, what he planted, and what he harvested. She'd require her students to keep lists of what they spent their money on. She'd ask them to write about what they "planted" in the metaphysical sense, and what they "harvested" in return.

Henry David's was also a very thrifty fellow. He dismantled the old Irishman's shack, even straightened the nails, and used these materials to build his "sturdy" cabin.

Beyond the tangible, what could her students "dismantle" and reuse? What had those who had gone before them left behind? What had a parent or grandparent or aunt or uncle left them that might help them build their own "sturdy" lives? And Hester wasn't talking about money or things. No, it had to be a virtue, a quality, a perspective, a good example of how not to live a life of "quiet desperation."

Once Hester actually taught *Walden*, she was hooked on Henry David and begged Al to take her to Concord, Mass.

It was a breezy autumn morning when Al and Hester visited the pond, the sun dotting the rippling surface with diamonds. A lone woman swam through the winking jewels, crystals dripping from her fingertips with every stroke. It was beautiful, and Hester insisted they hike the three mile trail. She wanted to take it all in, wanted Henry David's love of Nature to rub off on her, and Al.

Al, true to form, told her he'd wait in the car.

One thing Hester didn't like about herself at the time was her obsessive attachment to things. Al and she had money and real estate and things, lots of things. Though Hester often told herself she could be happy even if she didn't have what she did, she wasn't really, deep-down inside, willing to give any of it up.

They were living in the Victorian, updated with all the modern amenities. Each room showcased a portion of her hoard of furniture, rugs, rare lamps, vases, tapestries, etc. Atop the back fence was a collection of early American whirly-gigs. A gravel path led to the three car garage. Al's BMW sedan and her new Honda Odyssey and an overflow of antiques shared the space. Sometime Hester spent whole days out there just going through the stuff that wouldn't fit in their house. She had so much, too much really, and she knew it; but acquiring things filled her hours and kept her from thinking about how empty her nest had always been.

At the end of the hike around Walden Pond, Hester stood in the doorway to Thoreau's cabin. Al got out of the car and joined her. There wasn't much to look at, a desk, a chair, and a bed. Al took a photograph of her sitting on Henry David's bed.

"How could anyone live in such a pitifully small place and with practically nothing?" Hester said.

"Easy," said Al. "The guy was a real nut case."

Just like Al to come with something like that, she thought. But a part of her sort of agreed. Yeah, she got the part about Nature making you feel like you could transcend your earthly ties, but she just couldn't buy it. Of course, Nature was important to her. Wasn't her beautiful home surrounded by Nature? Nearly an acre of land, manicured and landscaped. Along the front porch wisteria grew on a trellis, and lilies of the valley bordered the brick walkway. In the back a blue stone patio was rimmed with black-eyed Susans and daisies. Yes, she loved Nature from a window, loved the way trees and flowers and a nice lawn boosted real estate values. But as great as Nature was, you couldn't really own it. You could plant a tree, but the tree could die. Possessions were more permanent. Unless your house burnt down or you were robbed, if you took care of them, you could keep your belongings for a lifetime.

Besides, she enjoyed shopping for things. She never knew what she'd find. How she looked forward to the weekends, getting out of bed early on Saturday morning, riding around looking for yard sales. In the afternoon she cruised up and down on both side of the river hitting the dealer centers. Sundays she went to the Silver Nugget or the flea market in Columbus.

What would she spot, buy, bring home, put someplace, show Al…even though he could care less? What would be such a steal she couldn't pass on it? The anticipation made her forget everything else, made it seem like she was on a great adventure searching for something that when she found it, it would make her happier than she'd ever been before. Hester never tired of the cycle, never felt buyer's remorse. What she did feel, every now and then, was remorse about what she didn't buy.

How different her life was then?

The ragged volume of *Walden* was growing heavy in Hester's hand. She looked at it warily. Again she opened it and paged through it. There was no copyright date. Parts were underlined, and there were notes in the margins, the writing so ornate she could barely read it. In the back there was a blank page with three notations followed by what looked like signatures. Hester wished she had her cheaters or a magnifying glass because, though, she thought she saw H.D. Thoreau below the first sentence, she couldn't be positive; and she could only dream that the two other lines might have been penned by R.W. Emerson and N. Hawthorne.

Wow, what would that be worth? Hester felt like pinching herself, but no way in hell could she get that lucky. She held the book up so the sun could hit it and stretched her arm out trying to see the writing more clearly.

God, it sure looked like Thoreau, Emerson, and Hawthorne all wrote something. She could make out separate words, a…the…castle…unity…you…words like that; but she couldn't read any of the sentences entirely. Now if she only had her laptop, she could search for similar editions, find out how much it might be worth.

Hester barely slept that night, but by morning she was over it. Who was she kidding? It would've been one chance in a hundred million finding an original copy of *Walden* signed by Thoreau and his two best buddies. No one would be stupid enough to throw that away. No, it had to be a fake, the creation of a counterfeiter or a jokester or some bored student who was supposed to be reading, not doodling. She put it in the drawer of the file cabinet next to Schwartz's "Read Between the Lines," got up, dressed, and went down to the river.

Today was cold. Winter was coming. She watched the muddy water rush by, and a lone turtle slog its way down the bank and get swallowed up by the current. She was no chanticleer. She had nothing to brag lustily to the neighbors about. She had no neighbors.

Hell, she had nothing.

Thirty

Cecilia Kurts stared at her pleasing image in her mirror and pondered what the appropriate length of time to mourn the loss of your beloved was. Though, truthfully, Lola Giordano had not, had never been her *beloved*.

But appearances were important, especially when Cecilia hoped to become the next educational guru, the next Lola Giordano.

Why shouldn't it happen? She was as smart as Lola.

No smarter.

For now, though, Cecilia had to wait for a lot of reasons. The will had to be probated. The deed to the beach house recorded. Anything else the woman might have left her, liquidated. She'd called Stark and Stark almost immediately to notify them of their valuable client's demise, and they'd assured her they'd expedite the process. Yet, here it was two months later and nothing finalized.

Sitting tight was killing her. If all she inherited was the beach house, she'd have to sell it. The taxes and maintenance were astronomical, and she had no money of her own, even keeping the Escalade was a burden. Thank God. Jimmy was such a softie. All she had to do was look a little down, and he was digging in his pocket to put a smile on her face.

Well, eventually she'd be alright and not need Jimmy Raymer to dole out money to her because the property was prime and worth at least a million and what was in it was worth over a half a million. If she cashed everything in, she'd be able to buy a lovely home and have plenty in the bank until her career took off. And she knew it would.

Eventually, she'd figure out a way to slip right into Lola's shoes. She needed to get Lola's publisher to take a chance on her, and that would require patience, and some clever maneuvering.

Be the tortoise, not the hare, she thought and winked at herself.

But then there was the other issue. She was almost thirty-two years old and single and had lived with a woman for the past five years. It wasn't rational under the circumstances, but she did want a baby. Having a child, loving that child above all else would prove once and for all, she was nothing at all like her mother, her peculiar, mentally ill mother, a woman who hadn't been able to care for herself properly, let alone for Cecilia. The irrational woman clung to Cecilia, demanded things from the girl, the girl had to give her, had to let her do to keep peace between them; but when Cecilia got a full scholarship to Rider College and left the small crummy apartment in Trenton to live in the dormitory, she realized quickly that she would never go back to her mother, never live in such squalor again. Why Cecilia found it difficult to believe the woman who claimed to have given birth to her actually did.

Cecilia, having freed herself from her past, now wanted to craft her future, and for it to be perfect she had to have someone she could love completely, something that would love her back, unconditionally. That would be a baby.

Lola? She'd only loved some of the things about her, not her, not who she really was. Still it might've worked out if Lola hadn't gotten so selfish and made it so clear she wanted nothing to do with having a family with Cecilia.

And Jimmy? Okay, there were things Cecilia didn't like about him either. He was too much of a pushover, too spineless. But Jimmy was raring to go, and the sex they'd had when they were engaged wasn't that bad. Moving into the Silver Nugget and sleeping with Jimmy was a whole hell of a lot better than she imagined it was going to be. Jimmy was a kind soul and cute, his body strong and well-proportioned. He worked hard even though he didn't get ahead. If he'd stop drinking beer, which she hated the smell of, and stopped sending money to his parasite of a father, then he'd be the almost perfect sperm donor.

So let it be written. So let it be done. Cecilia ran the brush through her luxurious mane and like a wild horse shook her locks free.

Thirty-One

Hester, chilled to the bone, pulled the old blanket around her and hurried into the office to check the radiator. Cold as freaking ice, again.

She shivered her way back into the closet and put on the few decent articles of clothing she'd found in the trash: a faded boy's flannel shirt, a pair of badly stained extra-large sweatpants, and one threadbare jeans jacket. She'd also scored fine red wool gloves when someone left them on her table and never returned to claim them. Still, she was chilly; and when she sighed with exasperation, her breath blew out in a cloud.

If she did set up today, most likely it'd be a waste. Too brutal out there even for the diehard pickers. It'd be a good day to drive to Rite-Aid and pick up something for her stomach. She'd felt so queasy lately and attributed it to her lousy diet of mostly hot dogs. Occasionally, she'd buy bruised bananas and apples from Bill, the farmer, who set up at the market every Saturday. On other days she rationed her basic foodstuffs: Saltines, generic brand peanut butter, and carrots, the cheapest vegetable in the produce section. Coke syrup might help or Tums, they weren't that expensive. She wrapped the blanket back around her, sat on the bed cross-legged, and tried to picture herself back in Pleasant Palms Trailer Park sitting on the beach in the hot sun.

Instead, a terribly embarrassing memory interrupted her reverie. It was a day just this past summer when she foolishly ran the Fourth of July 5K race at Washington Crossing State Park. She just signed the divorce papers and in an attempt to pull herself out of her emotional slump, she threw herself into a grueling exercise regime.

Unfortunately, she rushed into this race without enough training under her belt and on top of that it was torrid out, ninety degrees on the unshaded asphalt. Hester was barely jogging, doing a sort of run-walk thing. As she crossed the finish line, she was shaky from the heat. A volunteer handed her a bottle of water and a slice of orange.

"Lady, I think you've got a problem there," said a young woman who finished right behind Hester. Hester turned and saw that the fellow runner was looking at Hester's crotch area. Hester followed the woman's eyes.

"Oh! Oh no. Oh my God. Thank you," Hester said as she saw the blood. She'd thought the wetness had been sweat; but now she saw she'd gotten her period, and it had seeped through her pink running shorts. She didn't know what to do. She had nothing to wrap around herself, no one to turn to for help. She bolted toward her van which was parked a good distance away. By the time she got to the vehicle, found a rag to sit on, and turned on the air, she was dizzy and so sick to her stomach she almost didn't make it back to the condo.

That was three months ago, and Hester hadn't menstruated since. After the initial heavy flow, it'd been a short period, then nothing. Hester wouldn't say she was disappointed her period was over—look at the money she'd save on sanitary products—but she did feel sad that she never bore a child, that now she never would. Despite the fact that she'd screwed herself up back in college when she had the abortion, she had always harbored hope the specialist was wrong and, by some miracle, she might still conceive.

So this was menopause. Hester rubbed her stomach trying to get it to settle down. She hadn't expected the nausea, and she hadn't expected to feel so sexy. As sick as she was, the minute she sat still she started daydreaming about Jimmy. And she didn't want to, but it was like when she was in college and couldn't get Arty out of her mind. She'd even get wet down there. She was wet now. And here she thought she'd dry up like an old prune. So what was going on with her?

Hester propped herself up in the bed and picked up the latest book she'd found. She read the blurb on the back. It was based on a real life incident that happen in Florida in 1962. A boy put rat poison in milk and snuck it into his friend's house. His friend and the friend's little sister drank the milk and died. The boy admitted to the crime so the book was about why he did it. The title was "Disturbed."

Good title, Hester thought as she opened to the first page and began reading, only to find out the boy's last name was Raymer. *Creepy coincidence how Jimmy and this little psycho have the same last name.*

Hester kept reading. What would make a young boy do something so horrid? He had a normal family it seemed, and appeared to like his friend. Hester tried to concentrate, but Cecilia had turned on the television upstairs and the sound of it blared through the thin, uninsulated floor. Hester stuffed some toilet paper in her ears and again tried to read. It was no use, how could she make any sense of the words in the book with that stupid OxyClean commercial on, the fast-talker's voice beyond irritating.

Hester didn't know much about the mysterious Cecilia, but she was discovering the young woman had terrible taste in T.V. and certainly didn't use the remote control the way it was meant to be used. How many stupid commercials could one human being stand watching?

Sometimes it wasn't so bad, though, like when Cecilia was up in the middle of the night watching the Hallmark Channel, and the voices and music came to Hester quietly like the hiss of a snake slithering around in her brain.

Thirty-Two

Cecilia pulled-up in the U-Haul-It loaded with her things from the beach house. She turned off the engine, put a cigarette in her mouth, and lit it. The cabin of the truck clouded up with smoke. After a few more puffs, she closed her eyes and leaned her head against the steering wheel. The tip of the cigarette glowed like a ruby between her fingers.

It had been a long day and she was tired. The whole way driving across the state she'd been thinking about how good it would feel to throw out every piece of crap in Jimmy's apartment and start over. She couldn't wait to get rid of the beige pleather La-Z-Boy and the pillows with the roosters on them. She'd already taken down the cheesy, red pique valances with the white pom-poms.

"Theresa had some stupid idea they'd brighten the place up." Jimmy had told her.

Cecilia had thrown her head back and laughed. "Brighten the place up? They make it look like a clown's house."

"She was a clown, a pathetic clown of a woman," said Jimmy. "I'm glad she's gone."

"I'm glad she is too, Babe," Cecilia said as she climbed on the stepstool and took down the hideous valances.

I've got more good taste in my little toe, Cecilia told herself. But it wasn't just what was in the place. It was the place itself, too small, no view. The main living area looked out over the wobbly tables and the crumbling barn and pavilion. Then there was the noise on weekends, the dealers, pickers, the curious, the bored, and the broke. All riff raff. The rejects of the world who didn't have enough money to do what they really wanted to do so they went to the flea market.

Her own mother had put that idea in her young head, telling her every weekend they were going to the flea market to get some fresh air and a free history lesson. "And it won't cost us a dime that is unless we find something that we really must have." But they never did spend any money, not really. Her mother stopped at every table that had a "Dollar Table" sign on it, and it pained Cecilia to watch her mother agonize over whether or not to spend one measly dollar on an old toothpick holder or not.

Then there were the collectors. The elite customers who had their favorite dealers; who dressed in Versace or Gucci; who, if they weren't gay, usually had a handsome gay friend with them; who carried soft leather sacks and wore Ray Bans, who found slumming at the Silver Nugget a lark. Cecilia despised these elitists most of all. It was their money that kept the place going.

No, she did not belong in a place like this. But for the moment she had to put up with it. It turned out Lola had not given her the business, not one dime except for the house and its contents.

Bitch!

This was the scenario she'd been dreading. She had no alternative but to put the place up for sale—and because the economy was still in the throes of a recession that might as well be called what it was, a depression––at a price much less than she wanted. She'd also been told by the realtor to "thin out" what was in there. Her agent told her in a calm, firm voice, "This décor may have pleased you, Ms. Kurts; but if you want my professional opinion and if you want to sell this lovely property, then you must get rid of three quarters of what's in here. The stuff that looks like it belongs in a castle has to go first." And she swept her hand wide to indicate the whole of the living room.

That's what Cecilia had grown accustom to, living in a castle by the sea, not in a rickety dump of an apartment over a flea market office.

But she needed Jimmy's money, and now that the wheels were in motion down on Long Beach Island, it was time for her to get pregnant. Tonight would be the night. She was, she had to admit, sort of looking forward to it. Jimmy had cleaned himself up, new clothes, tight-fitting jeans, V-neck sweaters, new work boots, expensive ones. He always combed his golden hair back now, and it showed off his features.

Hmmm. Cecilia thought, I wonder what his mother looked like. She'd never seen any photos. Not of his father either, or even his sister. His sister? His deformed sister?

Oh no, now here was a problem she hadn't thought of. Did something run in his family?

His sister was probably deformed because his mother never took care of herself. Jimmy had told her how much she smoked and all the beer she drank. Cecilia thought this even as she lifted her head from the steering wheel and took another drag on her cigarette.

And Jimmy's father was a rotten husband. He was driving Jimmy's mother mad, so her nerves must've been frayed.

How could a healthy baby come out of a stressful marriage like that?

Initially, way back when she was tutoring him, when Jimmy told her his sister drowned in the bathtub, he neglected to say anything about the fact that she'd been born without legs. Years later, when they were living together and engaged, he spilled the beans and wept like a baby. How, she hated to see him cry. Yeah, she had cared for him. But what he'd told her had given her the creeps and had shifted ever so slightly her affection for him.

A shame things changed, she thought as she lowered the truck window and flicked out what was left of her cigarette. She'd stop smoking. She was still young, younger than Jimmy's mother had been when she had the deformed baby. She'd have to ask him to be sure.

Cecilia stared at the peeling paint around the windows of the building, at the T1-11, faded to the color of snot. When would she be free, when would she hold the reins of her own life? Going to live at the Nugget was going backwards. She'd be doing time again. Hell, living with Lola had been like doing time too, hard time.

Sure there'd been perks, but they came at a price.

"Go ahead, C." Lola encouraged Cecilia when she first moved into the beach house. "Decorate anyway you like. I want to spoil you!" So Cecilia went wild buying the most expensive and exotic things while Lola sat in her office and wrote out the checks. It thrilled Cecilia to have Lola spend all this money on her. Her biggest high came when something was delivered, and Lola came out of her office to sign for it.

All day, every day, there was the work, which Cecilia found easy and rewarding, and the buying, buying, buying. Quick trips to design centers in Manhattan, to furniture outlets in North Carolina, and when there was no time, the local Home Goods in Manahawkin would do. If the sun never set, Cecilia would've been grateful because when it did, it was time for paybacks. Lola got frisky almost every night, and it was always the same thing. Lola in her terrycloth robe came looking for her C.

"Where are you? Ready or not here I come." Her high-pitched voice sing-songy and childlike, feigning playfulness. "Want to see what Lola's got for you?"

Like Cecilia couldn't guess, like she hadn't seen it a hundred times already, and the first time had been one time too many.

Dramatically, the old woman would opened her robe. Cecilia had all she could do not to cringe at the sight of Lola's naked body, her flabby breasts, bloated stomach, the strap-on penis. No matter how dark the room was the damn thing picked-up enough light to make it glow.

Eventually, Cecilia got serious and hired two high-end designers, one from Brooklyn, the other from Philadelphia. She pitted them against each other by siding first with one about the faux bois dining set, and then with other about the gold-trimmed Murano sconces.

Such a combination could not work.

Cecilia told them not to worry. She wanted eclectic, and bold, "…not something you see in a magazine and not something anyone else has ever done."

The designers argued with her and with each other. Then Lola put in her two cents, "C, Honey, they're the experts. Maybe you should listen to them."

Shut-up, bitch, Cecilia wanted to shout, *if I have to do what I do with you, then I am sure-as-hell going to get what I want; and I want a dining set that looks like tree branches and antique sconces made of fucking gold-flecked Venetian glass.*

Such nasty thoughts exploded like fireworks inside Cecilia's skull, but she maintained her calm exterior, furrowed her brow slightly, put one manicured index finger to her pursed lips, and pretended to consider Lola's two cents.

"I see your point; but…" Cecilia said as she fluttered her long black lashes, "…I really, really think it will work. Please, can't we just try it?"

"The sconces alone are six thousand dollars, and …"

"And the dining set is three times that. I know, I know." Cecilia's voice cracked with frustration. "Money, money, money! Do you talk about it so much because you have so much of it? Really, Lola, you can just write another book if you run out. Please, I beg you, don't make it about the money, okay?"

Lola was standing in front of Cecilia. She was short and had to reach to pinch the young woman's trembling chin. "Okay, sweetie, calm down."

Those sconces were going to figure prominently in Cecilia's plan for the apartment so she'd be reminded every day of how she'd won that skirmish. After the handyman unscrewed them from the wall, she tore the pages out of Lola's unfinished manuscript, "How to Grow a Good Teacher," and stuffed them in the sconces before wrapping them in newsprint and boxing them up.

Oh my, was Cecilia glad Lola was gone. And just in the nick of time. Funny, how one change leads to another. If she hadn't seen

Jimmy that night, Lola would still be alive. Oh well. That's the way it went...all for the best.

As she stepped down from the U-Haul-It, she thought about sex. The only orgasms she ever had she'd given herself. She'd been close a couple of times with Jimmy; but just at the last second, just as she was about to come, it was over, and she'd be lying there disappointed and have to wait until she was alone to finish the job.

She tossed the cigarette butt on the ground and crushed it with the toe of her boot.

I'll quit smoking, fix up his arm-pit of a place, and try to teach my pal Jimmy how to make me come.

It would all work out.

Jimmy must have been watching from the window and ran out to meet her. He wrapped his arms around her, pulled her close, and kissed her neck. Cecilia playfully pushed him away and slapped him on the shoulder. She led him to the back of the big van and lifted the gate. He'd get his later. Now, she wanted Jimmy to see all of the wonderful things the dead woman's money had bought.

Thirty-Three

The Silver Nugget was opened on Thanksgiving Day. Hester layered on her clothes and the new, black wool scarf Joyce, now her friend, had given her and headed out before sunrise. She emptied the entire back of the van, and her goods barely filled one table. When she removed the cast iron doorstop in the shape of a cat, from the last container, she knew she was at a turning point. When this stuff was gone, she'd have nothing to sell except what she found in the trash. Today was her last chance to make real money.

Irwin and Ruth pulled in behind the table on Hester's right. Irwin was into mid-century, Ruth into late century. They towed around a "shitload," as Ruth put it, of furniture in a box van that use to be a bread truck. Since August, they'd taken the spot next to Hester every Sunday and on holidays.

Irwin, bald as a cue ball, had the face of a hound dog, long, boxy, flabby jowls. Ruth was not bad looking, her grey hair cut short and gelled into spikes, her eyes rimmed with black liner. She was thin and wore thick red leggings and a tight-fitting shearling jacket. She had some wrinkles, but who didn't at her age.

Hester looked over. Ruth was sitting in a lawn chair writing something in a notebook. The angle of the rising sun illuminated the pale hair that grew along her jaw line and across her upper lip. It reminded Hester of something that happened a long time ago when a teacher who was out on maternity leave brought her newborn into school. Hester was in the lounge and watched as the woman put her baby on the table and changed his diaper. When he was clean, she rolled him over and showed Hester how much baby fuzz he had on his back.

"He looks like a little blonde monkey, doesn't he?" she said as she laughed. "Go ahead, touch it. It feels like silk, doesn't it?"

And it did. The baby started to cry at Hester's touch so his mother whisked him away and stuck him up under her shirt to nurse him. Hester watched this swift movement in utter amazement, and with lacerating envy.

Hester had the urge to go over to Ruth and stroke the down on her face. Talk about crazy. Hester would never do anything like that, though, because she really was a little intimidated by Ruth and Irwin. They weren't down on their luck. Selling at the Nugget was a retirement hobby for them. Hester had heard from Joyce that Irwin used to work in finance in Manhattan. He'd given it up recently, and now they lived in a "huge" townhouse across the river in New Hope and traveled around buying stuff in their other car, a Range Rover.

They'd bought a few things from Hester and had quite expertly haggled her down on her price: a '60's wooden Dansk cheese tray, a West German Lucite clock, a Swedish cut-crystal vase, a Hawaiian Ukulele, a bolt of cowboy-themed bark cloth. Ruth really wanted to buy Hester's the three old, celluloid dolls. They were jointed, and their eyes opened and closed. There was the cowgirl, the cowboy, and the small blonde doll that reminded Hester of herself. Ruth's jaw dropped at Hester's price of ten bucks for one or all three for twenty-five. She wanted Hester to take five a piece, and Hester wouldn't let them go for that, even though she'd gotten them at the Fisherman's Mark rummage sale for a dollar each. That wasn't the point. They were so darn cute they were worth the twenty-five bucks. No, Hester decided, she'd put them on the file cabinet next to her bed before she'd let Ruth steal them from her.

After that, Ruth and Irwin were polite but remote. They'd briefly talk about their shopping adventures, but that was it. When Hester tried to have a conversation with one or the other of them, Ruth or Irwin didn't seem interested. Some Sundays, they'd set up and ignore Hester completely.

But maybe it wasn't about the dolls at all, though. Maybe they just didn't like the looks of Hester. She'd added a green skull cap with an Eagles team emblem; an extra-large, pilled, black turtle-neck sweater; and yellow rubber boots to her mish mosh of other people's cast-offs. When all of it was worn together, there was no denying it, Hester looked like a bag lady.

Where was the woman with the manicured nails, chemically-peeled skin, tweezed brows, lined lips, and powdered nose? Where was the scent of J'adore Dior? The glow of Aveda? The drama of Lancome? Hester tried not to dwell on the catastrophic metamorphosis she knew had occurred, on the fact that the once-lovely princess she was, had turned into a frog.

Then to Hester's left, a man in a VW van that looked like it'd been through a war pulled behind the table. Duck-tape held one headlight on. Rust had eaten through the fender. When the driver of this wreck got out, Hester found it impossible not to stare at him. He was tall, broad-shouldered, super tan for the dead of winter, and his hair was bleached platinum blonde.

"Hi," he said to Hester and stuck his hand out. "I'm Eric. I guess we're gonna be neighbors today."

"Yes, I guess so," Hester said as she raised her arm to block the bright sun coming through the gaps in the treetops. "Your first time here?"

"Hardly. Been coming to the Nugget since the day it opened. But I don't remember seeing you here."

"Well, I used to come here to buy, not sell. I just started selling here in late August."

"Just about the time I left to give Georgia a try. What a waste of time. No money down there. What a bust. Same as here, I guess. No money anywhere these days. Everybody wants something for nothing. You ask a hundred bucks for something worth two hundred, and they offer you fifty. It's not like it used to be. Not by a long stretch. Did I miss anything?"

"Hardly, like you said, everybody wants something for nothing. I sold plenty of great stuff for peanuts because I didn't know what I was doing. And now it's too late. This is the last of my good stuff."

"You haven't been buying?"

"No, I'm trying to save money to get an apartment."

"Well, you won't ever make enough money to live if you don't keep buying."

"I don't want to sell things at the Silver Nugget for the rest of my life. I want a real job."

Eric's face dropped. He stopped talking, went back to the van, and started hauling out his wares.

"Sorry," Hester hollered after him. "I didn't mean there's anything wrong with being a dealer. It's just that I used to be an English teacher, and now I'm not anymore. It was what I was good at."

Eric didn't answer. He was busy getting something big and heavy out. It looked like a metal cage and was almost as tall as he was.

Hester was disappointed with herself. Who was she to put this place down?

"Wine rack," Eric shouted over to her. "Pretty cool, huh?"

"Yeah, very cool." Hester was relieved he hadn't taken her comment personally.

"That's what I adore about this business. Some really amazing pieces pass through your fingers."

"Now that's a good way to look at it."

"Is there any other way to look at things? All this stuff is only ours for as long as we're alive. Once the grim reaper gets us all of it, whether we like it or not, will belong to somebody else. Me? I like knowing the story of where something came from, and I like knowing where it's going next. Like this gorgeous wine rack, I bought it from some old gentleman whose father had it shipped from Avignon after World War II. The poor guy is moving into a trailer park in Florida so he had to get rid of it. Now it's mine for the moment, but maybe today it'll pass through me to someone else. The story too. Provenance is important."

"Yes, it is, isn't it?" Hester agreed. What Eric said reminded her of the Rabbi in the Schwartz book. We are just "passing through." It was both a comforting and discomforting thought. Like Thoreau, she could take comfort, perhaps, even pride in her current frugal existence. She was no drain on the resources of the planet; that was for sure. But the idea that one day her very existence would be over, terrified her. She thought for the thousandth time of the dead woman under the tarp, the whites of her eyes, her slashed wrists.

"So about your job? I thought once an English teacher always an English teacher. What happened?"

Now how could she answer this without opening up a can of worms?

"I retired early. My husband wanted me to. So I did, and then he left me, took all of our money, didn't pay the bills, didn't pay the mortgage or the assessment on our condo. I got evicted, and, long story short, that's why I'm here on the other side of the table, so to speak,"

"Sorry to hear that. Must be tough."

She wanted to say, tough's not the word. Disgusting, infuriating, unbelievable were all better words to describe what she felt about the down-turn had life had taken, but she thought better of saying anything more to this man, a nice man, a man about her age, who seemed not at all repulsed by the fact he was talking to a frog.

When Eric was finished setting up his table, he asked Hester to keep an eye on his stuff and headed across the lot toward the food stand. He came back with two donuts and two cups of coffee. Hester hadn't had a donut in forever, and she hadn't splurged on coffee in over two weeks. Eric handed her the warm Styrofoam cup, she plucked a donut from the card board carrier, and bit into the delight. She hadn't had anything this sweet since the Chardonnay at Bull's. It tasted like fried and glazed heaven.

"Thank you so much. I didn't realize how much I missed confections."

"Who doesn't like a little sugar in their life? Or a lot of sugar? Right?" said Eric, his eyes bluer than the sky. "Oh, and I put cream in your coffee."

"Cream in my coffee? No kidding. That's exactly how I like it." A little white lie wouldn't hurt. Why look a gift horse in the mouth? "How did you know?"

"Educated guess. You look wholesome, like the kind of woman who'd be into milk products."

Hester laughed and said, "You are the first man on earth to call me wholesome! I love it. Me. Wholesome." She took the lid off the cup. She'd almost forgotten how much she loved that aroma. She took a cautious sip. The temperature was just right. She sat down on the back bumper of her minivan and savored the hot liquid. Heaven. A bite of the donut. Coffee. Donut. Coffee. It was all going down so easily, and then her stomach started to churn. She was going to be sick. She put the coffee and donut on her table, bolted toward the woods, and plowed into them as far as she could, before she vomited. She didn't know if anyone was watching. She hoped Eric couldn't see her. She sunk down by the trunk of a pine waiting for the queasiness to pass.

What in God's name was wrong with her? She couldn't afford to be sick. She pressed her palm against her stomach, which for some reason she couldn't suck in anymore. She used to be able to make it concave when she held it in, but not anymore. Was this another one of menopause's little jokes? You barely eat a thing and you still get fat? She'd have to get off her ass and get out there on the towpath no matter how bad the weather was.

Desperate to make money, Hester emerged from the woods. Eric was standing facing the back of his van with his hands in the pockets of his jeans. He'd put on a black knit cap. As she got closer, Hester saw a younger man sitting on the floor in the rear of the vehicle, leaning back on his arms and laughing.

She went to her table and, to look busy, started rearranging her things.

"Hey there!" Eric called to her. "You okay?"

"Yes, I'm fine. Thanks for asking," Hester replied.

"Come over and meet my partner," Eric said.

Hester immediately thought, *Oh? He has a business partner?*

As she walked over to Eric's table, the young man scurried out of the van, threw his arm around Eric's waist, and said, "Hi, I'm Angelo."

Well, alright, obviously she'd thought wrong.

Thirty-Four

"It's me."

"I know."

"Is it alright?" Jimmy whispered as he walked through the pitch dark to the bed.

"Yes, but only if you do everything I tell..." Before Cecilia could finish what she was saying, Jimmy was out of his pajama bottoms and under the blanket next to her. He kissed her cheek sweetly, then nuzzled his face into the warm crook of her neck, His lips on her clavicle felt like a butterfly had landed there. He moved his open mouth to her throat just below her jawline, and she felt his wet tongue.

So far so good, Cecilia thought as she turned and wrapped her arms around him. He swirled his tongue over her skin. Then he pulled away, turned on the lamp, and knelt facing her. Cecilia shielded her eyes from the light and propped herself up against her pile of pillows.

"Turn that off, please."

But Jimmy was busy pulling her camisole down, lifting her breasts, inspecting them as though they were eggplants and he couldn't decide which to buy. He settled on one, took it in both his hands, and watched it bulge up out of his fists.

Cecilia watched too as her nipple redden until it look like it might burst. Then Jimmy let go and her breast flopped like a water balloon against her ribcage. She looked down at it. She wanted him to touch her again, but he had his hands on his thighs, his eyes on her face.

Between his legs, his big battering ram of a penis stuck straight out.

Jimmy caught her looking at him and smiled. "Forget about me. Look at you. Look at how big they're getting. They must know what I'm going to do to them."

He hesitated for a minute, which was excruciating for Cecilia, before he pinched her nipples and rolled them between his thumbs and middle fingers.

Cecilia wriggled with pleasure. The rougher Jimmy got, the harder he pinched and pulled, the more excited she became. When she was almost to the point of screaming for him to stop, he let go of her nipples, grabbed her breasts and began milking them for all they were worth. All the while his eyes moved from one to the other. His mouth fell open. He looked ready to drink what he must've been dreaming might squirt out of them. Cecilia watched too, fascinated by his fascination with her hugeness.

Why wasn't he putting one in his mouth? God, how she wanted him to take her in his mouth and suck on her till she could feel that tingling in the back of her throat.

Oh, she was getting excited. The light—Lola never allowed the light on—made her feel like a porn star. Lola put on porn, but not this kind, not the kind that had a real penis in it like Jimmy's, that she could see was throbbing.

She was ready...now! Why was he holding back, torturing her like this?

His eyes riveted now on what he held, what he could've ripped from the wall of her chest if he wanted to, he pushed her breasts together and put both nipples in his mouth at once, sucking so hard Cecilia came like she'd never come before. She was in such ecstasy she screamed. Jimmy backed off for a second, straddled her, leaned over, caught one nipple between his teeth, and bit down. Cecilia came again. Again Jimmy backed off.

This time he grabbed her other breast and pushed it up to her mouth.

"Lick it," he commanded, and she did. Then she was holding her own breast and sucking on it, and he was sucking on the other one, and she came and came. When she couldn't take it anymore, she begged, "Stop!"

But Jimmy clamped his hand over her mouth.

"Shut up," he ordered.

And that made her come again.

Cecilia could tell Jimmy's body was on fire, ready to explode. She knew what he wanted and pulled him down on top of her, grabbed him, and put him inside her. He was hot, hard…alive.

Ohhhh…there was no holding back now.

And then it was over, and Cecilia felt such…she had no words for what she'd never felt before.

After a minute, Jimmy stood up, kissed her on the cheek, whispered, "Sweet dreams," and left.

Thirty-Five

Hester was reading *Walden*, "…throwing off its nightly clothing of mist, and here and there, by degrees, its soft ripples or its smooth reflecting surface was revealed, while the mists, like ghosts, were stealthily withdrawing in every direction into the woods, as at the breaking…"

But how could she concentrate with all the racket upstairs. The creaking bed, the heavy breathing, the moans. They were right on top of her, doing it. She put her book down, stuffed toilet paper in her ears, put the pillow over her head, and still she could hear them.

How she wished she could disappear. Poof! Be gone!

And the worst was, this was only the beginning. The first time. Her life would become hell having to listen to this every night. Every night!

It was like down in Florida in Pleasant Palms Trailer Park. Their double-wide was so close to their neighbor's, they could hear old Chet fart. It was the only drawback to being a snowbird and living for months in such cramped quarters because, really, the rest was like being in paradise, so close to the beach, she could hear the pounding surf and smell the ocean. It was a place where clouds danced, and the air quiver in the brilliant sun. Nostalgia for Pleasant Palms overwhelmed Hester. If she could walk to a beach, any beach, she was a happy camper. Yes, despite all that had gone wrong there, Hester still felt pretty warm and fuzzy about that trailer park. And in comparison to her current living arrangement, that double-wide was a palace. God, if she were only there now. How luxurious it would feel to have such space, a kitchen, a bathroom, a shower!

She wondered what was happening there now. The developer had demolished one whole lane of trailers, had stopped everything right at the Murphy's doorstep, had every right to stop things, considering the workers unearthed a dead body. Everything came to a halt. The deal was off. All of the owners were forced to return the developer's money.

So, technically, did she still own that unit down there? Or did Al? Again, the details of their divorce eluded her.

Why worry about that, though? Something was wrong with the Odyssey. She was afraid to drive it anywhere, let alone to Florida. Her insurance had most likely run out too, so driving anywhere was pretty much out of the question.

Still, if she did *own* it, at least she *had* something.

No, she couldn't think like that. She had to stay in the present, focus on here and now, save, save, save every red cent so one day soon she'd be back on her feet. When that day came, if that trailer belonged to her, she'd go there, pay off the assessments and fix the place up.

Hester took her blanket and pillow, went into the office, shut the closet door, shoved some books up against the bottom of it to block the sounds of Jimmy fucking Cecilia's brains out, and curled up on the sofa.

She put the pillow over her head again.

It was better, but not much.

Thirty-Six

Jimmy was behind his desk mesmerized by something on the computer screen. Hester was in the beige La-Z-Boy that had been demoted from the apartment to the office. She wasn't reading, but her favorite book was on her lap. She wasn't getting much sleep lately so it was becoming difficult for her to focus on Thoreau's insights for any length of time. The big chair was comfortable, and she could feel herself pleasantly drifting off when Cecilia, and a gust of early December wind, burst through the door.

"Did you tell her yet, Jimmy?" Cecilia said as she unwrapped her furry scarf from around her neck.

"No, Cecilia, not yet."

"Well, go on. Tell her."

"Tell me what, Jimmy?" Hester said.

"That we are going to have a baby!" shouted Cecilia.

"What? When?" Hester was surprised.

"Oh, I don't know when. What I mean is that we have officially started to try to have a baby. Right, Jimmy?"

"But you two aren't even married yet," Hester blurted out. Now why the hell did she say that? What business of hers was it what the two of them did?

The stupidest things in the world came out of Hester's mouth every time she was around Cecilia. The young woman was off-putting and unpredictable. She scared the bejesus out of Hester, who had no illusions about how annoyed Cecilia was by Hester's occupation of the office closet. But Hester could not afford to lose the roof over her head so she steered clear of the sassy, domineering Ms. Kurts.

Hester also believed that Cecilia would eventually break Jimmy's heart, again. Cecilia's grief over Lola's death had been dramatic, to say the least. Obviously, Cecilia loved Lola. Obviously, Cecilia was gay. Obviously, Cecilia's biological clock was ticking, but once the woman got what she wanted from Jimmy, namely a baby, she'd most likely be on her merry way.

Hester started to get up to leave before things went downhill.

"Don't go, Hester," said Cecilia happily. "We are so excited we just had to tell someone. Right, Jimmy?" Cecilia took off her coat and gloves and flopped down on the faded sofa. She picked up a nail file that was on the coffee table and began working on her pinky.

"Funny, you should bring up marriage, Hester," Cecilia reflected.

"Oh, I don't know why I said that. It was a stupid thing to say."

"I agree, Hester. Who gives a flying you-know-what if we're married? Lots of people who aren't married have babies these days. For your information, I, we, have no intention of getting married and every intention of having a baby. Right, babe?" Cecilia smiled in Jimmy's direction. He didn't look up from the computer, but nodded in agreement. Cecilia continued talking to Hester, "What you said made you sound so old-fashioned, Hester. How old are you anyway? Sixty-something?"

Cecilia glanced at Hester, then back at her finger.

"Fifty-two. It's only fifty-two," Hester said as if her age were a thing apart from herself. How she wished she could sink right through the bulging cushions of the La-Z-Boy and disappear.

Sun came in through the window, lighting Jimmy's slicked back hair, pinning the shadow of his profile to the wall. Hester stared at him.

Had she really had sex with him?

Sometimes it seemed like she'd dreamt it, probably because neither Jimmy nor she ever mentioned it. And they spent lots of time in the office together. And they talked about all sorts of things.

Over the past several months, Hester shared the whole sordid "novel" of her past life, well almost. She couldn't bear to tell him about her abortion or what she'd done to Nina before she buried her body.

Still, without even knowing the worst, Jimmy agreed she certainly had been on the edge of dangerous things married for thirty years to a hypocrite like Al. How had she survived?

Hester was grateful to Jimmy for his companionship. And slowly, but surely, Jimmy shared his past with her. Hester believed she couldn't have known him better if she'd been married to him. Why only yesterday, he shared the last chapter in the Horrible Harry and Terrible Theresa saga.

Jimmy told Hester that after he graduated from Trenton State College, he was busting his hump to keep the Silver Nugget from falling down around his father, Theresa, and himself. Out of nowhere, Theresa decides Harry should take her down to Florida. So they went. Even though that left everything at the Nugget on Jimmy's shoulders, he was glad they were gone.

"When they got back, though," Jimmy said. "Harry made himself a martini. A martini? For Christ sakes, where did he learn that? Then Harry asks Theresa if she wants one, and she acts like she didn't know what a martini was. After he gives her one she puts it to her lips like it was going to burn them. Then Harry told me Theresa and he were celebrating because they were getting married and moving to Boca Raton.

"So Harry says, 'Son, the Nugget will be yours, just send me a check for half of what you take in on the first of every month.' That was seven years ago. I haven't seen my father since, but I still send half of what comes in to some P.O. Box down there. The checks get signed and cashed. If it weren't for that, I wouldn't know if Harry was alive or dead."

Yeah, Hester got to know Jimmy pretty well, and she felt sad for him. What a selfish narcissist the poor guy had for a father, but, thank God, Jimmy seemed to be the exact opposite. He was nice to Hester, to Eric, to Joyce, to all the pack rats that hung around flea market. He didn't take advantage of any of them. She'd witnessed it herself and heard it through the grapevine, if Jimmy found out that a dealer hadn't made enough to cover the table rent, he let it go. Jimmy was that generous.

And look how loving he was toward Cecilia. Alright, he'd slipped up once, that one time with Hester, but beyond that he was as loyal as a puppy to that woman. You could see the affection in his eyes when he looked at her. Her wish was his command. Watching him, hearing him talk about Cecilia made Hester realize, regrettably, she'd never known what it was to be truly loved, and, unfortunately, the likelihood of her finding out now seemed slim to none.

No, Hester didn't really trust Cecilia, but she did trust Jimmy. She like him and admired him. He was a worker and a lover of all humanity. No matter how poor or raggedy, Jimmy Raymer didn't look down on anyone.

Cecilia looked up from her pinky and said, "So, Hester, do you have any children?"

Hester shifted her weight in the chair. She was so uncomfortable all of a sudden. The elastic on her large, grey sweatpants was too tight. God, it had happened to her. She'd officially turned into fifty-something and fat, her body expanding, taking on a life of its own, always hungry, always tired. And here was slim, beautiful Cecilia prying, "Well, do you?"

"No, I don't," answered Hester. She hadn't done a good job of hiding her irritation.

"Sorry, I asked," Cecilia shot back.

"That's okay, Cecilia. I didn't mean to snap at you. My ex-husband and I tried for many years to have a baby, but it just wasn't in our stars, I guess."

Not only was Hester losing a grip on her emotions and her body, but her mind seemed to be slipping too.

The other day when she was walking on the towpath trying to get up enough energy to run, she spied a large earthworm wriggling across the gravel. She squatted down and picked it up. It writhed around tickling her palm. It was wet from the grass and coated with clumps of dirt. She smelled it. It had the odor of the dirt. Then for no reason she could explain, she licked the dirt off the worm and let it go. It was a fairly insane thing to do and it worried her so she told Eric about it, and all he said was, "Rose of Shar'n."

"What?"

"Tell me you don't get it? And you *are* the English teacher."

She had to think for a minute. "Oh, 'The Grapes of Wrath.' Yeah, yeah, I get it, now; but she was eating...limestone? No, I think you're right. It was dirt."

Hester had grown fond of Eric, the way he surprised her with all he knew, the way he laughed at things she said, the way he cuddled so openly with pretty Angelo, the way...

Cecilia's voice interrupted Hester's thoughts. "So, Jimmy, is Eric going to fill in for you when we go to the beach house?"

"I didn't ask him yet."

Cecilia got up from the sofa, scooted her firm ass up on the desk next to Jimmy's computer and said, "Well, why don't you call him so we know for sure and I can make plans? I want to be ovulating when we get there."

Hester felt tears stinging her eyes. Now she really was thinking nutso thoughts. *Why can't I have a baby? Jimmy Raymer's baby?*

If she were younger, if she hadn't lost the chance a lifetime ago, if hell could freeze over.

Get off the cross, we need the wood...be happy for these young people. Maybe they are right for each other. Maybe Lola Giordano, not Jimmy, was the blip on the screen for Cecilia.

Hester tried to soften her heart toward Cecilia, even though it felt like the woman was capable of sucking the life out of anyone she encountered. Hester eased her fat body out of the La-Z-Boy. All she wanted was to go to bed and hibernate for the rest of the winter. She felt Jimmy's eyes on her and turned and met them.

"I wish you all the happiness in the world," Hester said as sincerely as she could.

"You're not mad at me, are you?" Jimmy said.

And Hester remembered that was always something he'd said to his mother.

"No," Hester assured him and watched as Cecilia turned toward Jimmy and said, "I'll have the manager open up the beach house. Okay, Jimmy? And he can stock the fridge with…"

Then Jimmy looked away from Hester at his former fiancé and exhaled solemnly as though releasing his last breath of love.

Thirty-Seven

As Jimmy was putting the overnight bags in the back of the pick-up, and Cecilia was still inside the apartment, Hester pleaded with Jimmy to let her run the Nugget for the weekend. She needed the money. It was the middle of January, the market was dead.

"I know I don't look like a Viking or a tight end, but I'm just as reliable as Eric, and he doesn't need the money as much as I do. Really, he won't mind," she said trying to convince Jimmy, one last time, it was a job she could handle, but he thought it'd be too much for her. Besides, Eric knew the routine and where everything was.

Jimmy stopped what he was doing and put his arm around Hester's shoulder. It made her jump. He hadn't touched her since Lola's body was discovered.

"Look, friend, rest until I get back," he said. "You look worn-out."

"Thanks for caring," Hester said dejectedly. Yes, she was worn-out, but she could've rallied to manage the Nugget for one blustery weekend when she knew barely anyone would show up.

Cecilia came out of the building and pulled the hood of her down Anorak tight around her face. She climbed into the cab and eyed Hester through the driver's side window.

"Bye now," Jimmy said. He got in the truck, turned it on, and drove out of the parking lot. Hester stood in the swirling dust and the cold, and watched the vehicle disappear around the bend of River Road. She closed her eyes against the airborne grit. She was glad they were gone. At least they wouldn't be waking her up tonight.

Since that day in the office, Cecilia made a habit of dropping into Hester's closet. Hester was pretty sick of hearing her say things like, "You know you would look so much better if you did something with your hair like dye it so it doesn't look so mousy," or "Why don't you let me give you a facial and get some of that dead skin off your face? Then your wrinkles won't be so noticeable."

That young woman had nerve, alright, zoning in on every one of Hester's little flaws. It was flat-out rude.

As the day wore on, after she had time to think, Hester decided what Jimmy said to her was pretty rude too. He added insult to injury. He didn't trust her to run the market, and he thought she looked "a little worn-out." Wasn't that just a nice way of saying she looked like crap?

God, maybe she should take some of Cecilia's advice.

She was in the office listening to the loose glass panes rattle in the wind, mulling all this over, when Eric came in.

"According to Action News a blizzard's coming," he said.

"No kidding," Hester said.

"Who knows? You know how wrong these weather people can be. Probably, we'll only get an inch, if that, but I better check to see if they closed everything up, upstairs." Eric rummaged in the desk for the key. When he found it, he said to Hester, who was trying to find her place in the *Walden*, "The little witch would have a conniption fit if something happen to all those flocked damask curtains. Angelo thinks they belong in a cathedral. I agree. Really, it is beyond me what she's trying to do with that apartment."

This was the first time Hester ever heard Eric talk disparagingly about Cecilia. It secretly delighted her. Someone else who wasn't head over heels about Jimmy's ex...current friend.

Hester chose her words carefully, "She's an enigma, alright. I've accepted that fact, and I guess you will have to too. But I really can't comment on what the apartment looks like because I've never seen it."

"Really? You live here, and you've never been upstairs?"

"Well, Jimmy is letting me stay down here only because I had no place to go so I can't really say that I live..."

"I know all of that; but, here you are, and they never had you up for so much as a f"ing glass of wine, or anything?"

"Never."

"Well, shit, put that book down and let's go, girl. What are you so engrossed in any way?"

"*Walden*." She closed it and held it up for him to see.

"Thoreau? Please, Hester, after the line about living a life of "quiet desperation," the rest is boring with a capital B; but I will say that does look like an old edition."

"Found it in the trash. Had mustard all over it, but I cleaned it up, even patted out most of the coffee stains."

"Did you get anybody to look at it yet?"

"What for?"

"What if it's a first edition or something? It could be worth a fortune."

"Now why would anyone throw away a first edition of *Walden*?"

"Ignorance, which accounts for a lot of the money we make. People are ignorant of what they have so they throw it away or sell it cheap, and we come along and because we are not ignorant we grab it and turn it into gold." Eric took the book from Hester. He stared at the worn cover and ran his hand over it. "Real leather."

He cupped the spine in his palm and let it fall open. Gingerly, he paged to the frontispiece and inspected it. "The illustration of the cabin in the woods is quaint, isn't it? Let's see, publisher: Reginald L. Cook, Thoreau Society Bulletin, Winter, 1853. I'll have to look it up later."

He turned to the last page and examined the three signatures. "I'll need my best magnifier to read these. Probably just some shyster trying to make a killing by forging those autographs. If this was the first edition of *Walden*, and it was signed by Emerson, Hawthorne, and Thoreau, it would be priceless. Thoreau is unique in the American literary canon. Of course, I don't have to tell you that, and you probably know about all of the bad stuff that happened to him after he finished the book."

"No," Hester said. "All I can remember is he grew up poor, went to Harvard, taught, helped his father design the best pencil of the decade, and, I quote loosely from the Norton Anthology, surveyed the land of other men without coveting it. I don't remember any bad stuff."

"His brother and he fell in love with the same girl, and she rejected them both. Henry David never got over her. His brother eventually died of lockjaw. A few years later he lost his sister, and then he got tuberculosis. For seven long years he withered away, alone. He wasn't even that old when he died. I can't remember exactly."

"Forty-five. He was only forty-five when he died," Hester said. "That's young now, terribly young. I must have known all of that and forgotten."

Eric closed the book ceremoniously and handed it back to Hester.

She took it from him and put it down on the coffee table, but she couldn't move her eyes from it. There was something about that book... Was it that the happy chanticleer's heart had been broken, that broke hers? To love and not be loved in return. Why, it was what shattered a person.

"Enough of the literary chit-chat for now," Eric said. "Let's advance to the Master's, or I should say Mistress's quarters. Wait till you see how tacky it is. Well, I'm not going to say another word. You just look around when you get up there and let me know how bad you think the train wreck is." He raised one devilish, finely-shaped eyebrow and laughed.

The wind was blowing like a son-of-a-bitch so Eric grabbed Hester by the elbow and pulled her along the side of the building. The little foyer at the bottom of the steps smelled like cat piss. She pinched her nostrils, and Eric cracked-up.

"And that's not the worst of it, Lady Jane," he said as he backed up against the wall for her to pass. She turned sideways, pressed her rear end into the paneling, and tried to suck her gut in; but it brushed against Eric right at crotch level.

How embarrassing! Hester swore to herself one more time she'd start doing sit-ups.

"Sorry, Eric, but I just seem to keep putting on the pounds."

"Hadn't noticed," he said, but his tone of voice led Hester to believe he'd totally noticed.

What Hester saw at the top of the stairs did surprise her. She thought her collecting had gotten the better of her, but this place looked like if one more thing came off the U-Haul-It and up the stairs, the official diagnosis would be a full-blown hoarding disorder.

There were marvelous pieces to see if you honed in on one object at a time, but if you tried to make any sense out of the overall contents, it made your head spin.

"Told you so, didn't I?" Eric was beside her with his hands on his hips.

"Train wreck is an understatement."

"'Oh, the inhumanity!' And the odor of that filthy litter box permeating everything. What *is* she trying to do?"

"Impress Jimmy with her money?" Hester blurted out and immediately regretted doing so. Now did she have to say something so catty? Damn, if she wasn't losing even her basic good manners?

"I'm sure he is duly impressed. I know I am. All I see here are dollar signs, lots and lots of dollar signs. 'Avida Dollars!' That's an anagram of Salvador Dali. He lived for money too. Look at that lamp, a Daum Nancy glass cameo, and next to it a Lalique Domremy vivid green art glass vase, and in front of that a Ming carved rhinoceros horn libation cup depicting plum blossoms."

"Wow, you sound like you memorized the catalogue."

"I love this stuff, but would I ever have a chance to own anything remotely like any of it? No. And here it all is in this crummy apartment over the even crummier office. You know what kind of money you are looking at right there on that end table. Oh, rough estimate, about ninety thousand dollars."

Even Hester, who in her past life had worried little about the cost of the things she collected, was bowled over by that figure.

"Well, I guess that Lola and Cecilia were more successful than I ever imagined," Hester said. "There must be tons of cash in professional development. Too bad I didn't know about that sooner."

"You ain't seen nothing yet, Sistah," Eric took her hand and pulled her around the white wool Thonet sofa, past the New England pie safe and the Shaker chairs, and down a long hall to the back bedroom. "I think this is the witch's den."

Hester laughed, until she got into the room and saw that nobody could've slept there. The flocked damask curtains were pulled back, but the room was still dark because it backed up to a stand of pines on Goat Hill. The bed was loaded with unopened boxes. Eric flipped on the rustic antler chandelier. A stack of early American quilts were piled on a Stickley dresser, nine small Bonheur and Gelibert bronzes took up the whole top of a French marble vanity, a Waltham tall clock towered in one corner, a Warhol of Reagan hung over the Eastlake headboard, and eight gorgeous faux bois dinner chairs were stacked up on the other side of the room. The hall bathroom was packed with stuff too.

"On to the main event." Eric was enjoying this, grinning from ear to ear.

"Ta da!" he exclaimed as he bowed toward what must have been Jimmy's bedroom.

Hester gasped. So this is *their* room, the room over her head. She had to admit, even though she tried hard to find fault with it, it was nicely put together. There was an ebony four poster with a coarse white linen canopy and white silk bedding, white sheers on the windows, the grey walls adorned with black and white photos of forests. Among them, she recognized two by Ansel Adams. The mirrored dressers and tables reflected the soft light of the crystal lamps.

"Holy shit!" Eric shrieked with surprise. "She must've had someone come in and help her with this."

"I have to admit I like it."

"Surprise, surprise! I do too. But I would've nixed the canopy."

Hester walked into the room and let her hand drag across the silk of the duvet cover. "Hmmm, imported, China, but the good stuff. The Swarovski candlesticks clustered on the dresser work perfectly. A Persian carpet? Just the right amount of color in just the right place."

Eric nodded in agreement. Hester was at the doorway to the bathroom. She flipped the light on and peeked in. The bathroom was fine, basic, but fine; and on the sink was an open EPT Pregnancy Kit. She flipped the light off, "Nothing special in there, Eric. Maybe we better go now."

"You sure you don't want to snoop some more."

"I'm sure." Hester's back ached and her legs throbbed. All she wanted to do was flop down somewhere and get lost again in *Walden*. She was on the chapter called "Higher Laws."

"Let me check the kitchen, and then we're out of here."

Hester started down the stairs. The steps were steep and when she looked all the way to the bottom she got a little dizzy. She turned sideways, grabbed the railing with both hands, and worked her way down. Eric was singing, "The north wind shall blow, and we shall have snow and what will poor…"

The next thing Hester knew she was at the bottom of the stairs in Eric's arms. "Shit, Hester, you scared the hell out of me! Are you alright?"

"What happened?"

"You fell."

"I was dizzy. I must have fainted."

"Not my business, Miss Hester; but if I were you, I'd see a doctor. He pointed at her bulging stomach. "I think you got something growing in there."

Thirty-Eight

Jimmy thought he'd be exhausted from two days and nights of nonstop sex with Cecilia, but he wasn't. He could've taken a whole lot more of Cecilia than she'd been willing to dish out. Not that he was complaining about the physical contact that did take place. Hell no. In one weekend they'd christened all four bedrooms; the hot tub on the deck, despite the bitter wind coming in off the ocean; and the massive kitchen, specifically the granite island.

The granite island, Jimmy thought, was the icing on the cake. It was Monday morning, and they were getting ready to leave the beach house to go back to the Nugget. Jimmy was packing the stuff Cecilia wanted to bring back to the apartment. He wandered into the kitchen looking for her and found her sitting on the island, naked and holding a cucumber. He had to admit he was a little shocked that she'd taken her clothes off when they were just about ready to go and that she was holding something edible, but it didn't take him more than a few seconds to start stripping. Before he could get his pants down, though, she leaned back on one elbow, spread her legs, and inserted the cucumber. Slowly in…slowly out.

Well, he couldn't believe what he was seeing. He'd heard about using food, and, like any guy, fantasized about it. But to actually see a woman fucking herself with a cucumber. Wow. It was too much, and he practically came just looking at her.

She threw her head back and laughed. Slowly in…slowly out.

He could see how wet the big veggie was getting. Slowly in…

He grabbed the cucumber, pulled it out of her, put himself in, and came before he could count to three. Then he worked with the cucumber until Cecilia told him to stop.

Well, he could've come a hundred more times like that, but she recovered in a split second, tossed the cucumber in the trash, and got dressed.

On the ride back to Lambertville, Cecilia didn't have much to say which rattled Jimmy's confidence, and he began second guessing just about everything he'd done that weekend. He should've eaten the cucumber right in front of her. Maybe that would've turned her on. He should've gone down on her while she was still on the countertop. He should've...what would Lola Giordano have done to Cecilia to keep her from getting dressed, getting in the car, and acting like what just happened was no big deal?

Had that woman Lola made Cecilia happier than he did? Christ, did he have to measure up to a ghost?

Sure, they'd done the deed enough times, but when it was over Cecilia just seemed so...unimpressed.

Jimmy was still mulling over this thorny disappointment that evening back at the Nugget as he whipped them up an omelet, did the dishes, and watched as Cecilia went to soak in the tub, alone.

And I wracked my brain to be creative, used every trick in the book.

God, he wanted to grab her and shake some sense into her. But instead he reached under the sink for the smelly cat food and poured enough in the three bowls to keep them from mewing at him.

As Cecilia's felines circled his legs on the way to their feast, another possibility came to him. Cecilia did nothing all weekend long but take her temperature, trying to determine when she'd be ripe for, as she put it to him, "your seed to be planted"?

Okay, so, maybe, she was preoccupied with getting her eggs fertilized. That he could understand. That made sense to him. He couldn't be jealous of Cecilia's ticking clock. He wanted her to have his baby. Then maybe she'd marry him, and finally he could relax. She would be his.

Still, couldn't she have thrown him at least one crumb of gratitude or appreciation? She hadn't. Not one word about how much she loved him or what a great lover he was, and he'd been too insecure to ask, too afraid she might say something he didn't want to hear, and would never forget.

Restless, feeling hurt and insecure, and beginning to think that, perhaps, he really was a lousy lover, Jimmy decided to go downstairs to visit Hester, the only other woman he'd ever done it with.

Thirty-Nine

Jimmy knocked on Hester's door and opened it. She was sitting up in bed and smiled when she saw it was him. He looked worn out and glanced at her sideways, and it reminded Hester of photos of Princess Diana and the way she'd be looking at the Prince, sideways and sort of victim-like. Jimmy's eyes were big and bottomless like hers, but much more striking because of their unusual color.

"Hey, so you had fun, Jimmy?"

"Yeah."

"Great," Hester said. "I'm happy for you."

"Then you're not mad at me."

"Well, a little, for not trusting me to manage the market."

"Sorry about that. It's just that I've always relied on Eric. Call me a creature of habit." Jimmy sat on the end of the bed. "How you doing?"

"Fine. Eric checked up on me. I really like that guy."

"Yeah, he's good people." Jimmy looked at his hands and ran the nail of his middle finger on one under the nail of his thumb on the other. Without looking up he said, "I want to ask you something, Hester; but I feel kind of awkward. It's about what happened between us that night in the back of…"

"I know, Jimmy, I should've stopped you. I'm much too old for you. I guess I was out of my head that night with all that had happened to…"

"Too old?" Jimmy interrupted. "I don't care how old you are. That's got nothing to do with how it was for you? All I want to know is how you thought it was?"

"Fine."

"Fine? That's it, fine?"

"What do you want me to say?" And Hester meant it. If she gushed about how she'd had the best orgasm of her life and hadn't been able to stop thinking about it, and he went and told Cecilia, she'd fall through some thin ice, alright.

It was obvious by the hang-dog look on his face, though, the weekend hadn't gone as well as expected. Which only confirmed Hester's suspicions that Jimmy had much deeper feelings for Cecilia, than Cecilia would ever have for him. Geez, he looked miserable sitting there probably trying to figure out how to make the woman he loves, love him back. Hester wanted to shake him, tell him to see the handwriting on the wall before it was too late. He was a square peg trying to force himself into Cecilia's round hole.

Just quit while you're ahead, Hester wanted to say. Trying to be somebody you're not for someone else, well, just ask her, it always ends badly. And so does thinking you can change the other person, that you can, by the sheer force of your will, get them to be, not who they are, but who you want them to be.

God, if Jimmy didn't remind her of herself. All his happiness hinging on Cecilia. His whole life revolving around her just like Hester's had around Al. Al, the big lousy cog in her wheel.

Stop, she wanted to holler, trying to get what you want. Want something...someone, else!

"Hester," Jimmy said, "tell me the truth. Seriously, you must've had tons more sex than I have. I need to know how I measure up."

Measure up?

Now she had to say something. "For crying out loud, Jimmy, people might be able to determine how they 'measure up' as lovers on some Richter scale of sensation, but there is no measuring at all when it comes to love. A hearts is either full or its empty. Love is, or it is not. And all the wild sex in the world will not make love happen. Take it from me. I've had plenty of wild sex in my life, but have I ever been loved by anyone. I hate to admit it, but sadly, no. The two men I was convinced I loved, never loved me back. No matter how much great sex I had with them, it didn't change the fact that they did not love me."

"Hester, Christ, I'm sorry to hear all that, but all I wanted to know was what you thought about…"

"Look, Jimmy, when I showed up here, I was at a real low point, literally, without a pot to piss in; but you were kind to me. When you climbed into the back of my car, I was terrified at first, but then something came over me. I don't know why, but I trusted you wouldn't hurt me. Your touch was warm and caring, and I was so down and feeling so alone, I gave in. Yes, in hindsight, I shouldn't have, but I did. No regrets, because I think it all happened for a reason. Though, honestly, I'm hard put to say what that reason is. Maybe one day I'll find out."

"Yeah, it was a bad night for me too, after running into Cecilia and everything, but as bad as I was feeling, when we were doing it, it just seemed so…natural."

"Yes, it did seem natural; and, I don't know, familiar. It was like I knew you, really knew you."

"But you don't really know me. Well, at least, not everything about me. I haven't told you everything."

"No one tells anyone everything, Jimmy. We all have secrets, things we did and can't go back and change, things we did when we were weak instead of strong. Believe me, we are all sorry for something we can't forgive ourselves for. We feel evil, when really all we should feel is human. We let our shame cut us off from others, even though everyone is exactly like we are, flawed."

God, shut up, woman, Hester thought, *you sound like you're teaching "Lord of the Flies."*

"Now you sound exactly like my mother, Hester. Damn, if I don't still miss her." Jimmy stood up.

"Not so fast, Mr. Raymer," Hester said like she was talking to one of her students, "Stop worrying about what Cecilia wants or thinks. Find your backbone, set down some ground rules. If she comes around, great. If not, let her go. Trust me, or you'll be living in the kind of hell I just got out of."

"Right…I hear ya," said Jimmy, but Hester could tell by the hesitation in his voice he would never have an easy time letting Cecilia go.

"And on another topic," said Hester. "I need a favor. I really hate to ask you, since you've done so much for me already; but you know my van is out of commission and I need to see a doctor."

"Why? Is something wrong?"

"I'm not sure, but Eric thinks something's up with my stomach because it's gotten so huge. According to him, he thinks something's growing in there. Me? I just think I'm getting fat on too many of those horrid hot dogs."

Hester had her knees bent so Jimmy couldn't see the shape of her stomach.

"May I take a look?" he asked.

"At my stomach? Don't be crazy, Jimmy. I'll just go to the clinic tomorrow if you'll give me a ride?"

"Please, let me take a look. I just want to make sure there's no emergency."

Forty

Jimmy really didn't want to look at Hester's stomach, but he felt responsible for this woman. He wasn't *involved* with her, but he *was* involved with her. She'd been living in his office since August, five months. And there'd been the sex. And she'd just said some nice things to him, trying to make him feel better, and it had for all of about five minutes.

Now, he was feeling more like the warped heel of a human being than ever because the truth was he'd only fucked Hester Randal because he was pissed after stalking Cecilia and seeing her with Lola. That was it. And now like the stupid ass he was, he wanted to know how it was for Hester. And she'd tried to build him up and give him confidence and make him into more of a man. The least he could do was try to make sure she wasn't dying right underneath him.

"It's not an emergency, its fat! But if you insist…" Hester flung the blanket off and lifted her tight turtleneck sweater.

Jimmy stared her white stomach. It looked huge. His first thought was, *it's got to be a tumor.* His second thought was, *what the hell am I going to do now?*

If Hester got sick, who'd take care of her? Not Cecilia, she would freak out.

The next morning Jimmy and Hester got into his pick up and headed north to the Cottage Hill Clinic. Jimmy pushed the pedal to the floor, eager to get there and get this whole thing over with. He wanted to turn the radio on and blast something like "Fast as You Can" through the cold air. Maybe it would help him clear his freaking head, but he didn't want to disturb Hester, who was staring straight ahead, her hands clasped calmly on her lap. She gave no indication she even noticed the reckless speed the pick-up had achieved. Jimmy was driving like a madman, and he didn't care.

Just don't let it be cancer, kept going through his mind.

Once inside the clinic after Hester completed two clipboards full of information, they sat side by side in silence in front of the blinking television.

After several minutes Jimmy snuck a peek at Hester's profile. He saw the beginning of a double chin. Her skin was blotchy, her hair flat in the back like she hadn't bothered to brush it. She looked pathetic, but still there was something about her that moved him.

Even though, he'd been preoccupied with Cecilia and tried not to think too much about this older woman, he had to admit he was drawn to Hester Randal. Sure there was the whole resemblance to his mother, but beyond that he felt something for her. He had tried again and again to forget that night with her, but he couldn't put it out of his head. He couldn't believe he'd done it, and he half-hated the idea and half-loved it. The memory of the two of them in that cramped, smelly van in the sweltering heat grossed him out one minute and tempted him the next. Even now it was like a song he couldn't get out of his skull.

Did he or didn't he want to take her by the hand, lead her out to the truck, drive to Raven's Rock or somewhere remote, and do her?

Oh, God, was he fucked-up or what?

Jimmy tried to stop thinking about Hester and to concentrate on Cecilia. How many times he'd come at that beach house! And he was finding fault with Cecilia just because she wasn't falling all over him.

Hell, she was home, in his apartment right this minute, wasn't she? When he got back, he'd lead her by the hand into the bedroom and…make sure she liked it.

"Ms. Randal?" the nurse called loudly from behind the desk.

Jimmy watched Hester follow the nurse through the door into the examining room and cursed himself for being such an idiot.

Poor Hester was the one having to face the real music, and all he could think about was himself.

What a self-centered bastard he was.

Forty-One

Hester's hand shook as she took the prescription for the vitamins and the referral to see an obstetrician from the nurse. The General Practitioner looked at the expression on her face and saw the tears welling up in her eyes and must have figured she was overjoyed because as he ushered her out toward the waiting room, he said brightly, "What a miracle to conceive at your age! The obstetrician will be able to tell you more, but to me it seems everything is going perfectly, though I'm a little surprised you haven't felt the baby moving around yet. You're at least five months along already."

When they got into the waiting room, the doctor looked at Jimmy and asked Hester, "Is this your son, Ms. Randal?" Hester, unable to speak, shook her head, no.

"The father, then?"

"The what?" Jimmy was on his feet.

Hester still couldn't find any words and nodded, yes.

"Oh...well then..." The doctor extended his hand to Jimmy and said, "I guess congratulations are in order. A healthy baby is on the way. Quite a surprise at Ms. Randal's age, but she's doing well considering she hasn't had any prenatal care yet."

Jimmy's jaw dropped. What the hell was this guy congratulating him for? The doctor left. Hester blotted her eyes with a tissue and walked out of the office. Jimmy followed her to the truck. They both got in.

On the drive back they passed fields of stubble, the skeletons of the trees brown against the bleak sky. Here and there crows dotted the landscape like black rocks. Hester did not need to do the math. Five months to the day, in the middle of the night, Jimmy had crawled into the back of her minivan and made love to her. There'd been no one else for a long time before, and no one else since.

This baby was Jimmy Raymer's.

Hester thought back to the last obstetrician she'd gone to. Al and she couldn't conceive so Al found this expensive specialist. The guy not only blamed their infertility on the fact that Hester had adhesions from her abortion, but blurted it out right in front of Al, whom she'd never told about her biggest sin. Al had been blindsided by this awful revelation, and Hester couldn't deny it had been another huge nail in the coffin of their marriage.

But now, looks like that smug specialist had been wrong.

For a second Hester wished she could remember the jerk's name. She'd love to call him up and tell him off. That is if she had a phone.

Well, the old Hester would've liked to have done that. The new Hester, the pregnant Hester, however, wouldn't worry about something as childish as getting even. No, pregnant Hester would only worry about one thing, her miracle baby.

This baby would not wind up in some filthy trash bin.

This baby *would* be born, and loved.

Case closed.

"So, Hester," Jimmy said as he handed her his cell phone, "let's get this whole mess straightened out right now. I don't know what that doctor was talking about, but you better figure out how you can get in touch with your ex-husband and tell him the good news."

Jimmy's words stung. Of course, he wouldn't think it was his. Of course, he'd assume she'd been with other men. Of course, he really hadn't paid much attention to all the things she'd told him about her past life with Al Murphy. On the verge of crying or screaming in frustration, Hester took a deep breath and calmed herself. Now was not the time to alienate Jimmy. Now was the time to form a strong alliance with the father of her baby. Her baby, their baby would need both its mother and its father.

But Jimmy persisted in his denial and said, "Go ahead, call him. Better sooner than later. Maybe the two of you can patch things up for your child's sake."

They were stopped at the red light at the junction of 518 and 29. Hester noticed a mutt sniffing at the base of a garbage can in front of Valpario's Deli. She wanted to explain to Jimmy calmly that this was *his* child, *his* responsibility, and she expected him to take care of her and the baby. She wanted to suggest that, perhaps, just perhaps, they could become a family, that she liked him enough, despite their age difference, to at least try. But hunger was clawing at her, and she was suddenly feeling faint.

"Pull into the deli. I need to eat," she said abruptly. She hadn't meant to bark at Jimmy, but oddly enough, he did as she wished and nearly hit the mutt trying to get into one of the narrow spots.

Jimmy followed her into the store and paid for the large Italian hoagie she ordered and a Coke for himself. They sat in the car while she ate, and he sipped on the soda. She was finished in no time and quickly sent him back in for pretzels. When he handed them to her, she opened the bag and waved it in front of him. He took a handful, and the two of them sat there like a couple of teenagers on a cheap date. When they emptied the bag, Jimmy again offered Hester the phone. "Now, will you call your ex-husband and tell him about this so I don't have to worry about you anymore?"

"No, Jimmy, I will not call my ex-husband and tell him about this baby because this baby is not his."

"Well, if it's not his, whose is it?"

"This baby is yours, Jimmy."

"Mine?" Jimmy looked at her squarely. "Come on, it can't be."

Hester straightened her back and met his gaze. "It is. The baby is ours."

The color drained from Jimmy's face. "But it can't be. We only did it…"

But before he could finish his sentence, Hester gasped, bent over, and hugged her stomach. Something inside her moved. She put her hands on the spot and felt around. Again! Her world was shifting.

"Oh my God! Jimmy, the baby moved! Oh, there it goes."

Without thinking, she grabbed Jimmy's hand and put it on her belly. "Here," she whispered.

And silently, they waited for the miracle to happen again.

Forty-Two

At the moment, Cecilia had Hester on her mind. She knew Jimmy had taken her out somewhere. Where? He'd been vague about. Cecilia wasn't jealous. There was nothing for her to be jealous about. She had Jimmy wrapped around her little finger. He'd do anything for her, and she knew it, loved him for it, loved him for the fact that he could give her a child.

Yeah, after that first night, she had really looked forward to trying to get pregnant with Jimmy. It'd blown her mind to be with a man again. And where did Jimmy get all *those* moves? She liked the way he didn't rush and stick his thing in her like it was *the* special treat. No, she was happy with the way things went, the way he'd gotten to her through her huge mammary glands. She didn't know her "girls" could do the trick on their own. Well, Jimmy had taught her at least one new thing about herself.

Yeah, this whole reunion with Jimmy had started out great. For weeks following that initial mind-blowing session, they'd had decent sex every day so why wasn't she pregnant yet? And then at the beach house. She'd actually looked forward to taking Jimmy there and sharing with him all that she'd given up so much to get. Lola would've spit nails to find out Cecilia was back with Jimmy and screwing him in every room in "her" place.

But then, it was tedious, having to constantly take her temperature and do it on demand. It was tedious looking at Jimmy's expectant face every time they did it. Was it good enough? Was it? She could see it in his eyes. God, more pressure. So she, as was her habit, took to inventing her own little ways of getting herself off, like with the cucumber. Yeah, that had been fun for about a minute.

Would it all be worth it once she had her child? God, yes. She could almost smell the sweet scent of her baby's breath and feel those chubby arms around her neck. She could see herself on the beach collecting shells with her little angel in tow. Yes, she wanted to be a mother, and she wanted Jimmy to be the father. She, at least, had some feelings for him.

And she certainly didn't have to worry about him running off with anyone, let alone that odd woman Hester. One look at her was enough to turn anyone off. She dressed like a bum. Her face was emaciated, her skin mottled, and her stomach bigger than Lola's had ever been.

But then the vision of a naked, freshly scrubbed Hester entered Cecilia's mind, and Cecilia could see that despite obvious signs of neglect and aging, Hester Randal was not really an ugly woman. Cecilia imagined Hester's narrow shoulders, her ramrod posture, her small breasts, her pale nipples, her light brown bush, probably sparse enough to see...

The shape of Hester's head was aristocratic, her features refined. She had wrinkles, but only superficial ones. A slight double chin, well, at least the potential for one, did appear when the woman looked down, but all else was pleasant to Cecilia's critical eye. And she detected a similarity between the shape of Hester's face and the shape of Jimmy's, though Jimmy's face was much larger and more striking.

Jimmy's face, in fact, had been what first attracted Cecilia to him. Even at ten Jimmy had been beautiful, the strong angles of his features there beneath his pre-pubescent pudginess. And those violet eyes. Cecilia could never tire of staring into them. True, his teeth were bad, had always been crooked; but teeth could be fixed.

And Hester could be fixed too. She had potential, precisely what Lola lacked. No amount of money, no fashion trick was going to fix what was broken there. As they say in China, Lola had been hit with the ugly stick.

Cecilia, however, could transform Hester, if only the stubborn woman would let her. Cecilia thought Hester was either shy, aloof, or stupid. The woman always took off whenever Cecilia came around; or if she did stay in the same room, she said practically nothing.

Cecilia, at first, thought Jimmy was nuts letting Hester live downstairs. She'd told him so several times. "You barely know her and she's been living down there for months. It's crazy, Jimmy."

And Jimmy would say, "Christ, Cecilia, she's not hurting anything."

But lately, Cecilia felt more light-hearted about many things including Hester's presence beneath them.

Lola's death being declared a suicide. What a stroke of luck.

Cecilia didn't realize until Lola was gone how stressful living with her had been. She'd been Lola's third arm, a deformity, a grotesque extension of the dictatorial businesswoman's body. And now, after the amputation, it was as though Cecilia had crawled out of a cave into the light and was just now regenerating her own missing parts.

Day by day, her mood lightened. She felt more kindly toward almost everyone. Being around Jimmy, his niceness contagious, made her want to be nicer, too.

What did she have to be grumpy about? Eventually, she'd have plenty of money, take over Lola Giordano's empire—who knew better than her how to write those formulaic regurgitations—and have Jimmy's baby.

Yeah, life was on the upswing for Cecilia Kurts, but she'd have to watch herself. She wanted a baby, badly, but she didn't ever want to be so in love with Jimmy Raymer that she couldn't leave him. No way was she going to spend the best years of her life at the Silver Nugget. And there was the rub. The stupid Silver Nugget. Either Jimmy would have to leave it or she would have to leave him…eventually.

Cecilia had Plan B, always had a Plan B…

She was in the kitchen chopping scallions for scampi when Jimmy came up the stairs. He didn't shout, hello, honey, I'm home, like he usually did. And that's what made Cecilia stop—the knife in her hand suspended in mid-air—and look up at him. She didn't like the mixture of shock and dread she saw on his face.

"What, in God's name, now?"

"Sit down," he mumbled and pointed to the sleek white sofa. "I have to tell you something, and I don't think you're gonna like it."

"You look like hell."

"Hester's pregnant." He blurted it out.

"Really? That's amazing at her age. I didn't think somebody that old could get pregnant. Just goes to show, you never know. Figures she'd get pregnant and not us. Right? And look how hard we're trying. I'll have to ask her, her secret."

"Please, put the knife down and come over here. That's not all."

Cecilia pointed the blade at Jimmy. "Just spill the beans, will you? I can't take the drama." And she meant it. She wasn't one for playing guessing games.

"Alright," he said and took a step toward her.

She stabbed the air impatiently. "What the hell, Jimmy?"

"Alright, I'll tell you the truth."

"I hope so. Why would you ever lie to me?"

"It's my baby."

"No way. What are you saying? You had sex with Hester?"

"Yes…once."

"Once? Are you kidding me? You're joking, aren't you?"

"I wish I was."

"Holy shit, Jimmy, she's old enough to be your effing mother."

"I know."

"When? When did you fuck her?" Cecilia slammed the knife onto the cutting board. A beam of sunlight glinted off the blade.

"In August."

"When in August? Goddamn it. When in August?"

"Not when you were here. It was the night I saw you in Bull's, the night Lola died."

"The same night? So you saw me for the first time in five years, and then you picked up Hester somewhere and screwed her?"

"After I saw you at Bull's, after you kissed me like that, I drove past Dina's. There you were with Lola. I watched through the window. I thought I saw you holding Lola's hand. It was too much for me, I snapped. Had too much to drink and Hester had been so nice to me at the bar listening to my troubles and all."

Cecilia leaned across the counter, stared at Jimmy, and thought, *what in the hell? Hester? Pregnant?* It was a lot to process.

What was this going to do to her plan? What was this going to do to Jimmy? To Jimmy and her? God, he looked pathetic to her all of a sudden. He'd probably been humping everything that walked since she left him. And she was wondering where he'd gotten all those moves.

She looked down at the knife and picked it up. "I'll think of something to fix this," she whispered, as if to herself, and went back to chopping the hell out of the rest of the scallions.

Forty-Three

Cecilia cleared out most of what was in the spare room, and Jimmy helped Hester move in. Hester's ankle bones had disappeared, her feet were swollen too, and her inflamed toes stuck out like breakfast sausages on skewers. It'd become painful for her to walk so she shuffled back and forth to the hall bathroom when she needed to, and once a day she went all the way to the living room and sat in the arm chair by the window.

Today, a wild storm was growling its way in from the northwest. In the arm chair earlier than usual, Hester tried looking through the window, but it was like trying to look through marble, the icy mix coming down in solid sheets. She could hear the wind and the snap of the breaking tree branches. It was as they said in New Jersey, one fucking fence-lifter of a squall. And she was in no mood to endure it.

She dreamt of getting away from the Silver Nugget, hiking into the wilderness, building a cabin, and, like Hawthorne's Hester, raising her child there.

But three hundred and seventeen dollars was all the money she'd been able to save. God knows, she tried, but things had to be bought and eaten and the market so dead these past months. Everything she had left to sell, she'd found in the garbage so what could she expect to get for it? Not much.

Oh, she had to face the facts, stop fantasizing. She could not raise a child on three hundred and seventeen dollars. Her desire to have a baby was about to be satisfied, and frustrated, at the same time. She couldn't take care of herself, let alone another human being. She'd have to rely on Jimmy. He said he would take care of the baby, but what would happen to her? Would he take the baby and make her leave the Nugget? She wouldn't allow it. She wanted to get all the details straightened out, but there it never seemed to be a good time to talk. Since Hester had moved into the apartment, Cecilia never left them alone, and she had so much to say, neither of them seemed to be able to get a word in edgewise.

There was the Trenton Shelter for Women down on Brunswick circle. She could take go there. She'd made donations to it every year. Maybe, they would remember getting her checks.

But did she have it in her to swallow her pride and be taken in as a charity case?

Her baby grew large in her womb, as her spirit shriveled. Her heart ached as much as her back. Her breasts and stomach were covered with stretch marks so deep it look like a wild animal tried to claw its way into her. Her legs throbbed. She either had heartburn or nausea, or both at once. She had to empty her bladder every half hour so how could she get any sleep. She couldn't. She sighed deeply trying not to wallow in this latest wave of pain and self-pity. Aborting her first baby had almost killed her, carrying this one to term was about to finish the job.

Cecilia came over and sat on a stool in front of Hester.

Oh no, thought Hester, *another one of Cecilia's ministrations.*

"Maybe *we* need a little foot massage to help with that water retention?" Cecilia, not waiting for Hester's response, picked up one of Hester's feet, and began kneading the sole, forcing the toes apart and the top of the foot into a flexed position. Hester sank back into the soft chair. Why fight city hall? Cecilia's knuckles rubbed deep into Hester's arch, her strong fingers pulling Hester's toes one by one almost out of their sockets. Hester had to give it to Cecilia: this was better than any foot massage she'd ever had, even at Zanya's Spa.

Cecilia began humming "Brahms' Lullaby."

Oh, please? Hester thought. *Cecilia can be almost wonderful, and then she has to go and ruin it.*

For weeks now Cecilia had been working on Hester. One day she gave her an oatmeal facial, the next she plucked her eyebrows, then a back massage, then a henna rinse. Hester's skin glowed, and her hair was now the color of polished chestnuts. She looked years younger, but the lift she got from seeing her new self in the mirror didn't last long. In the back of her mind, Hester was suspicious of all this attention from this odd young woman.

Was Cecilia being nice because she really *was* nice?

Hester had her doubts, but she could fret only so much about what the young woman was up to before the multiple and varied needs of her burgeoning body so exhausted her that she could barely think straight about much of anything.

Forty-Four

Cecilia was feeling pretty warm and fuzzy about Hester, and that was good. As she was stroking Hester's ankle she thought, *after she delivers this baby and gets back in shape, she's probably going to look really good. Why the henna rinse alone was a major transformation.*

And Cecilia did like the fact that Hester was much shorter than she was. Cecilia had never minded how petite Lola was. It had been an advantage being taller, broader, and stronger than Lola. It could be an advantage with Hester too.

Yes, Cecilia stared at Hester's comely foot, *I could picture us naked together.*

Even now she had the urge to run her hands up Hester's unshaven calves, the soft light hair visible even on this dreary day. If Cecilia could get her in the shower, she'd shave those legs, and a few other places, and then take her into the…

They wouldn't have to go to bed.

Right here in this chair would be fine. Cecilia could move her hands further and further up Hester's legs until, slowly, she'd be massaging Hester's thighs. Gently, firmly, she'd push them apart. Hester would most likely gasp and protest, but Cecilia would gently press one thumb into Hester.

"Relax, I won't hurt you," Cecilia would say while she spread Hester apart with her other hand so she could peek at Hester's gleaming swollen flesh. "This will make you feel better, relieve your stress, make the baby feel better."

And, maybe, hopefully, Hester would put her head back and moan and enjoy it as Cecilia went deeper and deeper, her thumb disappearing, her other thumb and fingers spreading Hester open even wider.

The novelty and shock of what Cecilia was doing to her couldn't help but turned Hester on, and when Cecilia was confident that Hester was ready, she'd...

Hester would love it. And so would Cecilia.

But Hester had on her old grey sweatpants. Cecilia could pushed the legs up only so far. Innocently, Cecilia caressed the woman's hairy legs. Then Cecilia rested her hands on Hester's knees and looked up at Hester. Hester was staring out the window, and Cecilia was about to suggest Hester take those crummy sweatpants off when Jimmy came up the stairs and flung his dripping wet slicker over the railing. "It's a real bitch of day out there," he exclaimed.

And it is in here too, thanks to you, Cecilia thought of saying as she went back to the ball of Hester's foot and pressed her thumbs into the thick pad of flesh.

Eventually, Cecilia turned and looked up at Jimmy, who was standing behind her, and said, "Don't make too much noise. I'm trying to get some of this swelling down. *We* need rest and need to keep our feet elevated. *We* don't want the edema to get worse. *We* can't have our blood pressure spike. *We've* got eight weeks, and pounds more of baby weight, to go." Cecilia obviously had been reading the pregnancy manuals.

Forty-Five

Hester inwardly recoiled at Cecilia's "we" reference. *There was no "we."*

True, Hester *was* beginning to care somewhat for the young woman who seemed so concerned about Hester's well-being. Gratitude, maybe, was what Hester was feeling, but that was far from the sort of connection implied by the plural pronoun "we."

Cecilia's personality was no longer some airy mist on the rim of Hester's existence. No, it had turned into a dense fog that socked in every waking minute of Hester's narrow life. Little by little, Hester's needs were getting lost in Cecilia's innumerable wants.

She wants my baby. The thought struck Hester like a frying pan to the back of the head. *"We" as in "we" are having a baby.*

Now, the move upstairs; all of the attention; the fancy, fresh, local food; the facials; hair treatments; massages made sense. Hester squeezed her eyes shut tighter, and a tear caught in the corner and ran down her cheek. She was too disheartened to brush it away.

That woman will not get my baby.

Hester would talk to Jimmy and make it clear, she would never allow someone else, let alone Cecilia, to raise her child. Never.

Forty-Six

When she figured out that Hester's pain could be her gain, Cecilia had been elated. Of course, there'd be negotiations, but Cecilia could see that things could be worked out rather expediently.

"Marry me," said Cecilia to Jimmy one windy March night when they were at Bull's dining on the crab cakes.

"Whoa," replied Jimmy, "now you want to marry me? Out of the clear blue sky?"

"Seven months of living together in that cramped apartment is not 'out of the clear blue sky,' Jimmy. Don't you think it's about time we made it legal? We've got a child coming, and we better start acting more responsibly. That is if you want to get full custody."

"Cecilia, get real. Hester will never agree to give me full custody of *her* baby."

"You mean *your* baby. You have as much right to that child as she does. More. You're the one footing the bills. The lady is not capable of caring for that child without you, Jimmy. And you can take her to court. If we're married, happily married, the judge will be much more amenable to the idea of you having full custody. Judges always prefer a baby be raised in a normal, two-parent family."

"You do have a point there. But I don't want any problems with Hester."

"Problems? What kind of problems?"

"I want Hester to be happy too."

"Christ, Jimmy, you are such a bleeding heart," said Cecilia. She turned to the steaming plate of crab cakes and mashed potatoes, and loaded up her fork. "I'll offer her money."

"For what?" Jimmy asked.

"For herself. So she can start over." Cecilia devoured the forkful. "I'll get my lawyer, Lola's old lawyer, on it."

"Cecilia, you're talking nonsense. You can't just buy a child."

"I'm not buying a child, Jimmy. Look, Hester is penniless. Until we moved her up with us, she was living in the closet of your office, before that in her car. It would be irresponsible for us to leave a puppy with her, let alone a human baby. And it would be insane to continue to let her live with us. After the baby comes, that apartment will be a zoo. We'll all be living like white trash. Think about it. Hester needs money so she can move out and get a place of her own."

"I'm telling you she will not leave that baby with us. She can move back downstairs or maybe get a place in town. We can share custody."

"And how stable is that going to be? Look, you and I are the ones who can give that baby what it needs. We can give Baby Alice everything she needs."

"So you know if it's a girl, I want to name her Alice? That would really make me happy."

"Jimmy, when it comes to you, there is nothing I don't know," said Cecilia, "and nothing I wouldn't do to make you happy."

And when Cecilia saw the look of relief on Jimmy's face, she knew she'd said exactly the right thing.

Forty-Seven

Hester pulled her shirt up. "Jimmy. Put your hand here. Hurry, the baby is kicking like mad."

Jimmy was standing next to the bed staring at Hester. The baby would be coming soon, and with each passing day he seemed to grow more anxious. He told himself, what he was feeling was probably normal, but that didn't make his nervousness any easier to take.

Shit, when was he going to face up to it? What the hell was he doing having a baby? Nothing he could feel about bringing this baby into *his* world would be normal. He could feel the dark and threatening truth about Alice's death lurking beneath his every thought. This black truth had been trying to kick its way out of him for fifteen years. No one but him, not another living soul, knew the truth about what really happened that afternoon.

When he got off the school bus that day, he was bursting with energy. He didn't run up the hill to the house like he said he did. No, he was too excited. He'd just met his new tutor, Cecilia, and had fallen crazy in love with her. What ten year old boy wouldn't have gone nuts over Cecilia Kurts? There wasn't a girl around as beautiful as she was. He couldn't get her out of his mind and didn't have the words to describe to anyone, let alone his mother, what he was feeling. He didn't want to go right home and have to face his mother and her questions. He didn't want anything to interfere with what was going on inside him, so instead of going to his house, he crossed River Road and went down to the bank of the Delaware to skim some stones.

He was walking south looking for better stones when he did notice something red tangled in the branches of the downed tree. It was a sweater, like his Mom's. But he didn't really think it was his Mom's so he dropped it and kept going. Then, under a bush he did see a pair of Keds, like his Mom's. Now he started to get a little worried. What were her sweater and sneakers doing down here? Had she gone for a swim?

"Mom," he shouted, "Where are you?" His voice was drowned out by the sound of the rushing water.

"Mom," he screamed louder as the brown, opaque monster of a river swirled past him. His heart started pounding. Something was terribly wrong. Where was Alice if his Mom had been swallowed up by this river?

But his Mom couldn't be in the river!

He ran up the hill, into the house, and through all the rooms on the first floor. Then he flew up the stairs. Outside the bathroom he heard splashing in the tub. He hesitated at the door.

"Mom, are you in there?"

More splashing. He went in. Little Alice was on her back in the tub, the water covered her eyes, but not her nose or mouth. She seemed oblivious of any danger, her chubby arms plopping up and down. Through the water she spied her brother and smiled up at him.

Thank God, she's alright, thought Jimmy.

But where was his mother, and why had she left Alice alone like that? He rolled Alice over onto her stomach so she could raise herself up on her arms like a seal. When he was sure she was safe, he went to search the house for his mother. He looked everywhere, even down in the basement behind the furnace, where he hated to go. He was still in the basement trying to think of what he should do next when Alice started crying. By the time he got to the first floor, she was screeching at the top of lungs. The sound pierced Jimmy's ears, and he put his hands over them to block it out. God, she was a screamer. He had to shut her up so he could figure out where his mother was. He ran up to the bathroom. Alice was thrashing around in the water, her face angry and red.

Jimmy lifted her up. She was heavy and didn't stop screaming, only wailed louder. She was twisting around so much he could barely hold onto her. Snot was running from her nose. She was heavy as a stone, a heavy wet river stone. She wound her head around in circles, her body was rigid with anger. She screamed and screamed and screamed. He tried to make her stop. He really did. But she wouldn't. She would not stop, so he…

Yes, oh my God, he did do it.

Jimmy shivered as he shook off the haunting memory and came back to himself.

"What's wrong, Jimmy?" Hester asked.

"Nothing."

He could see Hester was waiting for him to sit on the bed, so he did and put the palm of his hand on her abdomen. It was taunt like the skin of a basketball. The white scars of her stretch marks reached like tentacles up the sides of her stomach. Clearly her skin was stretched to its limit.

Hester put her hands over Jimmy's big rough one and said, "Just be patient. She'll do it again."

They'd seen the ultra-sounds. Cecilia had picked up the tab for it. The baby was a girl. Little Alice had two legs, ten toes, two arms, ten fingers, everything she needed, as far as modern medicine could tell; and Cecilia had spared no expense to determine that the birth would be perfect too.

Hester had the best obstetrician in the area and the best doula. The delivery would be at the Capitol Health Center in Hopewell Valley in a private birthing room that looked like a fancy bedroom. A private Lamaze coach would start working with Hester and Cecilia next week. Cecilia, not Jimmy, would be her birthing partner. Jimmy would be there, of course, but it would be Cecilia who would help Hester through her labor. Everything had been arranged, and everything had been made clear to Jimmy and Hester. There was nothing for Hester to worry about. Jimmy had heard Cecilia say it enough times.

Jimmy waited, staring at Hester's gleaming white stomach. Inside was his baby. One being living inside another, biding its time, waiting to begin its own life—it blew his mind. Hester, lying there propped up on pillows, reminded him more than ever of Agnes, so much so he wanted to light a cigarette and put it in her hand. Then she would look exactly like his mother did when she was expecting Alice.

Jimmy liked the warmth of Hester's hand on top of his. It sent a warm feeling through him like his heart was filling up with goodness again, the bad memory fading again. She looked ravishing to him, so alive, so ripe with life she was about to burst. He wanted to embrace her, caress her, make love to her to thank her for going through all of this so he could have what he wanted, Cecilia. He could've pulled back the covers and gotten in next to her and been happier than he'd ever been before.

But he knew he wouldn't. He couldn't have her now. No. Never. Not now or ever again.

Then the baby kicked. Jimmy's mouth dropped open. It was a solid jab just below Hester's barely discernible rib.

"Whoa! I felt it!" he said.

"Told you she'd do it again. You ought to be here in the middle of the night. It's like she's trying to kick her way out."

Jimmy slid his hands down to Hester's hips. He turned his head and pressed his ear to the spot where he felt the kick. "I can hear her heart beating."

"Yes, I know."

He closed his eyes and stayed in that position for a long time and thought about how lucky he was. That little heart was beating with God's good grace. It wasn't that he was particularly religious, but here was living proof he might have been forgiven for the horrid deed he'd done. He was only a boy then, but he knew what he did was very wrong. He'd cut short his sister Alice's life. He'd put her back in the tub, screaming and punching the air with her tiny fists. He'd held her down and let the water cover her whole face. He watched as her eyes bulged and her mouth fell open and the last bubble burst on the surface

It was murder. He'd murdered his sister. And he could never change that fact, but, if he could forgive himself, he could make it up to this new Alice. He could protect her with every ounce of his strength and make sure nothing bad ever happened to her.

Jimmy kissed Hester's abdomen where the baby had last kicked.

"That tickles!" Hester laughed. It was the first time he'd heard Hester laugh in months.

"You taste like a coconut," he said.

"Thanks to your *wife*."

Jimmy shot Hester a worried look, "She told you?"

"Yes, Jimmy, she told me you eloped, and she told me the rest of the plan."

"Oh, I'm sorry. She should've waited for me to talk to you. But you know how Cecilia is, there's no putting a muzzle on that girl," Jimmy said as he stood up.

"Jimmy," Hester said, "Cecilia told me, and I quote, 'I can't thank you enough for bringing our baby into the world.' She was leaning over me rubbing coconut butter on my stretch marks while telling me that my baby is hers too, more or less."

"Well, Hester, Cecilia will be the baby's stepmother," said Jimmy defensively, "and I think she'll be a good stepmother."

"Jimmy, I want to raise my baby. Nothing against Cecilia. I mean, she's really been great. She's gone above and beyond to help me, but I want to be our child's mother."

"You will be. You are," said Jimmy, trying to reassure Hester.

"I think Cecilia has other plans," said Hester. "She told me that since you two are married the baby will have a daddy and a mommy. And I said to her, 'Aren't I the mommy?' And she told me, 'Honestly, Hester, don't you think at your age you'll be more like a grandmother to the baby?' A grandmother? Jimmy, come on, I hope you aren't thinking the same thing Cecilia is, that I'm going to fade into the sunset like some old person and let you two just have my baby."

Jimmy couldn't help but be exasperated with Cecilia. She shouldn't have been talking like this to Hester at all. Now he was really in the middle.

"I am not the grandmother," Hester stated firmly. "I'm the mother, and I told Cecilia exactly that. I pushed her hands away, and told her, 'You can't cut me out of my child's life like that."

"Hester, no one is going to cut you out of our baby's life. Trust me," said Jimmy. "Now get some rest. Please. And don't worry about a thing Cecilia said to you. I'll talk to her."

Jimmy left, closed the door behind him, and wondered where in the hell *was* his backbone? He was going to need it.

Forty-Eight

Less rough today," Cecilia said as her hand loaded with coconut butter slid like silk over the skin of Hester's forearm. Cecilia was beginning her daily ritual of tending to Hester's dry skin and the lengthening tributaries of her stretch marks.

"Look, Hester, I spoke out of turn the other day, and I want to straighten things out between us. I don't want there ever to be anything bad between us. Jimmy told me how upset you were. Now to clarify: Jimmy and I are *not* going to take your baby away from you. I promise you. What I was trying to say to you the other day was that we, Jimmy and I, that is, are better equipped than you are to provide for your child. We can give the baby everything it needs to grow up strong and healthy. You are going to have to depend on us whether you like it or not. I only say this because it seems to be a fact. You really do have nothing..." Cecilia hesitated, and Hester imagined that Cecilia really want to say, fucking nothing, "to offer a child. I could be wrong about this; and please, correct me if I am wrong, but you are practically penniless. Aren't you?"

Truer words were never spoken. Hester had *fucking nothing* to offer a child, except maybe her heart and soul.

Cecilia yanked Hester's top up all the way to her neck, gobbed butter onto Hester's abdomen, and began rubbing it in.

"So the way I see it, honey," Cecilia said sweetly, "we all need each other. How did Hillary Clinton put it? It takes a village."

At that, Cecilia knelt on the bed, reached beneath Hester, and unclasped her bra.

"What the hell are you doing, Cecilia?"

"Trying to see what kind of shape your breasts are in. Don't be prissy about it. We're all girls here." Cecilia lifted the cups of

243

Hester's bra. "Wow, look at those stretch marks and dried out nipples! You should have told me how bad they were." It didn't take Cecilia but a second to scoop out two handfuls of the butter and start in.

Hester pushed the brazen young woman's hands away and rubbed the coconut butter in herself. Her breasts felt much better, but Hester was humiliated. A part of her wanted to get up out of the bed and smack cloying, mawkish Cecilia right in the face. If this person ever figured out a way to get Hester's baby?

It was unthinkable.

Cecilia wiped her greasy hands on a towel. "You'll see, sweetie," she said, "everything will work out for the best. If you let Jimmy have full custody, we'll have full responsibility for all of the bills, the doctor, the pediatrician, babysitting, food, clothing, shelter, school, college…you get the picture. You won't have to worry about any of that. You can just relax and enjoy you little girl. And by the time all is said and done, we'll be one, big, happy family." Then Cecilia bent over, kissed Hester on the forehead, and left.

One, big, happy family? Hester rubbed Cecilia's kiss off her forehead. *What the f...?* She rolled onto her side. *Over my dead body.* She closed her eyes tight and tried to fall asleep, tried to block out what was happening, what she feared was going to happen.

But the baby was moving so much Hester's insides felt like they'd been twisted into a knot. It was tough for her to take a deep breath, and then the head lodged in her groin and the pressure got so intense, she thought her cervix might burst into flames.

Hester was wide awake now and torturing herself further by imagining the worst.

Jimmy saying, "Now the baby will have Cecilia for a mother and me for a father. At least we love each other and are married. It's what every child deserves."

"Jimmy, God damn it, I'm the baby's mother." She saw herself trying to protest, but she was weak and her voice a whisper.

"Well, yes, you are technically the baby's biological mother." Jimmy's voice was firm. "But, Hester, let's face it, Cecilia is the real mother to the baby. You'll be more like a grandmother."

"You and Cecilia will not cut me out of my child's life, Jimmy." Hester would keep repeating it, trying to keep her voice from trembling with anger, and she would turn her hot, angry face away so Jimmy wouldn't see the beast within slowly taking shape slowly rising up so it could strike these insane young people down.

But he would've heard something in her voice that would make him back down a bit. "Hester, honestly, we have no intention of cutting you out of your baby's life."

She could see him reaching out, taking her face in his hands and turning her head so he could look in her eyes. She would see her face in miniature inside his violet orbs, see her future there. *Would it be as he said?*

Then Jimmy would add, "Please, don't be upset."

"Upset?" Hester would want to spit in his face, but she'd look away again, pretend she was somewhere else. She would pretend she was with her baby in her make-believe cabin in the make-believe woods.

Forty-Nine

Then, out of nowhere, Cecilia's demeanor radically changed. It was difficult to explain, but the closer it got to Hester's delivery date, the more light-hearted and down-right hilarious Cecilia became. Like the other day, when Cecilia was going to take Hester to their Lamaze class, she came out of the bedroom dressed in an old, puffy-sleeved, 1970's maternity top with a pillow stuffed under it.

"How do you like the new team uniform?" Cecilia said, putting one hand on her lower back and mimicking Hester's wide-legged walk. She moaned, grunted, belched, and even farted which caused Hester and Jimmy to crack-up.

Cecilia continued the shenanigans through the class; and when it was over, several of the participants congratulated her on being such a clown.

Driving home, Cecilia asked, "Did you have fun?"

"I didn't expect to," admitted Hester, "but, yes, for the first time in a long time, I had fun."

"Me too," Cecilia said, then added, "Hester Randal, you naughty old girl, you're making me fall positively in love with you."

Hester didn't know how to respond to that, other than to laugh nervously. Was she letting herself get sucked into Cecilia's vortex of illusions? Or was Cecilia honestly, actually, an okay person, even a friend, perhaps?

The next morning the first spring rain arrived. Hester lay in bed staring at the ceiling, watching a wet spot bloom near the light fixture. Should she get up and tell Jimmy?

The hell with it. She was too weary to move. Her eyes darted around the top perimeter of the room and landed on the flocked damask valances. They reminded her of something that would've been in one of those rooms above an old Wild West saloon. She remembered the day Eric snuck her up to the apartment. Eric hated those drapes and valances, hated Cecilia's taste in home decor, hated Cecilia, period. As fond as he was of Jimmy, it was clear Cecilia rubbed him the wrong way. You think they would've gotten along being they were both gay, or bi, or whatever. Hester touched her forehead where Cecilia had kissed her that one time.

Damn her. Hester insides involuntarily clenched. *Cecilia. Confounding Cecilia.*

Hester closed her eyes. Her mind drifted back to Lola Giordano's corpse with its open eyes, open mouth, blood dripping from the tip of its middle finger, the crime scene investigator's gloved hand feeling around in the bloody mud beneath the table. He held the double-edged blade up, a wet, red sliver of evidence, held it close to his face to inspect it then dropped it in a clear plastic bag.

And this poor woman killed herself, this woman who was Cecilia's lover. Hester could picture this Lola having sex with Cecilia. Then she tried to visualize herself with Cecilia, to imagine them naked in bed together, but she couldn't. She couldn't imagine being with any woman, no matter how beautiful she was, no matter how clever or rich. And Lola Giordano had indeed been both clever and rich.

Hester didn't want to dwell on Lola Giordano, didn't want to spend this day thinking about the dead woman, who'd been such an authority on all things when she was alive. The great Ms. Giordano had all the answers, kept on top of everything, except what was going on inside her own head. Why had Lola Giordano killed herself? It was a great mystery to Hester, who both admired and envied the powerful woman.

Or had she killed herself?

Cecilia would know. One day Hester would put that question to Miss C.

At noon, Jimmy pulled on his waders and slicker, and left to check the barn. The roof was in need of repairs, and he was going to have to strategically place buckets beneath the leaks or the whole floor would flood.

"April showers, freaking pain-in-the-ass," he mumbled to Hester, who was wobbling her way into the living room toward the arm chair. "There're reports the Delaware might overflow at high tide. When I'm done in the barn, I'll go down and take a look for myself." He grabbed a bucket from under the sink and left.

From the window through the bare branches of the trees and the mist from the rain, Hester studied the grim sky, the steely clouds heavy over the river. It was a dismal, lonely landscape, Jimmy moved through as he cross the road and the footbridge, and headed north on the towpath out of her field of vision. It was like he was walking out of her life, exactly like everyone else had.

Sometimes she had to pinch herself just to remember she was alive and what was happening to her not a nightmare, not a novel she'd written and fallen into, no fantasy or vision. No, this was her freaking existence! Here in this weird apartment with two curious, no grotesque, people she hardly knew and eight months pregnant and poverty-stricken! Could she bear it? Live through another day of it? Were it not for this child in her womb, the answer would've been no, and she would've gladly hiked to the CVS, spent her last dime on a double-edged razor blade, and slit her own wrists.

Fighting the pall that had descended on her—she had to for the baby's sake—she got herself out of the chair and tottered back to the bed.

She needed sleep, but it was nearly impossible for her to get comfortable. She picked up *Walden* from the nightstand. She had made it to the chapter named, "Spring."

"We loiter in winter while it is already spring. In a pleasant spring morning all men's sins are forgiven. Such a day is a truce to vice. While such a sun holds out to burn, the vilest sinner may return. Through our own recovered innocence we discern the innocence of our neighbors."

Some real food for thought. Thoreau sure knew how to dish it up.

'...all men's sins are forgiven...such a day is a truce to vice...our own recovered innocence...'

He's right, thought Hester. She'd spent far too much time "loitering" in the winter of her sins, wallowing in guilt. When it stopped raining, she'd go out for a goddamn walk if it killed her.

Cecilia brought her a glass of water she'd floated some cucumber slices and a sprig of rosemary in and said, "I was thinking how nice it'll be after the rain stops. I should take you for a walk on the towpath. What do think, honey, can you make it?"

"I was thinking the same thing." Hester put her book down and with considerable effort pushed herself up into a sitting position. "I can make it to the towpath. How far along it I'll get? I'm not making any promises."

Hester took the glass from Cecilia and their eyes met. Hester wanted to say something, but she couldn't find the right words. She thought, *'...through our own recovered innocence we discern the innocence of our neighbors.'*

Cecilia watched as Hester drank the water, then took the glass and placed it next to the *Walden*. She reached for Hester's hand, grasped it, and entwined her fingers through Hester's. "Don't be frightened," she said. "There's enough love for all of us."

Such a tender gesture, the words so sincerely uttered, and from such beautiful lips, Hester was breathless. Those lips, full of life, like two living things that had curled up on the young woman's face. Hester watched them open and felt herself rising up out of her heavy body and drifting toward those lips before she came to her senses. Perhaps Cecilia's kind words had rustled the bare branches of her heart. So as if trying to secure a permanent truce between Cecilia and herself, as if deciding that it would be nice to have Cecilia as her friend, she said, "I know you will be a good stepmother to my child."

"I promise I will," Cecilia replied. And it didn't sound to Hester at all like an untruth.

Cecilia lifted the blanket Hester was under, crawled in alongside her, and put her arm over the warm mound of Hester's womb.

Fifty

When Cecilia was around cracking an off-color joke or doing something quirky that made Hester laugh, Hester felt light as a feather about the future; but when Hester was alone, she fell into a panic.

Were Cecilia and Jimmy lying to her? Were they plotting to get her tiny blossom of a baby for themselves? Did they have a plan to get Hester as far away from the new little happy family as they could? These were her deep, dark worries.

It was early May, her time was coming soon. Cecilia and Jimmy had gone to the Flemington Factory Outlets to shop for baby things. Hester, sitting by the open window, spotted Eric heading for the office.

"Hey, Eric, got a minute?" she yelled.

"Yeah, be right up."

Hester would ask him what he thought. After all, he knew Jimmy and Cecilia much better than she. And even though he didn't care much for Cecilia, he wouldn't demean her capabilities as a parent, her trustworthiness, just because he didn't like her style. That wasn't Eric's style.

Eric helped himself to Cecilia's wine, made himself comfortable on the sofa, and after Hester explained Cecilia's rationale for Jimmy and she having full custody, he said, "Look, since I'll never have one, I've never given babies much thought; but if you want to know what my instinct tells me, well, I wouldn't do it."

"But Jimmy is the father and she is the stepmother now that she's married to Jimmy and whether I like it or not they do have the means to support the baby."

253

"Yes, but that doesn't entitle Miss C to take over raising your baby. If it weren't for Jimmy, she'd have no rights to anything. I mean, sweetheart, there's no blood tie there."

"But I'm signing over my parental responsibilities to Jimmy, not to Cecilia. And they both swore I would be a huge part of our child's life. Like a grandmother. They said I could live downstairs for as long as I wanted."

"Oh sure, that's what they're saying now? Look, sweetie, I don't want to get in the middle of anything. I've known Jimmy a long time. I like the guy. As a matter of fact, I've had a crush on him since forever. Tried like hell to get him to switch teams, but that is neither here nor there. As nice as I think the guy is, I know he'd cut off his right and left arm for Cecilia. But if you insist on going through with it, you better get everything they're promising you in writing. Cecilia is..." He seemed at a loss to describe her. "...is two-tongued. She knows how to get what she wants by talking out of both sides of her mouth. Sounds to me like she wants your baby, like once she got it, she'd throw you and poor Jimmy out with the bath water and have the kid to herself."

"But she's been so nice lately. I just can't believe she'd do that."

Eric picked up his wine glass, swirled the Merlot, held it up to the late afternoon sunlight and studied the ruby liquid. "Oh, she would do *that*. She most certainly would."

Hester was so large now, she made the chair look small. She clasped her hands at the base of her belly for support and let her legs fall open because any other position was painful. Light fell on her face, and her skin shone from her last facial. She sighed, out the window the white clouds were turning pink.

She wanted to protest, but she didn't. She let Eric's words sink in. *Cecilia would do that*. The awful thought made her want to weep. She rubbed her belly. If only she could rub away all that could go wrong for her baby.

"Her name will be Pearl," Hester announced.

A bit obvious, don't' you thing, *Hester*?" said Eric. "Though I must admit, a proper choice none-the-less."

"You know the reference?"

"I didn't just crawl out of a swamp, my dear."

"Sorry, Eric. I didn't mean anything…"

"No problem. I didn't crawl out of a swamp, but I do have thick skin."

"So you like the name?"

"Love the name. Love Hawthorne. The man was a genius, but, me thinks he let his dark lady, Hester, suffer too much for the likes of Mr. Milk-toast, Mr. *Dims*dale. Don't do the same for Jimmy. Remember Jimmy Raymer is not worried about his reputation, his flock, or Jesus. All he's worried about is making Miss C happy."

"But, Eric, let's face it, I can't take little Pearl, traipse up Goat Hill, and set up camp in the woods. A baby can't live like that." Hester thought of her mother and father, of her sister, of—even though it was a mess now—how lovely it had once been, of all the advantages she'd had. Her baby deserved that kind of family. If she thought any of them would help her now, she'd have crawled on her knees back to them.

"Can't you see, Eric? I have nothing to give her. For her sake, I have to let them have her."

"I could help till you get a job."

"You are so kind to say that, but I can't get a job."

"Why? You're smart. You're still young enough to teach."

"Yeah, I'm young enough and smart enough, but no one would hire me. Did you ever hear of Alexander Bruno Murphy?"

"Doesn't ring a bell."

"I was married to him. Google him, and you'll see why I'll never be able to teach again."

"I don't have any access here. You going to make me wait?"

"It's just that I'm embarrassed. I was accused of befriending students so my husband could molest them. I was found innocent, of course; but the State took away his pension and benefits, and mine. Everything else we had he liquidated to hire a lawyer. He was facing murder charges because he…I can't go into it all now. It's too upsetting. Bottom line is, I will never get a job in a classroom again. Never."

"Shit, sweetie, you are between a rock and a hard place? It's enough to make someone go crazy."

"Tell me about it. I'm afraid I'm really going to lose my head for good this time."

Fifty-One

Cecilia walked into the apartment, put her hands on her hips, and said, "Thank God, I got back in time to save our baby from stuffy air."

Like a testy jay, she flitted about the room weaving in and around all her treasures, opening windows, and turning on lights. She hurried into the kitchen and shouted back to Hester, "Don't you realize, Hester, that's why I quit smoking. What we breathe, our baby breathes?"

Hester, ignoring Cecilia, looked at Jimmy and asked, "How'd you make out?"

"Got a truckload of stuff for one little baby. God knows where the hell we're going to put it all."

Eric moved from the sofa to a chair by the Baker Pembrook table and poured himself another glass of Merlot. Jimmy stuck his hands in the pockets of his jeans and looked down at Eric. "Did I tell you Cecilia dropped the price on her beach house? She's still going to get around eight hundred thousand when it sells, but the good news is, when the lawyer finally went down and had the safe opened, there was fifty thousand dollars in it. He said it belonged to Cecilia because she'd inherited the house and contents. Can you fucking believe it? What luck, and when that house sells, we'll be able to afford to just walk away…"

"Jimmy, shut the hell up!" Cecilia hollered from the kitchen. "That's our business, nobody else's."

Hester couldn't believe what Jimmy was saying, couldn't believe the astronomical figures he was throwing around. A half a million in cash? And what was he about to say? They'll be able to afford to walk away from what? From her? From the Silver Nugget? She had to figure it all out. She had to know.

Hester felt dizzy from all the 'what-ifs' swirling around in her brain. She tried to get to her feet, but she was suddenly too weak. She collapsed into the chair, pain shooting up from her crotch, consuming her. Her hands flew to her pelvis, and she pressed them into the base of her enormous abdomen. If only she were alone, she would've put them between her legs and pressed them into herself where the real pain was, where it was mounting again, the pressure building, the feeling that she might burst open scaring the shit out of her. She struggled out of the chair and wobbled through the living room trying to get to the bedroom where she'd close the door, where she'd be alone and able to tackle whatever it was that was happening to her. Well, she knew what was happening, didn't she? But she needed to be alone, to squat and let this baby drop out into her world, no one else's. She was almost to the hall when pain rippled down her legs and slammed into the back of her knees. It was so intense she screamed and collapsed.

"Cecilia!" Jimmy yelled. "Hurry up, something's wrong with Hester." He went to her and helped her up.

"She must be in labor," Eric said.

"Ahhhh! It hurts." Hester clenched her fists.

"It's alright, honey. I'm here." Cecilia was next to her, slipping her arm under Hester's. "Back up! Give her some air. Remember, Hester, nice shallow little breaths. Puff, puff, puff. Just like we practiced."

Cecilia waited until Hester was through another contraction before she started walking her around the sofa toward the bedroom. "Let's get you into something more suitable for the trip to the hospital. Jimmy, call our doula."

They were in the hallway by Jimmy and Cecilia's bedroom when Hester let out a blood-curdling scream. Her water broke and gushed out of her all over the Persian runner. Hester slumped to the floor as another contraction gripped her.

"It's alright, Hester. Let's go in our bathroom and clean you up," Cecilia said. "Jimmy, get her into our bathroom."

Cecilia barked orders. Hester was keenly aware of Jimmy staring down at her. She was on her side writhing in pain in a puddle of amniotic fluid and these people were watching her. How fucking pathetic.

Jimmy had her under the arms and lifted her up. She was too weak to tell him to leave her the hell alone, too weak to tell big mouthed Cecilia to shut the hell up. Cecilia had her arm around Hester and the both of them were practically carrying her through their bedroom into their bathroom. They sat her on the closed toilet.

Jimmy left.

Cecilia peeled off Hester's sweatshirt, took off Hester's sneakers and socks.

"Your feet and ankles are so swollen. Good thing this happening now, old lady," said Cecilia.

Despite all of the confusion and her frazzled state-of-mind, Hester could not mistake the edge in Cecilia's voice.

Cecilia pulled Hester forward and yanked the back of her sweatpants down below her behind. "You know what a pain in the ass you are? God, I'm glad we are finally getting this over with."

Hester, between contractions, studied the younger woman's face dumbly. Was Hester imagining the cruel set of Cecilia's eyes? Her rigid jawline, down-turned mouth? Was Hester's mind play tricks on her because her body was out of control?

Cecilia jerked Hester into a standing position, yanked Hester's drenched pants and underpants down, pulled the silk shower curtain back, and threw them in the tub. Hester stood there naked as another contraction took hold. She turned away from Cecilia and grabbed the top of the marble vanity with both hands, supporting herself while she blew her breath out in small puffs. Cecilia put her arms around Hester from the back, put her hands on Hester's lower abdomen right above her pubic area and pressed, "Come on, old lady, you can do it. Good, good."

Hester turned, pushed Cecilia away, and lowered herself onto the toilet.

"I'm going to your room to get you some clean things. Do *not* stand-up." Cecilia commanded as she scooped the dirty clothes from the tub, hurried out, and shut the door behind her.

Hester, waiting for the next invasion of pain, stared at the mauve towels with silver monogramed C's on them. They were luxurious towels, probably Egyptian or Turkish. Her eyes wandered to the enormous tub. Hester remembered the day, not too long ago, when the guys from Penn Supply delivered it. There was a big to do because Tony from H&D Construction said it wouldn't fit in the bathroom. Cecilia insisted it would and for Tony to make it fit. Somehow or other he did, because here it was. It was cream-colored with Jacuzzi jets. A puffy white plastic pillow was on the corner ledge. Hester thought about how lovely it would be to get in the tub, put her head on the pillow, and let the water swirl around her. She could use that pillow now. Put it behind her back and lean it on it. She'd be more comfortable.

She reached over and picked it up. Beneath it was...a razor, an antique gold razor, the kind of razor that had been in Al's shaving kit. Was it *that* razor? Was it the razor that held the blade the crime scene investigator found on the ground beneath Lola's body?

Another contraction distracted Hester. The pain peaked rapidly, intensely. Hester bit her lip not to cry out. She didn't want Cecilia to come in. Not yet. She had to get that razor. She moaned and stretched her legs out in front of her. My God, the agony was unbelievable.

When it passed, Hester grabbed the razor and wrapped one of the fancy towels around it.

"Eric!" she called. She'd give him the razor, tell him to see if it was solid gold, tell him to take it to the police.

"What's wrong?" Cecilia burst through the door, Jimmy behind her. "Why are you calling for Eric? Have you lost your mind? Look at you, you're naked."

Hester stared down at her engorged breasts, her bulging mass of flesh as though she'd forgotten what it looked like. Cecilia was right. She couldn't let Eric see her like this, but she had to do something. How did *that* razor get into *their* bathroom? Oh, she didn't care what Eric saw.

"Eric!" she screamed as another spasm made her break-out in a sweat all over again.

"Shut-up!" Cecilia's face was an inch from Hester's, her hot breath gaging Hester. Cecilia backed off, threw one of Jimmy's clean undershirts over Hester's head and roughly pulled it down.

"Get up!" Cecilia ordered. Jimmy helped Hester up.

Hester looked at him. All the color had drained from his face. He avoided her eyes.

"Thanks." Hester's voice sounded to her like it was coming out of her navel. She was going crazy trying to ride the roller coaster of the cramps.

"Lift up your foot," said Cecilia.

Hester lifted one foot then the other so Cecilia could get a pair of clean sweatpants on her.

"Let's go." Cecilia tried to take the towel out of Hester's hand.

"No, I need it," Hester insisted.

"For what? You're going to the hospital."

"To mop the sweat from my face. See how I'm sweating. I need the towel."

"I'll give you an old one."

"Please, Cecilia, let me use this one. It's so soft on my face."

"But it's one of my Turkish…"

"Cecilia, please," interrupted Jimmy, "let her keep the damn towel. I'll get you new ones when this is over."

Cecilia's face hardened and her eyes narrowed. She didn't seem happy about the towel. She walked out of the bathroom, and Jimmy and Hester followed.

"Eric, thank God, you're still here," Hester was relieved to see Eric standing by the top of the staircase.

"Waited to wish you luck. Hope everything turns out all right."

"Eric, get over here and give me a hug," said Hester. "I'll miss you."

"You won't be gone long." Eric walked past Cecilia toward Hester and Jimmy, and stood in front of them. He seemed hesitant to embrace Hester since they never had before; but Hester reached her arms up around Eric's neck and pulled him close so she could whisper in his ear.

"I think one of them killed that woman."

"What?" Eric said.

"What's the big secret?" Jimmy asked.

"Nothing," Hester said, as she convulsed with another tightening of her abdomen that was so fierce it made her double over.

"Get her down these stairs and in the car," Cecilia hollered, "before she drops our baby on the floor like some wild animal."

Eric went down the steps backwards holding Hester's free hand, the towel clutched tightly in her other hand. How could she get the razor to Eric without Jimmy or Cecilia seeing it? Jimmy was close behind her guiding her hips, and Cecilia was right behind him. She could feel the woman's eyes burning a hole through the back of her skull.

Hester looked desperately into Eric's eyes.

Damn it, Eric, read my mind!

Fifty-Two

Waves of pain washed over Hester for the thousandth time, gathered again into a fist, slammed again deep into her groin.

I can't bear it any longer.

She wanted to scream, make it stop!

But then she'd think, *Pearl is coming. My baby is coming... how I want to see her, hold her.*

But these happy thoughts changed in a flash to... *I want this baby out of me! I will not...make it... through the next...*

"Please," Hester begged, "can I have something for the pain?"

The doctor was at the foot of the bed. Jimmy on Hester's right. Cecilia on her left, squeezing Hester's hand every time she thought Hester should be puffing her breaths.

"No," Cecilia said firmly, "we agreed, Hester. No drugs. The drugs could harm the baby."

It was an incontrovertible dictum from Cecilia.

"Hester, stop breathing and push." The doctor's voice sounded far off.

"I can't. I can't stand the pain. I am going to die from the pain."

"Hester, you won't die. I won't let you die." The doctor's words did little to comfort Hester. Hester could feel his hands on her feet. He lifted them both and forced Hester's legs to bend. Cecilia grabbed the leg closest to her and forced it back until Hester's knee was nearly in her armpit. The doctor motioned to Jimmy to help with the other leg. He stepped up next to Hester and did what he was told while the doctor stuck his hand inside Hester.

"There's the head. We're close now. Now you have to push."

"I can't. I'm afraid."

"Hester, get a grip," Cecilia snapped at her.

Hester tried to sit up. The pain was between her legs, up her rectum, and shooting down her inner thighs, but she pushed and it felt like her insides were coming out.

Please, God, please? Hester prayed and looked between her legs and saw the doctor's gloved hands holding something that looked like a slimy melon. He turned it over and there was Pearl's face! The rest of Pearl was still inside her.

"Oh my God!" Hester screamed and closed her eyes and pushed. The rest of her baby shot out of her quickly. The awful pain gone, already Hester began to forget how bad it was. The doctor put the glistening creature on Hester's abdomen and suctioned mucous out of its little mouth. The mouth started making sucking noises. Weeping tears of joy, Hester pulled the infant up to her breast and tried to maneuver her large nipple into the little rosebud of a mouth.

"Pearl! Mommy will feed you." And the baby found Hester's nipple.

Hester couldn't think about giving the baby to Jimmy and Cecilia now. She knew she had agreed to Cecilia's arrangement, they'd pay for everything, give the baby everything it would need, in return for full custody.

That was before she saw the razor, before her longed-for baby was in her arms, before her flesh and blood was at her breast. She had only imagined such closeness, such tender, protective feelings. No, she would not give up her own child. Money or no money. She would knock on the door of the Trenton Women's Shelter. Gladly, humbly, she would accept their charity.

As Pearl took her nourishment, Hester imagined her escape. She'd thank Jimmy for his help thus far, and Cecilia for her understanding and kindness; however, thank you very much, she would retain custody of her daughter. Of course, Jimmy and Cecilia would have visitation rights. Hester would gladly bring Pearl to the Silver Nugget anytime they wanted. She would even sleep downstairs in the closet if they wanted Pearl to spend the night.

Oh, thank you, God, I found the razor. Hester prayed. She could've made a fatal mistake and delivered her daughter into the hands of a murderer. One of them, a murderer? Or were they in it together? Were they both lying? Were they both insane?

Hester felt she might drift off to sleep. She had to remember where she put the towel with the razor in it. It was evidence. The police might be able to figure things, might be able to get to the truth. The razor was still in the towel. Where was the *effing* towel? Hester looked around the room. She remembered she'd put it down…or someone had taken it from…her eyes were getting heavy. With Pearl at her breast she shouldn't sleep. She had to take care of her baby. She saw the doctor between her legs. He was pulling the bloody afterbirth out of her. She felt woozy. Someone…Jimmy was taking Pearl.

Hester's breast popped out of the baby's mouth.

The baby was gone.

"My baby!" Hester screamed.

Jimmy ignored Hester, went to Cecilia, and handed the baby over.

"But, please, Jimmy, let me nurse the baby," Hester, fully awake now, begged. "Please, Cecilia, you know how important it is for the baby. How will my baby get the antibodies she needs? Cecilia, you went to the classes. You know, *my* baby needs *my* milk. Please, see my breasts are so full they ache." Hester could not hold back her tears.

Cecilia, nestling the baby in the crook of her arm, looked indifferently at Hester. Jimmy lowered his eyes as if to avoid looking at her at all.

It was, unfortunately, what had been agreed upon. Jimmy and Cecilia get full custody of the baby. Hester lives downstairs, pretends she's the baby's grandmother and can see the baby anytime she wants. Hester had not signed any papers, but she had agreed.

Now she struggled with this decision as she watched the young couple inspect the newborn, unwrapping it like it was a piece of antique Venetian glass, looking at it with such wonder, such incredulity and reverence, and—yes, it did look like it—love, like that baby was the most valuable object in the world, which is precisely what it was.

What was there for Hester to do? Maybe the razor meant nothing. Maybe lots of people who ran flea markets or shopped at them had old gold razors with double-edged blades. Maybe Jimmy thought using an antique razor was just the kind of thing the manager of a flea market did. Maybe Cecilia thought using an antique razor was the epitome of luxury.

If only Hester had had her cheaters with her, she could've seen if it was really gold, really the one that had been in the case. But she didn't have her glasses with her so she could not be sure.

So what could she think now? That the only thing evil were the thoughts in her head?

Face it, Hester told herself, *you are fifty-two years old. By the time this infant is fifteen, you'll be sixty-seven. Sixty-seven is too old to keep up with a teenager. You have no job, no chance of getting a decent one soon. Food, clothing, shelter? The Women's Shelter? Well, what would that be like for a baby? A baby whose father had a good job and whose stepmother was wealthy...extremely wealthy.*

These thoughts crowded Hester's mind.

After divorcing Al and before all of this, she had started listening to the famous radio talk show psychologist, Dr. Ethel Brannigan. Now that smart woman's words rang in her ears. *"It's not about you now; it's about your child."* Dr. Ethel always advised women who had a baby out of wedlock to give that baby up for adoption so it could be raised in a loving, happy, two-parent family.

Did Cecilia and Jimmy fit that description? Hester did believe, based on all he had told her, all she knew and thought of him, Jimmy Raymer, come hell or high water, would see to it that their Alice Pearl would be part of just such a family.

So, Hester concluded, she could deal with having nothing, not even Pearl, as long as Pearl would have everything.

Exhausted from the ordeal of giving birth, from the heartbreak of her daughter being taken from her, Hester closed her eyes and tried to comfort herself. She recalled the brilliant daylight on Walden Pond studding the surface with diamonds, the swimmer making her way through the glittering water. She remembered the clouds dancing like happy trolls across the dazzling Florida sky, the fiery red and orange orb slipping into the horizon, the sand warm on her back as the dome above her turned dark. She pretended she was lying there, letting the heat of a long-gone sun penetrate her disappointment. A million stars exploded above her. On this special Sunday, the sixth of April, could not just one of them be lucky?

Fifty-Three

Pleasant Palms Trailer Park was deserted and so overgrown it looked like a jungle. In the year or so since Hester left, it appeared not one ounce of maintenance had been done, weeds in every crack and crevice, grass high as an elephant's eye. The pool was a wildlife habitat, frogs napping in the shallow gutter, snakes navigating the stagnant water, an iguana sunning by the steps. The marina empty. The glass on the auditorium windows broken. The office on A1A locked, shade down.

Hester had been manipulated into leaving the Silver Nugget, as she feared she might. The few weeks she did live in the closet, she had to keep her breasts bound. The doctor had given her a shot to stop her milk from coming in, but every time Pearl cried she could hear it through the thin floor, and her flesh filled up and throbbed. Her heart ached too. The laughter of the happy couple pleased her one minute and made her head want to explode the next.

When they brought Pearl down to her, they both came. Cecilia's hovering made Hester jittery. Hester wanted to bite the young woman's hand off when she tried to adjust the way Hester was holding Pearl. Jimmy usually said very little, and the visits were curtailed the minute Pearl started to whimper, Cecilia whisking the baby away with such confidence, such a look of proprietorship on her face that Hester had to clamp her hand over her mouth not to let loose a scream.

Then one morning, Cecilia came alone and told Hester the happy couple had made an important decision. Hester could not stay in the closet any longer. It was probably against some law, but beside that it wouldn't be good for Alice Pearl to realize one day her "grandmother" had lived beneath her in a squalid closet like some poor tramp. So Cecilia would give her ten thousand dollars, if she moved back to Florida. Jimmy was in complete agreement and would see to it that the Odyssey was tuned up and properly insured.

"Grandmother? Why do you keep referring to me like that when I am and always will be Pearl's mother," said Hester, exasperated by Cecilia's thick-headedness. "I don't think we should lie to the child about the facts. True, I'm allowing you to be the primary caregiver for now, but one day I'll be on my feet and able to share the responsibilities. Cecilia, Pearl should know I am her *mother* and you are her *stepmother*."

"Oh, please, Hester. Let's not argue semantics. Pearl will always know the truth about everything. So let's get back to the matter at hand, namely, your move to Florida. Now, admit it, Hester. Won't this move be better? For you, for all of us?" Cecilia smiled a quick, curt smile.

"But when will I see my baby if I'm all the way down in Florida?" asked Hester.

"When we come to visit. Or you can fly up. You'll have the money to do that. Or I'll send you the money. We'll work it out. You'll see."

"Offering me such a large sum of money is extremely generous of you, Cecilia. And I would be appreciative if I could use that money for a place in Lambertville. It would be much closer and more con…"

"Lambertville is too expensive, and you know it. Besides you still own your trailer down there. Jimmy looked into it, and the park reverted back from the developers to the original shareholders. Why not live in a place you have stock in and is yours, a place where you have a chance to get ahead," Cecilia said, then added, "and why look a gift horse in the mouth? End of story."

Hester could see saying anything further on the topic was useless. Cecilia's steel-trap of a mind had been slammed shut, and Hester could almost see the army of lawyers lining up behind the most outstanding stepmother in the world, Mrs. Jimmy Raymer.

Momentarily defeated, Hester accepted the money. Cecilia gave her five hundred dollars cash and a check for nine thousand five hundred, a decent war chest. She'd retreat for the moment, make this money grow, and come back for Pearl.

So here Hester was, in Pleasant Palms, driving through the section by the Intracoastal, crossing over A1A, and parking in the weeds by the shuffleboard courts. The eight foot wire fence the developer installed around the demolition site was completely entwined with vegetation. The gate that had been open the last time she left her place, had three padlocks on it. To get to her unit, she'd have to find a way in.

She walked along the perimeter of the fence towards the surf shop and deli, up Coconut Palm Lane to Old Ocean Boulevard. When she turned north, luckily she found a spot where the fence had been cut low to the ground and bent back just enough for an animal or child to get through. Standing there, the boarded up Ocean Clubhouse behind her, staring at what used to be the neat rows of well-kept trailers, Hester was stunned by the damage time had done. Time, and neglect, had trashed the pristine park. Even if she did get inside the fence, how would she get through the impenetrable jungle of overgrown vegetation? And what if squatters were in there? And snakes, fox, alligators? An alligator could've gotten through that hole in the fence.

Going any further might be a mistake, but going back…there was no going back. She wasn't about to use any of the money Cecilia had given her for a room or an apartment. She had no alternative but to fix up her unit and live in it. When she got a job, maybe things would change. She knelt down, made the sign of the cross, took a deep breath, and squirmed in under the fence scratching herself up pretty good on the raw ends of wire. She crawled through giant philodendron and bristly weeds. Lizards scattered. A fog of mosquitos erupted. She made her way to a narrowed but passable lane and got to her feet. The trailers were besieged by vines and so dwarfed by bushes and trees, Hester feared she wouldn't recognize her place even if she was right in front of it.

The humidity was suffocating, sweat poured off her, her clothes were drenched; but she soldiered forward.

Had she gone too far? She turned, looked back, no way to determine distance. She was about to give up and break into whatever place she could, when she spied the Bo tree.

"Ah, old friend," she said, and her words seemed to make its leaves stir.

The key had been left in the Lambertville condo, and the sliding door was locked so Hester worked her way through a hulking gardenia, ripped a screen, opened an unlocked window, and crawled in.

She flipped a switch. Nothing happened. What the hell did she expect? The interior was as dark as a cave. She stood still and waited for her eyes to adjust. When they did, she got matches from the junk drawer and lit a candle.

What a relief! It could've been worse. The dirt and dust and lizard poop she could deal with, but no leaks, no water damage, everything looked about the same as the day she packed up her knickknacks, went to her car, and called the police. If she hadn't been so hell-bent on taking them with her, they'd still be here. Who knew?

It didn't take Hester long to bring the car around and move her handful of belongings into her unit. She went back out to Dollar General for bottled water, charcoal, bread, peanut butter, oatmeal— she'd eat it raw.

In the following days, Hester discovered that the only faucet in the park that hadn't been disconnected was the cold one in the pool bathhouse sink. She made several trips in the hot sun, two buckets at a time, until her sinks and tub were full. She threw everything that belonged to Al or even smelled like Al in a dumpster the demolition crew had left on Fishtail Lane and scrubbed every inch of the place until it sparkled.

Outside, she resisted the temptation to completely prune back the tangled vegetation. Something inside her craved wildness, and the shade provided by the behemoth plants made her feel like she was in a dim wood.

Most of the day it was hotter than hell, after all it was summer. Regardless, Hester busily spruced up her home and at night she barricaded herself in, finally Al's La-Z-Boy was good for something other than cushioning his sorry ass.

She thought often of Henry David as she tried to build her new life from what was left of her old one. How she missed that tattered copy of *Walden*. It'd been such a good companion to her.

When she was getting ready to leave the Silver Nugget, she looked everywhere for it. She asked Jimmy if he'd seen it, but he hadn't. She tried to find Eric, maybe he'd taken it. She drove around Lambertville looking for him, even went to the Cartwheel Tavern and asked about him. He must've been on the road. Nobody had seen him for weeks.

She put the Schwartz book, her shabby clothes, and her three dolls in a paper bag to take with her. The rest of the books she'd been collecting and sleeping on all those months, she piled neatly by one of the trash bins for the next poor soul who was down on her luck.

She nuzzled her face in Pearl's neck and tried to memorize the odor of her baby's body, the sweet smell of her baby's breath. She kissed her a thousand times before she gave her to Jimmy.

"Thank you, Hester. You will never know how much this means to me...to us. Little Alice Pearl will always know who you are. We'll never let her forget you." Jimmy hugged Hester gently. Cecilia did too.

Hester was crying, still not sure she could follow through on the promise, still not sure she wouldn't grab her baby and run.

It's for the best...for the best...for the best. She chanted this mantra as she climbed into her minivan, hating herself for being broke, hating herself having to take money from Cecilia, hating herself for...it was the past. She looked ahead and drove across the Nugget's lot and out onto River Road. The words of Yeats' "The Stolen Child" came to her:

"Come away, O human child,
To the waters and the wild
With faery, hand in hand
For the world's more full of weeping
Than you can understand..."

And weep she did. She drove straight through, twenty-one hours of weeping.

In a way it was a relief to be alone in Pleasant Palms, to have the solitude she needed to sort things out.

Pearl was with her father. Pearl was safe. That was all that mattered.

Fifty-Four

Hester tried to keep busy and fight what she knew had to be the worst kind of post-partum depression, the kind when you go through everything, and end up with nothing.

Attempting to follow Thoreau's example, she began keeping a journal and writing down every dime she spent. She recorded her activities: weeded; loosened soil; planted arugula, basil, tomatoes; swept patio. When she wasn't working around her trailer, she hiked the beach and logged her observations: silver fox with pup, small fruit on mango tree, green parrot, black snake, fading tracks of nesting turtle.

And every day Hester wrote a letter to Pearl and mailed it to Jimmy Raymer, c/o The Silver Nugget Flea Market. Always, as she dropped the letter into the mailbox, those final moments became frighteningly real again. She was driving down River Road shivering with regret, burning up with sorrow, her heart barren, her barren heart in her throat.

The worst for Hester, though, was the waiting. Around noon each day, she sat in front of the locked Pleasant Palms office and watched the mail truck speed by. As week after week passed, Hester could draw only one conclusion. Jimmy and Cecilia lied to her. They had no intention of keeping in touch, of letting her be a part of Pearl's life. She might never see her child again if she didn't go back.

Damn it, she'd go back!

But would anything be different?

Cecilia wouldn't be. Hester wouldn't be wanted there.

But the baby. The baby would be different. They change so quickly when they're young. That's what all mother's knew.

Would the baby even recognize Hester as the woman who gave her life?

No, that small mind would be dreaming only of her warm bottle, her soft cashmere blanket, her father's strong arms, the beating of his heart when he held her, which Hester hoped was often.

She pictured Jimmy, Pearl, and Cecilia, imagined them taking a little family trip to Long Beach Island, to Cecilia's castle in the sand. Hester had heard enough about it to picture the classic structure, the grey shingles, crisp white trim, the deck over the dunes from which Baby Pearl would get her first glimpse of the Atlantic Ocean.

Hester got up from the bench and hurried to the beach. As she looked out at the ocean, she thought, *eighteen hundred miles from Pearl.* It seemed a profound distance. At this exact moment, she did not exist for her daughter. Their time together had been brief. Hester tried to recall every detail, but many were fading, her daughter withering into a dream.

No, dear God, Pearl is not a dream. She is real. I gave Pearl life, and with great sacrifice, I also gave Pearl the best life possible.

What else could she have done, but leave her behind…with them? The lack of plausible alternatives did nothing to assuage Hester's torment. Even standing at the edge of the seemingly endless sea did little to help her put her life and this latest tragedy in perspective.

Yes, she was a useless clod, a blip on the screen of time. Many had suffered much worse than she. Many had done nothing to bring about their suffering, whereas she had fully participated in her downfall, again and again. And here she stood, letting waves of self-pity pull her further out than she'd ever been before. She had to do something to get her head back on straight.

Okay, so there was nothing else she could've done then, but now? An idea came to her.

Hester rolled the windows down on her van. The hot wind stung the skin of her face, but she refused to turn the air on and waste her precious gas. She drove to Barnes and Nobles out on Congress Avenue, bought a paperback copy of *Walden,* and drove back. Once inside her sweltering unit, she recorded the following in her journal: August 21, Walden by Henry David Thoreau, $13.95 plus $1.14 tax for a total of $15.09, (money well-spent on the anniversary of Pearl's conception).

She picked up the book, and the weight of it in her hand made her feel less awful than she had in months. The cover was not the rich worn leather of her old one nor was the frontispiece adorned with that quaint etching of H.D.'s cabin, but the words were the same and the words were what Hester needed to have. Reluctantly, though, she placed the volume on the table and put the receipt in an envelope with her other receipts. There were plans to be made.

She started her list. Tomorrow, go to Walmart for a phone card. If she called the Nugget's office, maybe Jimmy'd pick up. Then stop at the bank, open a new checking account with the nine thousand, five hundred dollar check from Cecilia. Once that money was available, Hester would purchase her ticket for a flight to New Jersey. See her daughter with her own eyes. Give the young Raymers a piece of her mind.

It was late in the day, one of those blaringly gorgeous afternoons. Hester pulled on her old bathing suit and went back up to the beach. It was breezy, the ocean transparent as jade, white caps riding the waves like bucking broncos. She walked out into the rough surf, the water clobbering her thighs and pounding into her stomach. She plunged in, swam past the break, and floated on her back, the water so calm and temperate it was like being in the womb of the world. Her favorite passage from *Walden* came to her.

"I found in myself...an instinct toward a higher, or, as it is named, spiritual life...and another toward a primitive rank and savage one, and I reverence them both. I love the wild not less than the good..."

Thank you, God, she could always count on Henry David for consolation, and to accept herself as complete, as simply heartbreakingly human, as both wild…and good, well, it was a tonic for all that ailed her.

Her spirit lifted.

But only momentarily.

Deep inside that crazy little head of hers lurked one nagging razor-thin doubt. Double-edged and sharp, Hester felt it beginning to slice open the skin of her serenity; and, oh no, damn if what little peace she had wasn't bleeding right the hell out of her.

The End

Made in the USA
Middletown, DE
04 December 2014